KATELYNN R. BUTLER

I am Become
by
Katelynn R. Butler

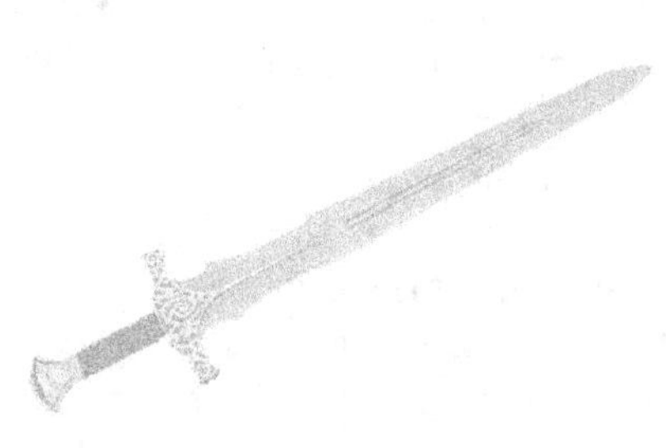

For Zach. You were right, the only way to fail is to
never try.

And for Mom, because you fostered my love of
stories.

Chapter One

Year 4069

I remember the stories my grandparents would tell me about the Great War, about the oppression of magic under the Coalition's totalitarian rule. Neither lived during that time, the war having ended nearly twenty years before they both were born, but each of their families had lived through its horrors.

They had also survived the many atrocities the Coalition inflicted upon the newly formed government – and people with magical abilities – before the New Allied Forces had been established. Because of this, they spoke of the war often. Their stories were so vivid it seemed to eight-year-old me that they had lived through it.

Their accounts of the war were what I requested to hear that day. My grandmother had just celebrated her seventy-eighth birthday a few weeks prior. I distinctly remember this because my grandfather had requested my help with throwing a surprise birthday party for her, and I had taken that job *very* seriously.

But on that day – a lovely spring afternoon – my grandparents were watching my baby sister and me while my father was in an important government meeting, and my mother was away planning an event for him. Neither of them wanted children underfoot, so they dumped us on our grandparents' doorstep early that morning with hardly even a "thank you" or "goodbye".

Not that I minded. My maternal grandparents had been my favorite people when I was a child. Not only because of their fantastical tales but because they truly loved me. I was not a political or status accessory for them. I was just their little Daux, their little deer.

We all sat out on their porch that afternoon. Amalie was seated in my lap, eating small gummy candies and getting sticky. My grandparents were having tea and cookies. I was given homemade lemonade because I would not grow to like tea until I was older. The warm breeze smelled of my grandmother's rose garden and the grass Grandfather had cut that morning.

I felt at home, at ease. Here at my grandparent's house, I only had to be myself. What is more, I was a curious child. My parents never wanted me to speak unless I was spoken to and prohibited questions about the war. No talk of magic, not even my own, which they tried their darndest to quash in me. They did not want me getting ideas unfit for a young lady to have. They did not want me to behave in a way that would reflect the very things they did not believe in.

Here, I could say whatever – and do whatever – I wished. So, I asked for stories.

On that beautiful spring day – Victorisday, the day of the week which was named to celebrate the end of the Great War – my grandmother complied and told them. Dark, dreadful tales that made me sorrowful; however, I still wanted to know. It was almost like I *needed* to know. In a way, I did.

I sat, sticky Amalie on my lap, enraptured with my grandmother's clear, beautiful voice as she told of families ripped apart. Of young women and men gunned down in public for no reason other than speaking their minds or having magic. Of the people fighting bravely for peace in a world filled with hatred and corruption. Of my great grandfathers and grandmothers fighting for their lives and the lives of their decedents. For the right for people with magic to be more than slaves, subjects of human experimentation, or enemies of the state.

Magic, in those days, was considered something to be feared. People born with abilities others did not – or could not have – created division among societies and even among families. The people had forgotten that magic had been given as a gift to the people by the Gods, who saw fit to leave us to our own devices once we learned how to fend for ourselves.

It was a wild, untamed thing that fed upon people's energy, but only became more powerful as people learned to wield it – birthing new magics that could only be learned by those who were born to parents who could wield them. Those who were born without magical ability began to fear it, and labeled magic as a curse from the Gods who abandoned their people.

"The Gods wished to leave us with something for us to remember them by," Grandmother said, letting the ghost of a flame dance over her fingers. "Elemental magic, as you know, is the most common."

"But some people have special magic," I nearly shouted with excitement, unable to contain my joy in this safe place. "Some families were blessed by the Gods with special powers that other people don't have."

"Right," Grandmother agreed, tapping her temple. "Like us, we can see things that others cannot. We can hear, taste, and smell. Our senses sharpen so we can survive."

"But it takes a lot of energy…" I whispered, remembering when my magic manifested itself in flame and a riot of color, sound, and smell. Before my father pumped me full of magical blockers, a substance to temporarily reduce a person's magical energy or for a longer period.

"Yes… and this magic – these special powers caused

much strife among the people of Eturnus," Grandmother continued.

This caused a rift among the people that lasted thousands of years, ultimately resulting in the formation of the Coalition. These world leaders established their totalitarian rule over most – if not all – the countries on the planet Eturnus, enslaving people with magic and laying waste with their twisted experiments as they tried to further their dominion over the planet.

The Great War ended long before my grandparents were born, but the anti-magic sentiments and devastation lasted well into their adulthood. The NAF and all its previous iterations had tried their best to unify and help their people but there were so many devastated and poverty-stricken families affected by the war. Many of the NAF countries had breakaway regions which defected into the Coalition's territories, blinded by the promise of wealth and power which was never awarded to them.

"Creating a fair, yet supportive government was difficult," My grandmother said, rocking back and forth in her chair. "Many people who had known wealth and influence wanted their way. Some still believed having magic was a blight on society and the world. It was difficult to keep those people out of power."

Grandmother's tone had become grim now and her face had a far-away look upon it. I supposed she was thinking of my father because that was where my mind had gone as well. He used his influence as Governor of Arcania to get what he wanted – whatever he wanted; even at my young age I could see that. I could see it in the ease with which he was able to procure magical blockers to render the magic I was born with obsolete, even though using them on one as young as myself had long been looked down upon.

My assumption would not have been too far from the truth either, as she envisioned people like him. People who had wanted to take advantage of the NAF's precarious position as a new and semi-unified front.

"It was a tumultuous time," she said when she finally spoke again. "And it seemed as though those people who craved power and influence over others would once again regain control."

"And that was when the NAF created the Placement Exam!" I interrupted without fear of a withering look or reprimand.

Grandmother laughed. "That is exactly right, my little deer."

The NAF also founded the Heliorious Academy, the Special Operations division: a defense and intelligence sector, and created the Placement Exam. All of which had been reworked often to match society's needs. The Placement Exam was invented to create easy assimilation into society after the Waring Times, as was the school, which was created specifically with magic users in mind.

It was somewhere I desperately wished to go. Somewhere to hone the magic I was being denied at home. But my parents would not hear of it. Nor would they entertain the idea of me joining the Special Operations division. Such a profession was unbecoming for a young woman or other such nonsense.

"Grandmother?" I asked, interrupting her yet again.

Both my grandparents turned to me with a smile.

"What dear?" she asked.

"Father says I am only a little girl and can't use my magic to help the NAF, is that true?"

I held Amalie in my lap tightly, not looking up at them, and praying that they would rebuke my father's opinion. I was merely ten years old with my whole future ahead of me.

"Now why would your father say that?" Grandfather asked kindly. I could tell he was trying to keep his voice even instead of showing his emotions.

"I don't know…" I responded, wiping Amalie's mouth with a damp cloth. "He says girls shouldn't be in charge of things. That important jobs are for fathers and men, and he hates my magic."

The frustration on my grandparents' porch was palpable. I had become accustomed to reading the room so as not to provoke my parents' disdain. My grandparents were angry, but not with me.

Grandfather knelt before me and lifted my sticky sister from my lap.

"Daux, what do you want to do when you grow up?" he asked.

I shrugged, still refusing to meet his eyes.

"Do you want to marry like your mother?" Grandfather prodded.

I shook my head vigorously and he laughed.

"Okay, what about your father's job? Do you want to be like him?"

My father worked for the NAF government as a governor but had been born into money and tradition. I knew he would convince people to do things he wanted and would bully them if they did not. Since I was a child, I did not understand these actions much. All I knew was that my father was mean, and I did not want to be anything like him.

"No," I said. "I want to be in Spec Ops and help people, as the NAF did, and teach people that our magic isn't bad or scary."

My grandmother smiled at me from her rocking chair.

"Then that is what you must do, my little Daux," she said, her voice rich with pride.

I grinned at her and stood to begin clearing the tea and lemonade cups from the small, white table when I noticed a tall figure.

"So, this is what you teach my children when I'm not around," my father snapped, scowling at my grandparents.

My grandfather, with Amalie still in his arms, started toward my father but he met my grandfather on the stairs and took Amalie from him. She immediately began to cry.

"Come, Daux," my father commanded. "We must be going."

"Charles," My grandmother started.

"I am not speaking to *you*," he said in a low, menacing tone, and I cowered at the sound, but hurried to his side.

My father grasped my hand tightly and began to lead me to his auto.

"Charles!" Grandfather thundered. Only then did my father halt and acknowledge my grandparents.

"Daux is capable of great things, you shouldn't keep her from them," Grandfather said. Even then I could hear the pain in his voice. See it in his face.

"Do not presume to tell me how to raise my children," my father hissed, green eyes flashing.

"Cha–" Grandmother began before my father cut her off.

"I will be speaking to Annette," he said. "We will have to find other arrangements for the children as I have deemed your company unfit for them. Sadly, you alienated Annette with your heretical beliefs, your daughter. Now you alienate her children."

My grandparents protested with vehemence, but my father dragged me toward the auto, ignoring them completely. I did not dare cry. Did not dare risk a peek over my shoulder at my grandparents. That was the last time I would see them as a child.

Chapter Two

Year 4079

The bathroom was cold that early Mournsday morning. It was strange that I remembered that little detail over others that day. I just remember the cool air and goosebumps traveling up my body as I gazed at myself in one of the many mirrors lining the plain white walls of the dormitory bathroom.

I stared into my reflection's eyes. My own eyes. Deep green, like the ocean. At the time I wished I could get lost in my eyes as easily as one could get lost in the deep, dark waves; but that was not to be. As fate would dictate, I could not lose myself to the ocean I saw in my irises and had to carry on with life.

My fingers gripped the cool ceramic of the sink and I considered sending a burst of flame through my fingers to shatter it. If all went well today, I could afford one demerit on my record – that is if the dorm caretakers even realized it was me.

But I did not shatter it. Like a good girl, I stepped back from the sink and tore my gaze from the mirror. Slowly, I removed the towel from my body and dropped it into the cleaning bin, then slid on my underclothes, battle suit, and holonav. Braided back my hair, fingers catching in the long strands. Then took a few deep breaths before exiting the bathroom.

It was time.

The commons hall was just as cold as the bathroom had been that morning. Hundreds of people were waiting in the large open space – their ages ranging from fifteen to nineteen – milling about, leaning up against the grey walls, sitting around the many practical chairs and tables set uniformly up and down the length of the room.

We were all here to be Placed. This year the Placement Examination was made up of a physical assessment and a simulated test that would tell us which position we were best suited for. Usually, our results would share an extensive list of options at the Placement Ceremony where we would accept our Placement; however, the prospects could be narrowed down to as little as two.

Heliorious Academy was one of the NAF-sanctioned academies which could host a Placement Exam. It was unique in the sense that any student – ranging from eleven to eighteen – could apply for graduation at any point in their academic career and take the Placement Exam. Should the Exam results show they are ready to graduate, they will be Placed alongside their peers. It is rare for students sixteen and under to graduate and be Placed so young, but it has happened.

NAF-sanctioned academies will also allow people from county schools to take the exam. These individuals were called "testers" by the Academy students and were often older and had less honed or less powerful magical abilities. Testers typically had more civilian jobs lined up than those of us who went to the Academy. We were trained from the moment we arrived on the grounds to be the most elite protectors, civil servants, STEM, and artists in all of the NAF. It was rare for a Heliorious Academy student to receive a mundane Placement.

My eyes roved over the large crowd. From my place at the entrance to the large room, I could see a few familiar faces from my classes; though, no friends, of which I only had one, if I were to be completely honest. Talia Edgegrieves. She and I both hoped to be Placed in the Special Operations division.

Special Operations – or Spec Ops for short – was a prestigious department of the NAF military. They specialized in everything from frontline combat to behind-the-scenes stratagems. I had the same goal as Talia. We secretly hoped to be on the same four-to-five-person team in which Spec Ops operated, as we had become close during our time at the Academy.

Best friends. Talia was my very best friend.

Disappointment flooded through me when I did not see her. While we had not planned to meet this morning, I had hoped I would be able to catch her before the exam. Being with her during these nerve-wracking moments would have brought some comfort. That and the letters 'D' and 'E' were next to each other in the alphabet, so I had hoped we would be in the hall around the same time.

But that was not to be, because soon the proctors began filing into the large space.

The proctors began separating the testers from the students and from there began calling examinees in alphabetical order by surname. It felt like an eternity before I was called back. Just waiting and waiting for the call that would seal my fate. And finally, it came.

"Deveraux, Daux!" A proctor called.

My heart leaped into my throat, but I refused to let the fear show on my face. Stoic, I made my way towards the proctor and the rest of the examinees that had gathered. There were quite a few I did not know, either from different classes or outside of the school. We were all quiet as the proctor lead us to the Arena for the physical part of the exam.

Perhaps they were all as nervous as me.

A few people – testers – let out low whistles as we made our way through the large doors. I had to admit, the Arena was quite large. It was about one-hundred-and-twenty meters across and forty-five meters wide, creating a massive space for fighting or other physical activities.

"All right, my name is Jane Láska," the proctor said, turning towards us. "As you have probably figured out by now, this is the physical portion of the exam. Are there any questions?"

A girl to my left raised her hand.

"What if we aren't planning to go into a career that requires fighting skills or strength?" she asked.

Every student at Heliorious Academy went through rigorous physical, magical, and mental testing to prepare them for anything the world had to throw at them, even if they had the option to obtain a non-combatant or more cushy position. Testers could take these kinds of courses at other academies but were not required to do so.

"This is merely to test your physical ability, we do not expect you to be on the same level as that of Academy students," Proctor Láska said, then paused. "Miss?"

"Date Kumiko," the girl supplied.

"Miss Date," the proctor repeated. "Are there any other questions?"

A couple of other people asked whether we would be fighting one another, participating in an obstacle course, or taking part in a competition. The proctor waved off the last inquiry, stating that was not expected of testers or students; however, testers would be assessed on fighting against other testers and taking part in a small obstacle course. Academy students would be facing fellow students in full-on combat. This was to take advantage of the Academy students' training; the automated and enchanted arena floor would be manipulated in their area to test their ability to fight in unfamiliar terrain.

Kumiko gulped. I received good marks in my physical, weaponry, and strategy classes. This I could do. After some chatter amongst the examinees, Proctor Láska called for silence. Then her assistants separated the testers from the Academy students and directed each group toward our respective sides of the large arena.

From there, our attention was directed to the weapons rack, which was a huge wall lined from top to bottom with various weapons. None of these weapons would truly cause more harm than a bruise or a small cut; they were relatively safe, even the projectile weapons. We were to choose one each.

"Choose wisely," Proctor Láska said as we all selected our weapons. "You don't want to end up in a fight with a firearm when you are more familiar with melee weapons."

A few people sheepishly handed ill-picked weapons back to the assistants and reconsidered their options.

I chose a simple sword. Lightweight, but well-balanced for a fake weapon. My best scores had been obtained when using my trusty rapier, which I had modified to transform into a bow or shield at the press of a button. Despite the modifications, I preferred the comforting weight of a well-balanced sword in my hand to anything else.

All the Academy's students were required to know how to use, and modify, different weapons so we would be as experienced as possible. We each had one or two categories we preferred, typically. Some flashier students claimed to be comfortable using a multitude. Among those claims were weapons with more than three functions, some of which were combinations of war hammers that could turn into machine guns. I found these claims outlandish and humorous as modifying a war hammer into a controllable firearm was incredibly difficult.

After we had each picked a weapon, Proctor Láska's assistants began handing out small, circular objects.

"These are sensors," the proctor explained. "Attach all

five of them to your battle suit. One over the heart, the abdomen, between the shoulder blades, and on each thigh. These sensors will send a signal to our databases if they have been hit by your opponent's weapon."

A few students raised their hands to presumably ask what I was thinking as well when the proctor interrupted.

"The sensors will be synced with your opponent's weapon when I and my assistants have observed all of your sensors to be in their correct places. Does that answer your questions?"

The students lowered their hands.

Once we had finished choosing our weapons and attaching our sensors, the proctor announced that this year's arena battle would be one-on-one matches, analyzed from the stands above, by multiple recordings, and the sensors.

"The rules are as follows," Proctor Láska began. "Each pair will fight until one person admits defeat by signaling me and my assistants, each of their sensors has been hit, or the match is determined as complete by my standards. Attacking another examinee who is not your opponent constitutes an immediate disqualification, and you will have to reapply next year. The use of holonavs is prohibited and my assistants will be coming around to make sure each one is deactivated before the exam begins. The use of magic is allowed but will not trigger the sensors. Any questions?"

Holonavs – or Holographic Navigational Devices – began as simple navigational tools. Through the years they had evolved into what we now have, a highly encrypted multipurpose device that still retains its original function at its core. In this instance, the proctor would be worried about the video feed being leaked to an outside source for cheating or a distraction such as a loud noise coming from a video or song played through the holonav's speaker.

There were no further questions. A silence fell over the group as each pair was announced by Proctor Láska and her assistants. When I stepped toward my opponent, I realized I would be fighting a hulking boy nearly twice my size, and I was not a short person. I recognized him from my weapons-building class but did not even remember his name. Thankfully, he did not appear to be brutish, as he smiled awkwardly at me and shrugged. Still, I would not go easy on him, and I felt he would extend the same courtesy.

I steeled myself, gripping my dummy sword tightly in my right hand, as I waited for the signal to start the match. I took a deep breath. In. Out. In Out.

Immediately I allowed a surge of magic through my body, sharpening my senses. Sight, smell, and sound all sharpened. The minutest movements of my opponent became visible to me, and I could see the nervousness in his body language.

Then came the signal. It was a loud, piercing sound.

I barely permitted myself to wince, and we were off. My opponent was a two-handed wielder, using a large war hammer-type weapon. He charged towards me like a bull, and I leaped to the left, out of the way. Getting in close to attack would be difficult, but he had a limited range. Attacking from behind would be the easiest, then the sides. The front only if it was necessary to hit his heart sensor.

My opponent was fast, but his attacks were slow due to his bulky weapon, and I easily dodged them. The plan was to let him charge me until his stamina ran out. And while I was dodging, I would have considerable opportunities to attack his sensors.

I wove in and out of his attacks, striking out at his sensors whenever I had the opportunity and avoiding his war hammer when I did not. It was easy to do when I could see his muscles tensing up through his battlesuit before each attack. Like I was predicting his movements.

Whenever possible I would hit him in the places that did not have sensors. I did this merely to slow him down, to weaken him, which the quickly changing terrain assisted with. At least it did at first.

Though I had been on the high ground, the topography switched at an almost imperceptible rate, and I was now far below my opponent and he had a much longer reach. I had no intention of harming him for fun, but as the blazing sunshine quickly changed to the icy bite of a snowstorm, I knew I would have to be far less careful with my attacks.

My opponent swung and missed as the ground beneath me rose to a considerable height, allowing me to slash successfully at the sensor on his left thigh. Abruptly, the snow switched to a monsoon, and my footing washed out from under me.

As I tumbled toward the head of the war hammer, my heart sank as it swung directly at my heart sensor. Luckily, a large gust of wind blasted into my opponent, causing him to slip on the muddy ground, missing my sensor completely. Though the weapon nearly crushed my head before I rolled out of the way.

I struck out once again with my sword as the climate became arid, caking the mud to my battlesuit in heavy clumps. My weapon connected with the sensor in between my opponent's shoulder blades and his opposite thigh, and I watched as the muscles in his back rippled as he swung backward. Whirling, I prevented him from hitting my heart sensor, but this move exposed my back, and his war hammer slammed me to the hardened ground, smashing right between my shoulder blades.

A strangled sort of gasp escaped my lungs and it must have startled my opponent, because he jumped back from me, taking his hammer with him.

I grinned in triumph and twisted abruptly on the ground, striking out with my sword straight into his abdomen. When the sensor indicated the hit, I leaped to my feet and advanced on him, avoiding the pairs of fighting students all around us.

Finally, when I thought I had gained the upper hand, having hit four of his five sensors, the arena's topography changed again, causing me to stumble. My opponent saw this as an opportunity and attacked once more, and though I saw it coming, I was unable to dodge fast enough.

He swung his hammer, and it connected to my left thigh with a sickening crack. Pain seared through my leg, and I cried out. The red light on the sensor glowed, signaling his hit was successful.

Surprisingly, my cry of pain stunned him once again, and he dropped his weapon. Reacting quickly, despite the agony in my leg, I lunged with my sword right toward his heart sensor.

He barely had time to react before the tip of my weapon connected with the sensor and it lit up, automatically signaling our match over.

As we shook hands, he apologized for hurting my leg. Then he helped me limp off the arena floor. I could not blame him whatsoever. He was sure to be full of aches and bruises from the attacks I had inflicted upon him.

I merely smiled and told him there was no need for an apology before taking a seat next to some others who had finished their matches to watch the rest of the examinees.

A pretty girl with coiled black hair smiled at me as I lowered myself down gingerly beside her, heavily favoring my left leg.

"I'm Riannan Daniau," she said, holding her hand out for me to shake. I shook it and smiled wearily at her.

"Daux Deveraux," I replied.

"I know," she said cheekily, her eyes twinkling.

"You know?" I asked, slightly incredulous.

"Yep. You're one of the top students here; most people know who you are."

Ah. There it was.

"My reputation precedes me it seems," I sighed, attempting to stretch my injured leg. That was one of the reasons I had so few friends and acquaintances. Most assumed I was "too good" for them or believe I assumed that about myself.

"But I know who most people are," Riannan chirped, "That's my magical ability." She tapped her temple. "I have a great memory, photographic and otherwise."

Most students at the Academy had some sort of magical ability while still being able to use other magics. My ability was called foresight, which allowed me to hone in on my target's movements and attacks and enhanced all my senses. This aided me in combat and in situations where observational skills were required.

"You were excellent in that match with Emíl," Riannan chattered on. "Though I'm surprised they didn't assign you someone else. He's not very combat-oriented. He wants to take over his mother's bakery when she retires. He told me once his dad wanted him to go here, so he could decide for himself what he – that is Emíl – wanted to do."

That information was surprising. But Riannan did say she had a good memory. And now I knew my former classmate's name.

"Well, the matches are made in the system, not by the proctors," I told her.

"Yeah, but they would know that beforehand and would see his scores. They could have switched up the fights."

"That's true," I mused. "But I shouldn't be given special treatment because I have top combat scores."

"No, all I meant was that it would have been more exciting to watch!" Riannan exclaimed.

She evidently thought she insulted me. I gave her a small smile to reassure her and let her keep chattering. It was kind of cute.

"Thank you," I said, blushing a little at her compliment.

Her grin was more than dazzling, bright white teeth against warm brown skin.

Soon enough, the rest of the Academy examinees were

trudging off the arena's fighting grounds to join us on the sidelines. A majority of them had done well in their battles, despite half of them losing; however, many had also done poorly from observational standards, even though they had won their match.

As we walked from the arena to the second testing area Riannan and I discussed who we thought did exceptionally well, and those who were lacking. She even let me lean on her while we walked to not injure myself further limping to the testing hall. I felt as if I were quickly making a friend.

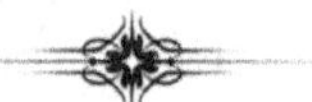

After the first portion, I finally understood why graduates were weary of the second half of the exam. The arena required so much physical and mental energy that I was completely exhausted. Besides the fight leaving me drained, my leg was killing me. One would have thought that I had lost the fight with the way it hurt.

I honestly did not know how I was going to take the second portion of the exam. I could barely walk without help at the moment, let alone think my way through a complex test. Thankfully, we were led to the medic station instead of the exam room. In the med-station waited several healers who immediately began assessing everyone and providing stim-pacs as well as light treatment to those who required it, like me.

I hated stim-pacs. The small, spherical medication always left a bitter tang in my mouth, but I took it anyway. Its soft, outer shell felt like jelly against my tongue, and the bitter liquid inside gushed out as soon as I punctured the shell with my teeth. Resisting the urge to gag, I quickly swallowed the mouthful of medication.

I was grateful despite the taste and thanked the young woman for applying med-spray to my more severe bruising. She grinned at me and Riannan before producing hard candy from the pocket of her tunic, pressing one into our hands before moving along to the next person.

Giving patients candy was such an antiquated gesture, but we were glad to receive them. I quickly unwrapped the candy from its brightly colored paper and placed it in my mouth, eager to chase the taste of the stim-pac away. The candy tasted like berries and cream and washed the bitter tang of the pac away quickly. A startling crunch came from my left, and I turned to see Riannan chomping on hers. She laughed at my astonished expression, and I laughed too.

We sat there in companionable silence, or I sat in silence while Riannan chattered at a breakneck speed, nursing our bruises while the medics fluttered around the exam takers like butterflies in a field of flowers. It was so relaxing, just sitting there listening to someone else talk that I almost fell asleep. But I was jolted out of my daze by Riannan pulling me to my feet.

"They're shooing us out for the next group," she explained, releasing me.

"Oh," I said lamely, blinking at the students and testers alike shuffling from the room.

"C'mon." Taking me by the hand, Riannan pulled me through the crowd and into the brightly lit corridor.

Then, surprisingly, she pulled me into a tight hug. Her coiled hair smelled of sunshine and coconut, and its fluffy volume tickled my nose. I stood there for a moment, thoroughly shocked before returning her embrace. I was concerned about the mud and dirt on my battlesuit, but Riannan's was just as filthy.

"It was wonderful to meet you, Daux," she beamed, pulling back from me. "Give me your contact info so we can stay in touch?"

"Y-yes, okay," I agreed, holding out the holonav on my wrist. "It was lovely to meet you too."

As our contact info synced into each other's holonavs I looked about the room. Several students and testers alike were doing the same thing as us. It was heartwarming to see, and I was glad for not the first time that the Placement Exam was not exclusive to the students of Heliorious Academy.

"There," Riannan said when our holonavs finished syncing. "All set. I'll ping you later! We could meet up for coffee or something sometime. Emíl's mom's bakery has the best coffee and pastries!"

"That sounds great," I agreed, flushing at her enthusiasm.

I wondered what Talia would think about Riannan.

Would she be jealous? I wouldn't want that. But she was always telling me I needed more friends or at least a partner. I nearly shuddered at the thought. I was so not ready for a romantic partner, even though I was nineteen. She could make a good addition to our dream Spec Ops team though.

"Well, bye then!" Riannan chirped, hugging me once again.

"Goodbye," I replied, slightly dazed.

And then she was gone, in a cloud scented with coconut. I blinked for a second, gathering my bearings. I had just made a friend.

Chapter Three

The aches and pains the stim-pacs and inflammation sprays had alleviated hours before returned with a vengeance, leaving me prostrate on my dorm room floor. I could not even bring myself to go down to the dining hall or the showers; though, I was probably smelling quite ripe and was most certainly covered in dirt. That Emíl fellow certainly had a strong set of arms. I heartily regretted being unable to dodge the attacks he landed.

"Shower or eat?" I grumbled to myself, struggling to push myself into a sitting position when a familiar knock sounded at my door.

Though my muscles screamed at me to stay seated, I stood to answer the door, relief and happiness washing over me when it opened to reveal a smiling, freckled face. Talia… Her honey-brown eyes and impish demeanor were like the first breath of fresh air I'd taken all day.

"Hey," she said holding up the two bags she was carrying under her arms.

Her short brown hair was damp, and her skin was free of any dirt she would have been coated with inside the arena. She didn't look at all worse for wear, unlike me. Her physical exam must have gone a lot smoother than mine.

"Hi…" I replied, moving to take one of her bags.

"Ah, ah, ah," she sang, snatching them away. "You go shower, I'll set up in here. You're filthy."

Begrudgingly, I acquiesced and dragged my weary body to the showers, grumbling all the way. When I returned, freshly washed, Talia had laid out a spread of snacks across my bed and was hanging upside down off the side.

"Heya," she said when I entered the room, her eyes alight.

"I see you've made yourself comfortable," I joked, tossing my dirty battlesuit into the hamper next to the door, then hopping onto the bed.

"Of course!"

Minutes later, my comforter was littered with snack wrappers of every variety imaginable. I did not even want to think about the crumbs. A good shakedown before sleep would be necessary.

We talked about the first portion of the exam and how it went. Talia, who was more experienced with long-range weapons, picked off her melee-oriented opponent within minutes of the start of the exam. It did not surprise me one bit that she could do so, her aim had always been better than mine.

Fighting skill was a must-have for any Spec Ops hopeful. If you want to even be considered you need to have a wide range of physical abilities and have the ability to wield magic. Another aspect that could help Placement in Spec Ops was a unique magical ability. From what the public was told, nearly everyone in the organization had one.

The general public was not told much about the prestigious organization, mostly for security reasons, but those of us at the Academy heard the heroic stories of those who came before us. And of course, many alumni visited the school or even taught there once they retired from Spec Ops. They were always happy to regale us with tales of daring missions across enemy lines, research and development so complicated our heads ached trying to understand, and explosive battles with Coalition forces.

While those feats were impressive and tantalizing, they were not the only reason I wished to be among the Spec Ops ranks.

Magic.

My magic was the reason. Other people's magic was the reason. The right to use it, to even exist with it. I wanted to protect, enforce, and extend those rights to other places. The way my parents rejected such an integral part of me, even going too far as to try and obliterate it with blockers – an injectable substance that affects the neural pathways in a human's mind that allows them to use magic, dampening the power temporarily or blocking it completely for an indefinite period – molded my worldview.

Knowing the history of exploitation and oppression people with magic faced instilled a strong sense of justice in me. And how I moved forward in my life after receiving a scholarship to Heliorious Academy at thirteen.

I could help people in a legislative position or the regular military… But the desire to do so using the gifts I had been born with was just as strong. Because of that, the instructors at the academy believed my abilities would be better suited to Spec Ops, which was the way I was immediately directed towards in my coursework.

To join Spec Ops… I had never wanted anything more than to be a part of the very organization that was responsible for so many people being liberated from the Coalition and their cruelty. Not only that, but it would be a direct slap in the face to my parents and their hatred of anything magic-related.

"So, who do you think's gonna be on your team?" Talia asked – breaking into my thought – with her mouth covered in the flavor dust from her bag of chips.

"Like we're even going to be Placed in Spec Ops," I teased.

"Of course, we are! With our scores and magical prowess, they have no reason not to Place us there."

Talia and I both possessed the ability to wield Elemental magic; the most common type of magic one could manifest. Most could use more than one, but often they were able to master control over only one in their lifetime. My ability leaned more towards flame than any other of the four, and Talia's leaned towards wind. This explained my temper and her mischievousness.

Beyond Elemental magic, there were special abilities passed down from parents to children, such as my foresight which came from my mother's side of the family. Most at the Academy had a special ability, but it was just as common to only be able to wield Elemental magic.

"Sure," I agreed slyly. "Sure."

"So then," she continued, stuffing a sweetbread into her mouth, chips finished. "Who do you think is gonna be on your team?"

"I've never really thought about it," I answered honestly, picking apart the bag of chips I was eating.

"Never?" She sat up in shock, scattering her wrappers onto the floor. "What about me?"

"Well, that's a given!" I laughed. "But other than you… I've not really thought about anyone else."

Which was true. Talia was the only person I *wanted* on my team. We, of course, would need other members but to them, I gave no thought. If Talia and I could be on a team together, then I would be happy to have anyone else on my team.

"Ooh, I know! Zima Angelov!" Talia joked.

Scratch that… Anyone *but* Zima Angelov. The young man was a legend in Spec Ops and a hero to hopefuls throughout the academy. Well, some hopefuls. There were those of us who heard rumors of his terrible personality and that he was a team-breaker – someone who is incompatible or unwilling to work with other team members.

He was only a few years older than I but had quickly risen through the Spec Ops ranks. His entire team had been murdered while they were on a covert mission across enemy lines. There had been rumors that they were killed on his watch, but no one outside of Spec Ops knew what had happened. After that, he began making a name for himself in Spec Ops, earning the name Zima, meaning "cold", for his unwillingness to join a new team or get close to anyone. Also, his rare ice magic ability. He was a *legend.*

I did not know him to say if he truly was a team-breaker or not, and despite his legendary status, I knew I would rather have anyone but him on my team. Someone as uncooperative as him… I was unsure if I could handle being on a team where I could not completely trust the whole group.

"I met a girl today," I said, attempting to shift the conversation away from the Spec Ops legend. "Her name is Riannan and she's got a memory ability."

"Ooh?" Talia's honey-brown eyes sparkled mischievously.

Slapping her arm gently, I grabbed a brownie and ripped open the package. "Not like that, dummy."

"Like what then?" She sounded slightly disappointed.

"She might be a good addition to our team, is all."

Talia stared at me for a moment before pushing herself to an upright sitting position, knocking more wrappers onto the floor. I was ready for the words about to come out of her mouth. After hearing them at least a hundred times since we met on my first day at the academy, I knew when she was about to give me "the speech".

"You know, you need to let yourself have a little fun," Talia began, like I knew she would. "Meet someone, go on a date. You don't talk to anyone besides me; all you do is do schoolwork or train. We're about to take the biggest step of our lives and all you've done is prepared for this moment."

"Talia," I interrupted brownie momentarily forgotten. "I have told you before. I am not interested in dating *anyone* right now. I want to finish the exam and finally get Placed.

If I do this, then I'm out from under my parents' thumb, forever. I can have my sister live with me, and she can be safe. We both can. I don't have *time* for frivolous things like crushes or dating."

Talia frowned, crossing her arms, but when she spoke her tone was not unkind "Gods, why'd I have to pick a stick-in-the-mud for a best friend?"

Sadly, the brownie was lost in the ensuing pillow fight and I had to replace my comforter with the spare in the closet. After that, we cleaned up the rest of the mess and lounged around, continuing our earlier discussion.

Talia thought of quite a few people she'd like on our team. First, she suggested Gwyn Hier, the wraith – a magical ability related to shadowmancy that allowed the person to morph their corporeal form into shadow itself. She had several classes with him and thought he was cute. Not that it influenced her decision to want him on our team. Of course not. That would be utterly ridiculous.

There were several names mentioned on both our parts, those with stealthier magical abilities, healers, or all-out berserkers like Félix Guerrero – the teen prodigy. Kajikawa Himawari, the shadowmancer, would make an excellent addition to the all-girl team I hoped for. Ultimately, it was decided that as long as we had each other, it would not matter whom we had on a team.

Except for Zima Angelov. I'd rather stab myself in the foot.

Later on, when Talia was sprawled out on my bed – snoring like an ancient smokestack train – I sat in the swivel chair at my writing desk, cheek against my knee, observing her as she slept.

Like a creep.

When I first entered the academy at thirteen, Talia took

one look at me during dorm orientation and decided I was going to be her best friend. I resisted her at first… She was exuberant, outgoing, and friendly. Everything I was not, with her puckish freckles and twinkling brown eyes. I never knew what she saw in me.

I was not friendly. Polite, yes. But friendliness did not come easy. Making friends meant making attachments, and making attachments meant something that could be taken away from me. Not that I didn't want friends – I did, desperately – but not knowing where to begin making them and a healthy fear of rejection always held me back before.

Talia was different.

She was someone my parents would never have approved of. The Edgegrieves did not move in the same circles – while in public service like my father, her dad was on a much lower rung than the Governor of Arcania, which was in the Province of New Palogenia where the capital city of Heliorious resided. Her mother was an ex-Spec Ops operative, something my parents looked upon with disdain due to the magical requirements of the selective branch.

Talia, who was so like her parents with her reckless nature – an attribute to her affinity for the elemental magic of wind – and inability to take "no" for an answer had barged into my dorm room and hardly left since. And it was easy to let her stay.

If she were to wake up now, she would tease me for staring at her. And I would smile and take the ribbing. Because having friends meant you put up with weird, but grateful, stares and good-natured teasing.

Despite her insistence that we would one-hundred-percent be Placed in Spec Ops, and on the same team no less, I felt a sinking feeling in the pit of my stomach when I gazed upon her sleeping face. In my heart, I knew it was merely anxiety. Foresight was a sense-enhancing magic that allowed me to read the actions of my opponents as though I were predicting them, among other aspects. It was *not* the ability to see the future.

But I still could not shake the feeling. Even when I crawled into bed next to her. Even as I fell into a fitful slumber. And in the morning when I awoke to a grey Trialsday sky, Talia's hand was grasped tightly in my own as though I was afraid to let her go.

Chapter Four

Talia left my room in a whirlwind that morning, as she usually did when she slept over. A heavy sleeper, and as chaotic as her element, she never woke to her many alarms or to me moving about in my room. When she did, she always rushed, leaving a mess behind as though a tornado had passed through the space. I never minded, and she never forgot to wrap me in a bone-crushing embrace before she left.

As required, the examinees met back up in the Hall a few hours later. Riannan found me easily, her cheery expression brightening my exhausted mood instantly. Her sunshiny attitude was infectious. I was glad to see her and told her so in a low voice as the Proctor's assistants called roll.

She nudged me with an elbow and sly grin, answering as her name was called.

Once everyone was accounted for Proctor Láska ushered us into the exam room. It was large, though certainly not as big as the arena. Each wall was lined with pods, reminiscent of cryogenic pods featured in old science-fiction films. Rows of the same pods were lined down the length of the room as well. If I had not known better, I would have assumed we were going to launch into outer space.

"This is the second half of the Placement Exam," the proctor called, signaling us to pay attention. "Here you will be tested on several topics, social situations, your magic and possible abilities, and more. We will be recording your answers and brain activity via the transcribing network set up within these pods. Your holonavs will continue to be shut off during this portion. Are there any questions?"

If anyone did have any, they were likely too exhausted from the day before to voice them and kept silent.

The proctor moved on, their assistants leading the groups of people to their assigned pods. A few were given calming-pac for claustrophobia before they entered their pods, dreamlike expressions on their faces.

Riannan separated from me and gave my hand a reassuring squeeze before her pod closed on her.

My own loomed before me, its glass cover reflecting my nervousness. Despite the pleasant time I had just shortly before I, again, wished to drown. The distorted reflection I saw filled me with dread. My eyes were wide and glassy. I again thought of the ocean. Of floating. Of drowning.

A tap on my shoulder made me jump, startled. I turned and saw a proctor's assistant.

"Ms. Deveraux, do you need a pac?" she asked me.

Ah. She thought I was claustrophobic. Rather it was the fear of my failure, but it would not hurt to take something. Not that one could fail their Placement exam, but the fear of the unknown and of not completing the goals I set was nearly debilitating.

So, I nodded to the assistant, and she handed me the small pac. I placed the sphere in my mouth, punctured the soft outer shell with my teeth – allowing the liquid center to flow, and swallowed. It felt like ice as it made its way down my throat, then I felt numb. I was floating.

The assistant opened my pod, the oblong door swinging slowly upwards, and helped me inside. As the door closed, encasing me inside, I leaned into the cool, soft gel-like foam and let myself drift away.

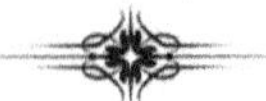

It was a bright, clear afternoon and I was seated at an outdoor table at a café, a pretty server was bringing me iced rose lemonade and scones. The sun was shining, and it was warm. A light, sweet breeze that kept outdoor patrons – like me – from overheating.

I thanked the server and tipped her generously. As I ate and drank, a small novella appeared at my table. It was one I had been meaning to read for some time but was unable to get my hands on. As I began to reach for it, there was a commotion across the street.

Calmly, I turned to look at what appeared to be a group of four young men and an older man. The young men seemed to be agitating the man, who was disheveled and dressed in the customary garb from the highland country of Eidolon. A country the Coalition had just seized a year prior that bordered New Palogenia on the large continent we shared.

He must be a part of the refugee community. I thought, placing the book back on the table.

This was not a couple of friends roughhousing with each other. It seemed like the young men were aggressive, and their harassment was becoming more physical as the encounter escalated. When one of them struck the man, I immediately stood from my seat to confront the group.

The server was at my side in a flash, imploring me to stay at the café.

"Please ma'am," she begged. "I can get you a table inside if that man is bothering you."

I was baffled. Did she seriously think that the man's presence was bothering me and not the boys attacking him?

"No, the table is fine," I replied, turning away from her. "I am just going to sort out that situation."

As I began to head across the street the server grabbed me by the arm.

"Wouldn't you like to come inside and read your book?" she asked her smile now sickly sweet. "I'm sure I could tempt you with some sweets."

No matter how much of a sweet tooth I had, none would tempt me to ignore someone being mistreated. Nor would the prospect of a book I had been meaning to read.

I looked around at the café's other patrons, but they were either engrossed in reading material, in each other, or moving inside away from the scene.

"Just ignore it," a portly man growled in my direction. "He's just a damned immigrant."

Shocked, I stared at his back. Did he just say that? I could *not* believe his audacity. I shook myself free from the server, who was practically throwing herself at me to get me to stay, and stormed toward the group of young men. Again, before I could cross the street a party of elderly women stood from their table and began chattering at me.

"Please, come sit with us!" one demanded.

"Yes, yes, leave those poor boys be," said another.

"We have questions to ask you!" the smallest one squeaked.

"A girl shouldn't insert herself into men's troubles anyway," declared the leader of the group.

As they gathered around me, I noticed more and more patrons trying to block my path. Men, women, and servers. All these people trying to keep me from going to the man's aide. Trying to drown out the cries for help he was now issuing.

I was so disgusted that I had begun to taste the bitter tang of bile in the back of my throat. How could these people possibly think this way? Every part of it was so backward and dehumanizing. I was not about to let them stop me.

Brusquely, I shoved my way through them, slapping one man's hands away when he tried to grab me by the waist. I reached the group of young men in a matter of seconds, shouting at them to stop their attacks.

They turned toward me abruptly, one of them gripping the man's red hair in his fist.

"Let him go," I demanded.

The four looked at each other and grinned.

"Don't think so," the tallest said, turning to face me again.

"Then you will be charged with assault," I said, trying to reason with them before escalating the situation physically.

"No, we won't, no one cares about *them,*" he sneered, gesturing to the Eidolon man, and the other three laughed.

"You will," I insisted and slid effortlessly into a defensive stance. "But you will be dealing with me first."

The tallest one scoffed while the others jeered at me. I could take them. They were barely older than me if that. I would not even have to hurt them. Not *too* bad.

The stockiest one charged at me with a roar, and I immediately was reminded of the arena fight I partook in earlier.

Realization and relief washed over me in an instant. The whole scene froze, the laughing boys, the crowd at the café, my attacker. Once I realized this was the exam simulation, I was able to decide whether to finish this scenario or not. The system had already recorded enough of my decision to score me, but I was not finished yet. Even if he was a figment of my imagination, I wanted to help him. I was angry at the simulations. At their bigotry, the way their sneering faces began to resemble my parents. I wanted them to pay.

I would *finish* this.

The simulation started up again and the boy hurtled toward me. I did not dodge his attack outright, letting him think he would barrel into me. But this time, I ducked right and sent a jab combination directly into his left side. He let out a yelp and lunged for me again. Jumping backward, I sent out a kick, connecting my foot with his jaw. He went sprawling to the ground, unconscious.

Cries of outrage arose from his group of friends, and another raced toward me, his fist pulled back, ready to strike.

I dodged him and grabbed him by the collar of his shirt. My arms deftly triangled around his neck as I kicked his legs from underneath him and squeezed.

He choked and struggled while his friends watched in shock and disbelief. Eventually, he went limp in my grasp, and I let him fall to the ground. The remaining two lunged for me in a double-team attack, which I was prepared for.

But I was unable to successfully dodge both of them and ended up taking a hit on the side of the head from the taller one. Thankfully, I managed to trip my other attacker and I was only dazed for a second before I righted myself.

What put me at another disadvantage, was that the one I tripped earlier had recovered from his fall and both boys were now circling me. If I were to rush at one, the other would surely grab me from behind. On the other hand, if I were to flee, they might give chase, allowing me to outrun them. But the possibility of the gang turning back on the man was too strong. That is exactly what I did *not* want.

But my decision was made for me when the Eidolon man grabbed the leader of the group from behind.

"Run, miss!" he shouted, his pale face reddened with the strain. "I don't want you to get in trouble because of me. I can handle them."

The simulation was rebelling against me. It wanted me to run, change my decision… give up my resolve.

"Not going to happen," I growled, turning just as the shorter boy had pounced.

My right fist shot out and connected with his ear, staggering him a bit. I then went for an uppercut to his jaw with my right, which he blocked. The attempt was feeble, but my attack was weak on purpose.

Before he could recognize the feint, my left fist slammed into his jaw and his eyes rolled back in his skull as he crumpled to the ground.

The leader shouted profanities at me and the man before running off, presumably in fear. With only himself left – now totally outnumbered – I let him go. Once he was out of sight, I accompanied the man to a civil station where he filed a report.

The young man had also headed to the station, and I was nearly charged with assault. The Eidolon man wished to press charges against the boys, and his injuries immediately discredited the boy's story. So, their case was thrown out in favor of the evidence the man and I brought forward. Now fully resolved, the scene began to fade to black.

Darkness surrounded me yet again. The surface I lay upon was cold against my skin. My body felt bruised all over and my bones creaked as I tried to move. Grit glued my eyes together. I had to rub them gently so they would open.

When I could finally open my eyes, it was still completely dark. I could not even see my hands in front of my face. Gingerly, I began to feel around, trying to discern where I was. I quickly realized I had been laying on the floor of some unknown building.

Feelings of desperation and fear began to creep up as I started crawling around on all fours to search for a light source or anything to discern where I was, and if I was safe. Even if I activated my foresight, it did not exactly allow me to see in the dark. As I was searching, a floodlight flashed behind me.

I jumped and whirled to see what it illuminated.

There were two people. That was all the light showed me; nothing beyond its borders was visible. Hedging closer, I attempted to get a better look at them. When I was as close as I dared, I could see that a man and a woman were bound to metal chairs with manacles around their wrists, ankles, torsos, and necks. Upon closer inspection, these manacles were not just holding them in place, they were connected to the chairs themselves and had visible wiring winding around them.

Another smaller, light flashed on near my right, startling me. It illuminated a handgun on a small table.

Then another light flashed on to my left. The small table this light illuminated held a vial of clear liquid.

"Choose or they die, Daux." A disembodied voice called.

"What?" I questioned, voice hoarse, looking around for who could have spoken.

"Choose or they die," the voice repeated.

"Who are you?" I asked, still straining my eyes to find the source of the voice.

It was no use. The darkness was blacker than black, and the floodlights did nothing to alleviate it.

"Choose," it repeated. "You have five minutes."

A frustrated sigh escaped me, and I activated my foresight. I still had trouble with the darkness, even using my magic, so I quickly began searching around the room for the voice.

"You are wasting time, Daux," it said coolly.

"Where are you?" I shouted, continuing my search despite its warning. I was going to make this person let me and these poor people out of here.

"You have three minutes left before the innocents die."

When it spoke, the woman began to spasm as if she were having a seizure. I rushed to her and knelt, asking in vain if I could do anything to help. She and the man were gagged.

Low moans of pain slipped past her gag, and I realized from the smell of burning skin and singed hair that she had been electrocuted, though not fatally.

"Why are you doing this?" I shouted frantically at the voice, still unable to place where it was coming from.

"To test you," it replied simply.

"Why?"

"We believe you know."

But I did not. Why would anyone capture innocent people and torture them? Unless they were psychopathic, I could think of no other reason.

The man began to spasm and shriek through his gag, and I scrambled to my feet.

"Okay! Okay!" I yelled, "You want me to choose, I will choose!"

The small table with the vial on it seemed the safest option and I ran to it, grabbing the bottle with trembling hands.

"You have chosen Thallium," the voice said coolly.

I nearly dropped the bottle. Thallium: a colorless, odorless, and tasteless poison. It was slow acting and provided a painful death.

"What do you want me to do with it?" I asked, my voice barely above a whisper.

"Administer it, of course."

"To whom?"

"One of the innocents," it began. "Only then may you leave."

"You can't be serious!" I shouted, slamming the bottle onto the table again.

The voice let out a low, colorless chuckle.

"Oh, but we are, Daux…" it purred. "You have another five minutes, or both of the innocents will die."

"Can I choose the gun instead?" I asked.

"You have made your choice and there is no going back."

I hissed a curse under my breath and picked the vial back up. Both the man and the woman looked at me with fear in their eyes.

I took a few steps toward them, and they began to struggle against their bonds. My stomach churned at their expressions. The man even wet himself. There was no way I could kill either one of them, not to save myself. But I could not just let them both *die*.

When I reached them, instead of administering the poison immediately I searched for a way to release them; however, the manacles had no space for keys or release mechanism in sight.

Electricity began sparking from each chair and the man and woman screamed. Even through their gags, I could hear their anguish.

I then had an idea. The voice demanded the poison be administered to an innocent or the man and woman would die.

I… I was innocent.

Before I could change my mind, I unscrewed the vial and swallowed the contents. If I got out alive, I could seek treatment. They would live.

"An unexpected choice, Daux," the voice said, and the manacles released the man and woman from their chairs. "Too bad for you, you will not reach civilization in time."

A door hidden in one of the walls slid open, sending blinding amounts of light into the very dark room. We all flinched in pain at the sudden brightness. When my eyes adjusted somewhat, I helped the man and woman with their gags and stood to lead them from the room.

"Why did you do it?" the woman croaked.

"What do you mean?" I asked.

"Why did you take the poison?" she reiterated. "You heard them. You won't be able to get to the antidote in time."

Ah. That. Though thallium was a slow-acting poison, I had already begun to feel stomach cramps. Sweat began to drip down my forehead. My anxiety was beginning to take over.

"I would not let either of you die to save myself," I responded, taking a few shaky steps toward the door. "And who knows, they could be lying."

With a look of gratefulness and compassion, the woman took my hand and walked out the door with me.

"We'll get you out of this," the man said from behind.

"Out of what?" I asked, turning to look at him over my shoulder.

"This simulation," he said as if it were obvious. "We can't let you die in here. You saved us."

The woman, still holding my hand, was nodding in agreement.

"It's time to wake up Daux."

That was when the simulation stopped. I was not going to die, and no one was in danger. Relief washed over me, and I chose to end the simulation immediately.

It's going to be a lovely day today. I thought with a smile as I watched my small son playing in his sandbox through my open kitchen window. We were going to go over the days of the week and months of the year again. He was doing so well that he could remember them in order at just three years old.

The Days of the Week poem was a bit tricky for a toddler, but saying it along with him seemed to be helping him to remember it. I was proud of him

"Godsday, Mournsday, Trialsday, Warsday, Sorrowsday, Gravesday, and Victorisday:

One for the Gods who left

One to mourn the dead

One to remember the trials and tribulations of our forbearers

One to remember the Great War

One for the grieving parents

One for the thousands whose lives were taken from them far too early

And one for the outcome of the war, so we never take

our freedoms for granted."

It was a pre-schooling requirement that children know the days of the week and months of the year. Children were also required to know other basic skills like using the bathroom unassisted and polite interactions with other people. Once we went over the days of the week, we would sing about the months of the year: Gynisis, Serenitie, Katalyst, Leumièr, Vybrance, Melodie, Bienveillance, Victoris, Aurrath, Trenquillity, Reflexion, Gloireaux, Reyquiem.

There was no poem to go along with the months of the year, so to help my son remember them we would sing them in order. Strangely enough, I could not recall his voice singing the months along with mine. I had been doing this with him for a few days. Why could I not remember the sound of his voice?

I looked down at my heavily pregnant belly and felt... unsettled.

I don't have a son... I frowned as I rubbed my stomach. *Do I?*

I was very obviously pregnant. I did not doubt that. But I did not remember giving birth to a child or having a partner to create another child with. I had never been interested in having children after my terrible childhood. So, having a loving partner and son made me incredibly happy. Didn't it?

"What is wrong with me today?" I asked myself aloud.

Of course, I was happy. I had no reason to question it. Of course, I had a son. I had a family. I had never been happier.

Then why could I not remember? Why could I not remember my son's voice? Why didn't I remember giving birth? It was supposed to be painful. Surely, I would remember something like that. Neither could I remember my marriage to my partner. Maybe we decided not to marry? I should remember that too, though. I could not even remember what they looked like.

I glanced at my son out the window. he was still playing peacefully, oblivious to my turmoil. He looked exactly like me. Golden hair, green eyes, even the same shape as my lips. I could see nothing of another person in him.

That can't be too unusual, can it? I thought. *First children often favor one parent over the other.*

But I could not shake the thought that something was off about the child. Or the fact that something was off about my pregnancy. Or that I had the strange impulse to try and forget my nagging thoughts and begin thinking normally again.

That was not so strange in and of itself, but the impulse would not go away. It was almost as if it were not an internal impulse… but an external one. As if some outside force was pushing me to forget whatever was worrying me.

No matter how hard I thought though, I could not remember what I had forgotten. I could not remember why having a son was strange. Why being pregnant was wrong. Why my marriage, or lack thereof, was odd.

Amid my musings, a strikingly beautiful man walked inside. His eyes were thickly rimmed with dark lashes and were the color of the icy, winter-blue sky. His hair was incredibly black against his pale skin. A broad grin was on his full lips and his eyes lit up when he saw me.

This stranger crossed the room and knelt in front of me, taking my hands in his.

"How is my darling wife today?" he asked. His voice had a soft, almost tenor-like quality to it.

Hearing him speak almost put me at ease. A rush of affection ran through me as he lifted my hands to his mouth and kissed them. This was, unquestionably, my husband. I loved him with my whole being.

But something still unsettled me. Why could I not remember his name?

Why could I not remember him if I loved this person

as much as I did? Why could I not remember giving birth to our child?

I was so, so confused.

He must have sensed my uncertainty because his face fell and his hands clenched tighter around my own.

"What's wrong, love?" He asked, worry and concern coloring his voice and expression.

Numbly, I shook my head, unable to form words. I would sound senseless if I told him what I was thinking. But I did not think I could act like I knew what was going on. At least not convincingly

"Nothing," I managed, with what I hoped was a reassuring smile.

"Is it the baby?" he asked, sounding more troubled than before.

Upon reflection, perhaps my smile was overkill.

"No, no," I shook my head. "At least, it's not anything bad. I think I am just tired."

Though still worried, he seemed placated by that and kissed my hands again.

"I love you, Daux." He squeezed my fingers gently.

Before I was forced to say it back a clattering came from the back door and a shrill cry of happiness filled the house. My son, *our* son, came hurtling into the room to his father and into his arms. My husband hugged him tightly and kissed the top of his head.

I smiled at their affection, regardless of my fear and confusion. I had longed for such a family, the one I was unable to have in my childhood. This was like a dream.

Wait... Is this merely a dream? I thought, my brow furrowing.

It was not possible. It was much too real. The fatigue of pregnancy, the kisses my husband placed on my hands, and the sound of my family's voices and laughter. There was not even that strange outline of darkness surrounding my vision which only appeared while I was dreaming.

No, this could not be a dream. But it was not real, that much was for certain.

But what I would not give for it to be... I thought sorrowfully.

My husband and child turned to me, each holding out a hand for me to take. And I did. I grasped their hands as if they were the only things tethering my body to this planet, and forced myself to wake up. I was not meant for this life – idyllic and sweet. The simulation ended without incident.

I awoke in a dark room. I heard muffled breathing. Sobs. Then I realized the room was not dark – my eyes were covered. When I tried to uncover them, I found my hands were bound. I immediately recognized it as another simulation, but it was far too soon to end it. I had not been in long enough for them to record any decisions.

Instantly I felt a sharp tug on my bindings and was free. I yanked the blindfold from my eyes and saw in the dim light dozens of people, my parents among them. Talia was behind me. Nearly sagging with relief at the sight of her honey-brown eyes and freckled face, I thanked her for freeing me, but she held a finger to her lips.

Then the pieces of the puzzle clicked together. In this simulation, we were all being held prisoner, and Talia and I were the only ones free. We needed to get these people out of here. Talia was here to help, as she always was. If Talia was anything, she was reliable.

And she was the only person who would be of the most help in this situation. With her affinity for wind, she was as stealthy as she was destructive, which was in my favor. But that seemed to be the only thing in my favor. The room only had one exit, and there were elderly and children among the prisoners.

And what was worse, my father was there, likely

judging me in silence. As if he believed this was my fault. He probably did. But that was no matter. Not when there were lives in danger. I would not let probabilities under my skin.

It made sense that he was captured along with the rest of us. His position as one of the thirteen governors of the NAF allowed him a lot of influence in the public and political sphere. The thirteen governors represented the thirteen territories of varying sizes and populations, and Arcania was one of the largest, presiding over more than half the Province of New Palogenia.

Governors were chosen through a similar process to the Placement Exam simulations and were in office until they stepped down, retired, or passed away. How my father was elected through this process was something I could not understand as he hated what the NAF stood for, but something must have changed in his viewpoint after he was tested. Otherwise, he would not have been able to take office.

The power my father and the other twelve governors had was only checked by each other and their lawmaking and voting powers. But there was another governing body that kept the governors in line, and that was the Chancellors of the NAF. They were also a body of thirteen people – elected similarly to the governors – who had the final say in many of the governors' decisions and all military campaigns against the Coalition.

This meant my father's capture was politically motivated and had to have been tied to the Coalition. Which troubled me greatly considering his ideas about magic and his secret alignment with the Coalition. Of course, they would target him as the Governor of Arcania. But was it possible they knew of his leanings?

Talia and I crept about the room, searching for any exits or weapons we could use to defend the captives. There were none, save the barred cell door. We both let out a sigh of defeat.

"What should we do?" I asked her.

"Why are you asking me? You're the one with great problem-solving skills." She brushed her short brown hair out of her eyes.

"I need help, Tali," I explained calmly. "There is no way I can get all of these people out by myself."

"Duh, right," she sighed, tapping the heel of her palm on her forehead. "Okay, well, let's start by releasing a few of the stronger-looking prisoners in case a guard or someone else shows up."

I nodded in agreement. We quickly began to free the strongest-looking people in the small room and explained the situation to them. They were all quite receptive to what was happening and remained relatively calm.

The chaos started when we began to free the other people with us. My mother was in hysterics and my father was incensed, shouting about everything under the sun. Thankfully, I had saved them until last, though that only seemed to worsen their moods.

Before I could begin to try and calm them a tall, dark woman with coiled hair stepped up.

"Shut up and calm your wife, Mr. Deveraux," she said. "We're in a life-or-death situation right now and we can't have either of you endangering anyone."

My father glared at her, but thankfully shut his mouth and tried somewhat unsuccessfully to calm my mother.

I breathed a sigh of relief and thanked the woman, who waved me off and introduced herself as May.

Once we freed all the prisoners in the room, we began to sort everyone into groups.

Each group had at least four strong adults or teenagers; the third and fourth groups were mostly elderly and children. All four of the groups were made up of about fifteen people, including a healthy adult to lead them. When all the groups were formed, the leaders of each group met up to discuss our plan to escape.

I lead the first group, which included my parents. Talia led the second, May led the third, and a large man – Finn – led the fourth.

"I think our best bet is to overpower a guard when they enter the room," May suggested, and Talia agreed with her.

"But if we wait too long, we may be discovered," Finn argued.

"Either way," I interjected with a wave of my hand. "We need to escape. Someone needs to open that door because there is no way to do so from the inside. Perhaps we should create enough trouble, so a guard comes to us?"

The other three looked at me quizzically and I returned their looks with a bland smile. "My parents should be willing to kick up a fuss."

Their gazes shifted behind me to my father and mother, then back to me and they all nodded, faces grim.

"When the guard comes in two of us will overpower them," I began. "Then I will take my group and scout ahead. Talia's group will wait for our signal then the rest of you will follow behind her."

"But what about the old people and children in our groups?" May asked. "If we are attacked then our groups will be the ones to fall first."

"I agree," Finn agreed. "We need to move to the middle and be in between Talia and your groups for better protection."

Their points made sense. With the elderly and children in the back, I initially thought that they would be better protected from an ambush from the front. But if there were an attack from behind, it would be better for them to be in between the two stronger groups for protection.

"That sounds safer," I amended, thinking through our options. "Okay, once Talia and I have cleared the area for frontal ambushes, your groups will fall into place between ours."

"Okay." May nodded. "Let's get going."

With a tight throat and a stomach full of apprehension I walked with the others toward my parents. I knew they would not agree to help anyone here willingly, even if they got to complain. We had to engage them in an argument or upset them in some way to begin our plan's first phase.

"Father," I began, but I need not have been so concerned. He had already begun shouting as soon as I opened my mouth.

"Daux, I will not be kept in the dark. I demand to know what is going on and how you got us into this mess," he yelled.

I fought hard not to roll my eyes. Of course, he blamed me. I had been correct in my earlier presumptions.

"Father," I said again. "I have no idea how we were captured or why. There is no need for all this blustering."

That did it, as I knew it would. His normally handsome face turned blotchy and red with anger. What I did not expect was the slap.

My neck popped loudly as my head turned with the force of his palm hitting my cheek. My father had not laid a hand on me since I was a child. Not since my magic manifested. Before I could even recover from his assault, Talia was on him, shouting and repeatedly trying to strike my father. Finn and May had to pull her off him. My mother was shrieking, May was shouting at her to shut up, which only served to make her scream louder.

This was going better than expected. A small, cat-like smile curved my mouth upwards, despite the pain in my face and neck. It was only a matter of time before the commotion we had caused brought at least one guard down to control the situation, and we would be ready.

Quickly, while my parents were occupied with Talia and the other team leaders, I explained our plan to several of the able-bodied adults with the instructions to pass the information along to all who could follow. Word spread quickly among the people, and they began to regroup, clutching children or old folks to their sides.

Within minutes two armed guards burst through the door and began shouting for order. And within a few minutes more we had them overpowered and bound. I had taken the liberty of relieving them of their keycards, handing one to Talia and keeping the other for myself, since we were heading the escape.

I told my group to wait for my command before following me. Once I scoped out the hallway, I returned to the room for them.

"If you don't hear anything in about two-to-three minutes then it will be safe to follow us," I told Talia before addressing the other two groups.

"Once Talia and I have led our groups out, you're to follow within two minutes of each other. Then we will all meet up in the corridor and the last two groups will merge into the middle of Talia and mine."

I waited for the nods of the two group leaders before heading out, keeping my parents at the back of the group. I stationed two large men with them so they would keep silent. We could not have them ruining the whole escape operation on account of their selfishness. Once we had made it around the end of the corridor, I signaled for everyone to halt. In my head I had been counting to one hundred and twenty, waiting for Talia to make an appearance.

A sigh of relief escaped me when she showed up a few seconds later, her group following close at her heels. Talia gave me a reassuring smile and began directing a few people into a formation.

Again, I had been counting, looking for anything that could hinder our escape. So far, nothing; though, that did not mean something was not there.

Soon enough, Finn's group appeared and was herded in between my group and Talia's. I instructed my group to form around them slightly, creating a barrier between any possible attacks from the front. All the while I was counting another one-hundred and twenty seconds.

May's group exceeded that amount of time, and I was beginning to worry when they also rounded the corner, unharmed. I slowly let out a huge exhale, reminding myself not to hold my breath.

Once the last group was herded into the middle, we set off, Talia created a protective barrier in the rear.

Carefully and quietly, we crept along the dark halls, somehow remaining unseen by our captors. It was entirely too suspicious. There were not even security cameras that I could see in this area, even with my foresight activated. That did not necessarily mean there were not any, but it made me wonder: if there really were no cameras, then why? And if there were, then why was no one stopping us from escaping?

We had already made it through several doors with our stolen keycards without getting caught, and I grew more anxious every second. Why was the response time to our scuffle in the cell so quick, when we were practically waltzing through this building like we owned the place? A growing feeling of dread began to spread throughout my body. Something was very, very, wrong.

We were not just being *that* stealthy. There was no way.

Someone had to have planned this. But who? I was unable to get to Talia, not without alerting the others to my panic. That would be disastrous. And I could not trust the others, not fully.

I was positive an ambush was coming, or something much worse. Someone in the cell with us had to be in on it. This escape attempt could be so easy. It was *much* too easy.

Dammit! I thought. *I should have thought of this sooner!*

How could I have been so naïve? Of *course,* someone was a traitor. Surely, there could still be a way to protect everyone and escape. There had to be.

But as soon as we made it into the next room guards descended upon us.

My first instinct, along with the other able members of my group, was to attack. But something held me back. I wanted to know who was responsible for this. The guards may harm those people but would hold back. So, I kept to the rear. Keeping myself in between the defenseless and the guards.

Talia's group surged forward and into the fray, but she kept back with me, watching. Only fighting those who came too close. Magic – special abilities, and elemental alike – sounded throughout the room along with cries of pain.

They kept coming. And coming. Our fighting members were beginning to exhaust all their magical energy and stamina, as were Talia and I when a stream of armed soldiers began to pour into the space.

"*Stop!*" I screamed to my companions, halting my attack immediately.

But they did not. And the guards opened fire.

Three were killed before our group put their hands in the air and surrendered. Ten more were injured. A few were children. Screams and sobs filled the room. I felt sick. Furious and sick. Whoever was responsible for this would pay.

My father came up behind me and placed his hand on my shoulder. Naturally, he would be hiding with the weaker members instead of helping us fight our way out. I turned my head to look at him and he was smiling, which was odd. My mother was next to him, smiling too, her mouth a red slash against her pale skin. Then they walked to the front of the room where the guards stood, guns trained on us, without their hands raised.

I wanted to scream at them to stop, to stay back, but the words would not leave my throat. My father greeted the chief guardsman, who was marked by the obvious crest on the bulletproof vest he wore. The chief shook his hand and handed him a pair of handguns. *His* handguns. The antique ones he was so very proud of.

My mind was reeling. I knew my father was dishonest. I knew he was a bully. I knew he was demeaning and abusive, but I never thought he would sell me out. Never had I thought he would sell out a whole group of innocent people.

"Why?" I yelled, storming to the front of the room with my hands raised.

"Why what, Daux?" he asked in his oily-smooth voice.

"Why have you done this?"

He laughed. It was a dark, sickening sound.

"I offered the Coalition something important in exchange for mine and your mother's safety," he said, cocking one of the guns. "I knew you would never accept the protection I could grant you this way, so I left you out of the deal."

I scoffed. He was right of course, but he still could have tried to protect me. Or anyone else for that matter.

"Sorry darling," my father sneered, aiming the gun at me. "It had to be done."

And he pulled the trigger.

But I saw this coming. I jumped left, out of the way of his shot before he could pull the trigger. A pained scream rang out behind me, and with a sinking feeling, I realized he had hit someone. Turning to look, I saw that it was only a wound to the leg and not something more serious. The man hit would be able to survive if I could just help them escape. An injury was a sacrifice I was willing to make to save everyone's lives.

Before he or his guards could react, I charged my father, knocking him to the ground. I grabbed his gun, grappling with him, but he would not let go. My arms screamed in pain as I tried to wrest the firearm from his grip.

It went off once, twice, and a third time into the ceiling before I wrenched it away from him and placed the barrel on his forehead.

My mother was screaming at the guards to shoot me. I would have found the situation humorous had it not been so dire.

Luckily, they would not be able to shoot me without harming my father. They could not risk that. They needed him for whatever plans they had to carry out. For now, I was safe.

"Drop your weapons," I shouted at the guards, pulling back the hammer of the gun. "If you don't, I will shoot him."

I knew that if I shot my father, then everyone else could die; however, if he died, then the Coalition would not get what they needed. And if my father were to live and get away from me, then we would all die anyway.

"You're bluffing, Daux," my father scoffed.

"Am I?" I asked and aimed the gun at his abdomen.

I pulled the trigger and he screamed. My father cursed me and writhed where I held him down. My mother was shrieking.

"Drop your weapons!" I commanded, pointing the gun back to my father's head.

Warm, red blood – my father's blood – was soaking my legs. I did not care. I could not think of it at that moment. There were innocent people to save.

The clatter of weapons settling on the stone floor was the only thing that pulled my gaze from my father's, his eyes filled with undiluted rage. They had all obeyed. So, I was confused when I heard another gunshot and felt a searing pain in my left shoulder.

I looked down and my father pulled his other gun out and shot me. Foolish. I should have taken it away immediately, but my focus was on the one he had previously trained toward me.

Blood gushed down my shoulder as I waited for the next shot from my father. But it did not come.

He seemed to be in terrible pain from the wound I inflicted on him and was having trouble aiming. I realized he had probably tried to aim for my heart but missed due to his wound.

Lucky me. I thought and tossed the gun I had taken away from my father to Talia who had made her way to the front. Talia pointed the gun at my mother, who had not stopped shrieking. She stopped when she noticed Talia aiming at her.

With a sinister grin, I dug my index and middle finger into the gunshot wound in my father's abdomen. Ah, yes. There was the wickedness he had tried to instill in me. Screaming in pain and horror, he dropped his second gun, and I grabbed it, placing the barrel at his head yet again.

"I know if I shoot him, you will probably kill us all," I shouted, making eye contact with my father again. "But if he dies, then no one gets what they want. If you let all of us go, without trouble, I will leave him at your borders in no more harm than has already come to him. That way, we all get what we want."

My father cried out incoherently, but the chief gestured to a guard, who used his keycard to open the facility exit. I stood and pulled my father to his feet, ignoring his groans of pain.

With the gun pressed into his side, I lead the way out of the compound, gesturing to the others to follow.

I forced my father to move outside, pushing him with my left arm, before realizing I was not feeling any pain. I should be feeling pain. My shoulder had been shot. It should be immobile. What was going on? It was impossible not to be feeling pain at this moment.

I had to be dreaming. That was it. I was dreaming. Nothing this horrible would happen in real life. Could it?

Wake up, wake up, wake up, I chanted in my head as I marched everyone out of the compound.

The continuation screen popped up. Just as I had thought, this was not real. A mere simulation. A figment of my subconscious. I was not injured. My father was not a traitor. No one was dead. With a surge of relief, I ended the simulation.

Chapter Five

This time, finally, I awoke for real. My palms slammed against the glass of my simulation pod. The coolness of it was sharper than any sensation in the simulations. Even the pain. I could feel the sweat running down my body in rivulets as opposed to the mild sense of perspiration I had previously experienced.

Oh, *Gods*, I wanted out. Out of this *thing*. The pac I had been given had already worn off, and I began to feel like the walls were closing in on me, crushing me. My lungs strained to bring in more air than they were capable of containing and my head spun violently.

As if they were acting of their own accord, my hands began to bang against the glass. I would tear it down if I needed to, rip it open, but I just wanted *out*. And out I fell, knees and palms landing hard on the tile beneath me, bruising them.

Medics swarmed into the room as others began exiting their pods, some in the same condition I was in. Two pulled me to my feet, offering all kinds of sprays or medications. All I wanted was to lie down and forget.

Those simulations had shown me things I never wanted to see. Had me experience scenarios I never wished to experience. It felt like something inside of me had broken open and salty ocean water was pouring into the wound. I was going to be sick.

Thankfully, as I turned my head to empty my stomach, I was able to avoid vomiting on anyone's person or their shoes. Nor was I the only one to become sick. That would save me from embarrassment later.

Quickly and efficiently, medics injected me with anti-nausea medications and handed me an anti-anxiety pac. Operating as if I were on autopilot, I bit into the sphere and let the cool liquid run down my throat, nearly calming me on the spot. A floating sensation took over my body as I was led from the room.

When I made it back to my dormitory, I did not manage to rest as the medics instructed me to. My bed, which had aided me nicely in sleep since I had started the Academy, was no longer comfortable. None of my many books could distract me. No games to play, nor friends to talk to as Talia lived in another dorm and would possibly be conducting her simulation or in the same state as me.

So, I merely lay there, staring up at the ceiling. Some instructors had said that the psychological side effects of the simulations would be uncomfortable and may even produce feelings of severe anxiety or depression; though, these side effects would merely be temporary.

I hoped this was true. While the pac had helped, I still felt… empty. As if the whole ordeal I just experienced was for naught. As if nothing mattered even though I wanted it to.

Hopefully this doesn't last… I thought as I lay wide awake, exhausted, staring up at the ceiling.

Warsday, Sorrowsday, and Gravesday passed along with several medical checks after the Placement exam. Thankfully, I was given a clean bill of health and sent on my way. Though I had not experienced anything so bad as the first night after the simulations, I still felt a twinge of that hollowness in my chest threatening to overtake me.

The medics merely told me to check back if my symptoms persisted.

It will be fine, I had thought. *This happens frequently enough. They should know what they're talking about.*

And that was that. I had other things to concern myself with. However, those *other things* included informing my parents of my upcoming Placement Ceremony. They would, of course, receive the official notification from the Academy, but I knew they would cause me any grievance they could if I were to neglect to inform them myself. I knew they would not accept a simple message from my holonav.

So, I did. I chose the finest stationery I owned – a thick, cream-colored paper with the family seal embossed on all four corners, a lovely stylized letter "D" for our surname backed by ancient great swords and fire-breathing wyverns. Then I picked up my ink and pen and wrote them for the first time since I had been accepted into the Academy.

Each stroke of my pen was difficult. The scene from my final simulation kept replaying in my mind. My father's cold, dead eyes as he aimed his firearm at me. The sadistic satisfaction I got from digging my fingers into the wound I inflicted upon him.

I would not lie to myself: I hated my father. I hated him with my entire being, but that simulation scared me. Though I knew he was a selfish, egotistical arse, I was *shocked* that my mind would conjure up such a scenario. What upset me the most was my reaction to it. I *wanted* to hurt my father. I *wanted* to scare my mother. Their fear and pain gratified me.

Was it because they were the villains in that scenario? Or was it for some deep-seated issue I developed? I typically disliked violence. Sparring was exhilarating and a good release for the emotions I kept stored away, but I actively disliked causing harm. If the situation called for it – as was the case in my first simulation – then I had no qualms about participating in a fight; though, I did not care for harming people.

So why did I *like* hurting them? There was probably some psychological explanation in which my subconscious mind decided to punish my parents for their wrongdoings and years of emotional abuse. Or it was just a simulation.

Either scenario was possible I supposed, though the latter was preferable.

Vigorously, I shook my head and finished the letter to my parents, signing and dating it – Victorisday the fourth of Katalyst – then sealing it and marking the address before I left my room to take it to the mail center in the lobby. From there, the letter would be transported via a combination of a transportation spell and tech to my parent's letter receptacle. This function would need to be reset by the transportation magic specialist after a specific amount of uses, and thankfully I got there in time before the reset. Hopefully, they would be in to see it. If not, they were bound to complain about it coming late when they came for the Placement Ceremony.

And they would not miss it. Their social standing was very important to them, even if they were ashamed of me and my magic.

The walk back to my room was uneventful, and the rest of the evening I spent in there was even more so. I declined my dinner – I did not wish to interact with anyone, even Talia who had messaged me numerous times with silly images and invitations to join her for dinner – and sat in my room, staring at the ceiling yet again. All I had left to do was prepare for the Placement Ceremony and wait for my parent's reply to my letter.

I did not have to wait long. Their response came in bright and early Godsday morning and was as short as it was swift, which I expected. Though a brief missive, it felt like it weighed hundreds of kilograms in my hand. I would have preferred not to open it, but I did.

It read:

Daux,

We will be expecting a formal invitation from the Academy before our departure. Thankfully you graduated from that uncivilized excuse for an academy before you were old enough to disgrace your mother and me. We are hopeful you have given up the notion of joining Spec Ops or any other magic-related position, as it is not befitting to our family.

Expect our arrival soon,
Your Father

I audibly snorted when I read the letter, if one could call it such. Yes, he *would* be worried about me embarrassing him instead of my scoring and accomplishments; still concerned about status rather than my desire to join Spec Ops. I anticipated nothing less. Before I knew what I was doing the letter was crumpled in my hand. I looked down at it, shrugged, and threw it in the recycling.

I had a Placement to prepare for.

It was mere days before the Placement Ceremony that my parents and sister arrived. My sister Amalie – seven years my junior – greeted me enthusiastically with a hug and many congratulations. My parents were much less animated. Times, places, seating, and guests were my father's concerns. My mother complained of my slightly tanned skin, split ends, and lack of makeup.

The latter was hardly my fault, as their arrival had woken me early in the morning and I had no time to prepare before having to greet them in the spartan dormitory lobby. As for my mother's other complaints, I regularly wore sun protection and had a hair appointment later in the day. This seemed to placate her, but she still scolded me about other minuscule things regarding my appearance.

To answer my father's demands, I had a list from the

Academy printed with all the necessary information sans the guest list for confidentiality reasons. He seemed irritated by that, for he and my mother prided themselves on their social circle. But there was nothing to be done about it.

Amalie, who was holding my hand, gave me an understanding – yet apologetic – smile and a reassuring squeeze. I was glad for her presence. I often wondered how she remained so sweet-spirited while being raised by our parents. Often, I hoped I had some sort of influence on her, but our communications were monitored, and I never visited home. I wasn't allowed.

She seems to have turned out okay, though. I thought with a hint of undeserved pride.

"Daux, darling," my mother drawled, running her fingers through the few dead ends I had on my hair. "I do hope you worked towards at least a *traditional* career. Such as the military, like me, or something in government that will be useful to your father."

I bristled at her words but kept my plastered-on expression as polite as possible. They never approved of my desire to join Spec Ops. They were secretly Neo-Traditionalists – a group of people who held to the Coalition's ideals of exploitation of Eturnus and shared its hatred of magic, believing it to be a curse from the Gods. My parents hated *my* magic in particular. Hated that they could have created me so flawed in their minds. Of course, my mother would now try and push me towards a military or non-combatant career now, before my Placement of all times.

She probably felt more out of control than she ever had.

"You know how your father would love you to work towards taking over for him as governor of the province one day," she continued, ignoring my discomfort.

"That isn't exactly how that works, Mother…" I started but was swiftly brushed off.

"It's all in the name, dear," my father interrupted,

never once looking up from his messaging screen on his holonav. "They will see 'Deveraux' and associate us together. You would barely have to campaign. And you're a Deveraux, you would pass the competency and law exams with flying colors."

I was not entirely sure what my father meant by his last statement, because he certainly disregarded quite a few of our laws to get his way. Also, yes, I was competent in the law and cultural aspects of the nations that combined under the NAF, but that was merely because I studied hard. I kept my mouth shut on that topic.

"We will see what my results are at the ceremony," I said, ignoring my mother's ocean-eyed stare.

My heart was thundering in my chest and sweat was gathering beneath my clothes. I had not been this nervous since I left for the Academy at thirteen. It was funny how only a stare could bring these feelings rushing back.

"Well, I hope it's in intelligence," Mother quipped, tossing her shiny hair. "That's what I did, you know. Hardly had to get my hands dirty. *And* I was able to snag a good husband."

Despite my fear, I had to physically restrain myself from rolling my eyes. *Father?* A *good* husband? Had she forgotten all the times I tried to get between them during their arguments? Had she forgotten the night one of their fights triggered a dangerous outburst of my magic when I was only five years old?

It appeared that she had.

"Intelligence would be a good foothold into a government position later on," Father agreed. "And it would keep you from using your curse. I cannot believe they are still pushing magic-based courses at the Academy, much less in our other territories."

I bit my tongue yet again. He was one of the NAF's thirteen governors and yet he continued to hold on to his horrifying beliefs that magic was somehow a curse from the

Gods. A punishment. Mother's magic was all but redundant after years and years of blockers. They had tried the same with me.

I could not for the life of me, understand how someone could hold such an important position in our government – a government which was created during a civil war to defend people like me, people with magic – and still think something so beautiful, so awe-inspiring was a curse.

"Mother?" Amalie asked, interjecting herself into the conversation.

"Yes, Amalie?" Our mother replied, barely looking up from her holonav device which she used to plan her many events. At least she had gone back to ignoring my appearance.

"I'd like to stay with Daux at her dorm," she said. "If I may."

"Darling," Mother began, without affection. "We already have a nice suite in the city, and you'll have a room all to yourself."

"But I would like to stay with Daux," Amalie insisted, clinging tighter to my hand.

My mother rolled her eyes and glared at my sister. Instinctively, I tensed ready to push Amalie behind me if our mother started in on her. I'd been doing so since she was born. Since I was just seven years old.

"Amalie, sweetheart, you haven't even asked Daux if you could stay the night with her. That is incredibly rude."

Before Amalie could respond I interjected: "I'm fine with it, Mother. I have plenty of room."

Open-mouthed, my mother seemed at a loss for words. Father finally looked up from his holonav in exasperation.

"Annette," he drawled. "It's fine. She'll just be in the way at the suite anyway."

Mother's mouth snapped shut, and she plastered a sickly-sweet smile on her red-painted lips.

"Of course, dear," she simpered, fluttering her hands

around my sister in sham affection "Amalie, we will send your things from our rooms. Have fun with your sister."

I rolled my eyes and watched as Father offered Mother his arm, nodded curtly to me, and walked away without another word.

Gently, I squeezed Amalie's hand and smiled at her.

"We've got some time before dinner," I whispered conspiratorially, staring at our parent's backs. "Why don't we walk around a little? I can show you some of my favorite places?"

Amalie grinned – it was bright, like sunshine – and we set off.

For hours I showed my little sister monuments of the civil war, monuments of the people who fought to claim freedom from oppression, a small bakery I frequented – and bought her a treat – as well as a beautiful flower garden I often ran in. She chattered insistently during my hair appointment, asking all sorts of questions about methods and tools. It was the most amount of time we had spent alone together since I had left for the Academy, and I enjoyed every moment of it.

By the time my dormitory served dinner, we had returned, famished and slightly sticky from our walks and the heat. The sweets had not deterred our appetites one bit. We feasted on deliciously fire-roasted vegetables, baked and curried meats, and large slabs of flatbread until we could hardly walk.

When Amalie and I arrived back at my dorm room her things had already been delivered, as I had expected. We received no note from our parents, which was also expected. Amalie did not seem disheartened by this and excitedly flitted about my dorm. I sent her off to the showers with a laugh and promised to show her around after.

After we both showered, we raced through the long corridors, giggling uncontrollably as we ran past other residents and their families. We ran and ran until Amalie got a stitch in her side and had to be carried back to my dorm room.

It was quite an experience getting Amalie to prepare herself for bed. I had never seen her so excited. I, myself, had never had a sleepover before coming to the Academy and meeting Tali so her excitement was no surprise to me; however, it made me that much sadder for my sister.

To have no friends – or family close in age – is a very unhappy predicament for a child to be in. It was one I had also dealt with. That, coupled with the fact that our parents provided us with little to no opportunity to make or visit with potential friends, was frustrating. I had no idea if they did so intentionally, or because they were too absorbed in themselves to notice, but such a life made it difficult to relate to those around me. I imagined it was much the same for Amalie.

Despite the surge of anger, which I had anticipated feeling toward my parents, I merely felt a numb sort of disappointment. The way they treated Amalie was no different from the way they treated me. I had hoped once I went away to school that they would care for her more than I did, perhaps even showing her affection every so often. But that was not the case.

It was apparent in the way Amalie leaned into me as I brushed and braided her hair before bed that night, or the way she had clung to my hand the whole day – as if I would disappear if she let go. My poor, poor sister. Her life was nearly devoid of care and love. I determined that as soon as I was able, I would persuade my parents to let her live with me.

Thankfully, she had not manifested any signs of magical ability, which is very common even in families whose magical genes are strong. There were no blocker syringes in her luggage. Unless they were using blockers with effects that lasted months rather than days or weeks. I was too afraid to ask.

By the time I had worked up the courage to do so, Amalie had fallen asleep. It was a long before I could, and I used that time to prepare for the upcoming ceremony. Nothing grand was expected on my part, but I at least wanted to be ready. And so, I practiced my Placement lines until I could hardly keep my eyes open.

As gently as I could without disturbing Amalie, I slipped into bed, wrapping a blanket around my shoulders. She had cocooned herself in nearly all of them. I smiled. She was so adorable. Her face was the last thing I saw before I fell into my deep slumber.

Chapter Six

Amalie and I spent the next few days joined at the hip, despite other graduates' siblings attempting to get her to join them to play or eat. I encouraged her to make friends; though, she refused, insisting I was the person she came here to see. I gave up after she began to get frustrated with me.

Our parents did not spare a moment of their time to check up on either of us. Which Amalie was okay with, despite my irritation.

"We don't need them," she had said, grinning up at me with her sunshine smile. "We're having fun all on our own."

And we were. But that did not detract from my annoyance. By the day of the Placement Ceremony, they had still not contacted me to check on her, and I was at my limit with them.

When Amalie and I made it to the Ceremony Hall, we were both finely dressed and presentable. Even my mother would be unable to find fault with either of our appearances.

The Hall was a massive, oblong-shaped building with a ceiling made of thick panes of colored glass. Its walls were sloped outward to give it a rounded effect on the inside as well as the exterior. Inside rather plain, pale ecru-colored marble made up the floor, stairs, and decorative columns.

The seating started on the highest row and ran down into the ground where the stage was built into one wall. It was built this way to resemble the theaters of ancient times, in which the actors' voices could be heard from anywhere in the audience.

Dressed in a deep purple tea-length gown, Amalie made her way to sit with a group of adolescents who were also staying with their siblings in the dorm. I had no idea where my parents would be sitting, and this group was near the stage, so I would be able to keep an eye on my sister.

I – as per tradition – was dressed in my armor. Graduating students are either required to wear their uniforms or if they were combat-oriented students, their hand-crafted armor. We were required to learn how to create our protective gear and weapons in case we needed repairs during a critical mission or battle.

The rich, blood-red colored armor I had crafted was designed after knights' armor, but of a more durable and flexible material. Its surface was detailed with mythical creatures such as wyverns, winged dragons, and chimeras in a pale, platinum gold. Taking inspiration from the ancient blacksmiths, I molded these creatures into my armor to instill fear into potential opponents.

I had also worked small, lace-like designs – from the same gold color – into the metal giving the armor a shimmering effect when I moved. A durable type of chainmail was worn underneath for an added measure of protection.

In all, it was the most ostentatious armor in the Ceremony Hall, besides the matching bright teal and gold plate armor two identical boys across the hall wore which they had decorated with gorgon heads and serpents, and another young man who wore armor that reflected as though it were made of a prism.

The former two were the Spyros twins, whom I never had classes with, but stories of their terrifying special abilities reached me nonetheless. One brother's magic allowed him to temporarily paralyze his opponent, and the other brother's ability could strike fear so primal it could incapacitate on the spot. Just like the tales of old.

The latter boy was also someone I recognized; I had taken my armor-crafting class with him. Jax Aldridge. He was nice, friendly to a fault, and a total pacifist – though his light manipulation ability was anything but gentle. I wondered why he joined the Academy when so many of our courses were offense and defense-related. We were not friends, but that was probably my fault. I never let anyone but Talia get close to me.

The flashy armor we had all crafted would be a problem if we had not been instructed to install a cloaking mechanism in our armor during the construction. This concealed the colors and designs to allow for more covert operations.

My helmet was forgone for this occasion, seeing as my face would need to be more recognizable than my armor. However, my handcrafted transforming rapier was kept at my side. I could not bear to leave it in my dorm room. It was too gorgeous, with its delicately crafted hilt and sharp edges, to not show off.

The sword was crafted out of the same light-gold material as my armor decorations and was easily transformable with the simple mechanisms I had installed to transform it into its other two forms.

Overall, I felt striking. Amalie gasped when she caught sight of me as I prepared for the ceremony. She insisted I use a deep red lipstick mother had once given me – which was nearly a perfect match for my armor – and I did so to please her. I was glad I indulged her. The color contrasted dramatically with my pale skin and golden hair tying the polished, but wild look my armor created, together.

Heads were turning at my ascension to the stage, but I was unsure whether that was a good thing or not. Tremors began in my hands, but I willed them back. Truthfully, I was more nervous about the Placement than being stared at, even if I was unused to so many eyes on me at once.

Once I took my place with the others in my program, I caught sight of my parents. They were surrounded by acquaintances and colleagues who were here for their children or family members' Placement. From where I stood, I could see my mother's pinched expression and my father's surprisingly uninterested one.

Perhaps she can't find fault with my appearance today after all... I thought, slightly amused.

Mother's opinion did not matter to me today, though. I was going to be Placed. Despite my anxiety, there was an underlying current of excitement jolting through me. I was going to be *Placed.* Now I could choose my path in life. And I could have the opportunity to take Amalie with me.

The only thing which could have made this moment more perfect was Talia and I being accepted into Spec Ops together. My eyes scanned the crowd on the stage and through the large expanse of graduating students, I caught sight of my very best friend dressed in her black fighting leathers.

Talia's honey-colored eyes met mine, and she gave me an enthusiastic thumbs up. I returned her gesture with a grin and stood up straight. The headmaster took the podium and the Hall fell silent. Headmaster Rajani Kader was a tall, dark woman with short black hair and striking features – one eye scarred and blinded on her left side. She was the type of woman to command attention with her presence alone, and she used that to her advantage, as she did now.

"Welcome, all, to Heliorious' one-hundred and third Placement Ceremony," Headmaster Kader said, her voice clear and strong. "Our students, and testers, have all worked diligently throughout their educations to be here today. Throughout our history, we have worked hard to provide an education that will benefit every member of our society. I hope that, with the successes of these future Placed here, this school and union will continue to prosper."

As Headmaster Kader bowed her head, applause erupted around the room from students, testers, and their families. Once the clapping and shouting had died down, the headmaster held up her hand in a two-fingered salute and began to chant the words to commence the Placement. Soon, the entire hall was filled with the sound of thousands of voices – some more enthusiastic than others – chanting and urging the ceremony to start.

"The Gods are gone, but we remain.
Their power is gone, but ours remains.
When we are gone, our power will remain.

The children are here, and we are with them.
Their power is here, and our lives are fading.
Let us Place them up so their power will remain."

Abruptly, the voices cut off and the spotlight shone on one of the testers. I grinned a little at the theatrics and the startled reaction of the girl who was chosen to be Placed first. She stood and the room erupted into applause yet again as she took her place by the headmaster.

"What is your name?" Headmaster Kader asked the nervous girl.

"Katalina Martín," she said into the podium's attached microphone.

The crowd was raucous with applause and Talia caught my eye again, jumping and cheering with many of the others on the stage. Soon, the headmaster found Katalina's scores on her holonav and put the poor girl out of her obvious misery.

"Martín," Headmaster Kader began, "Good scores in empathy and a scientific background... But poorer scoring in defense and offense..."

She paused. A heartbeat, but it probably felt like an eternity for Katalina.

"The algorithm recommends your placement in the medic branch; does that suit you?"

Katalina's face brightened and her back straightened, a grin spreading across her face.

"Yes!" She exclaimed, nearly bouncing. "My grandmother wished I would become a medic, like her."

"Very well," Headmaster Kader said with a wry smile. "You are on the correct path to do so. Katalina Martín, do you accept your Placement?"

"Yes!" The girl cried, barely containing herself in her excitement.

The headmaster's smile widened. "Your credentials and contacts will be sent to your holonav; now go and celebrate with your family."

Without waiting for the headmaster to finish speaking, Katalina rushed off the stage and into the arms of her awaiting family, who had left their seats crying and cheering.

Amid the din of cheering and applauding people, the spotlight landed on several other testers and Heliorious academy students, Headmaster Kader announcing their placements. Some – a very small amount – rejected them and received alternative paths, while others accepted their placement with joyous enthusiasm.

Then the spotlight landed on Talia. She shot to her feet and pushed past her seatmates to the front of the stage, excitement written in every line of her body. When the headmaster asked her name, Talia nearly shouted it at the top of her lungs. I could see her, bouncing eagerly on her toes for her placement. We knew what it would be before it could even be announced.

"Spec Ops on a four-person team," Headmaster Kader said over Talia's shout of delight. "Do you accept your Placement Talia Edgegrieves?"

"Hell yes!" Talia said, gripping the side of the podium tightly.

The headmaster waved her off with the parting statements of credentials and contacts being sent to Talia's holonav. She ran off the stage dancing and shouting as loudly as she could, which could not be heard over the riotous celebration of the crowd.

But several students and testers later, two members were added to Talia's team: the pair of armor-clad twins I had seen upon my entrance to the Placement Hall. She clapped and cheered with the rest of the crowd, but I could see the disappointment on her face when they were announced as her teammates and I was not. A position they each accepted.

Then the spotlight came to rest on me, and my heart stopped beating in my chest; my lungs could not draw in a single breath. I had waited for this moment since I had enrolled in Heliorious Academy, and now… It was here.

I stood robotically and made my way to the podium to stand next to Headmaster Kader. Tremors threatened to shake my body, but I refused to let them, holding myself as still as I possibly could.

"What is your name?" The headmaster asked for the umpteenth time today.

A deep breath. Then another. In and out.

"Daux Deveraux," I said into the microphone.

After a moment, she pulled up my stats on her holonav. I saw them: excellent marks in defense, offense, and strategy. Empathy, self-sacrifice, leading ability… My heart began to pound in earnest as if to apologize for stopping earlier.

And she said: "Spec Ops, to a five-person team. Is this acceptable to you?"

My pounding heart, which was in my throat, suddenly dropped to my toes and deep into the earth. Through the thunderous cheering from the crowd of Placed, their families, and friends I saw Talia. Her face was shrouded in disappointment. All sounds were muted against the roaring in my ears, and my eyes began to tunnel.

"Daux Devereaux," Headmaster Kader nudged me. She had finished reciting the traditional line and must have called my name a few times. "Do you accept your Placement?"

Another look out into the crowd, and I saw my father's slightly annoyed expression along with my mother's tense disapproval. Amalie's concerned face. And finally, Talia's slightly tearful nod of consent. I could not reject the Placement I worked so hard for because I was unable to be on the same team as her. That small nod and watery smile were all I needed.

"I accept," I said, willing my voice not to crack, and the headmaster patted my shoulder, repeating the words she had said to the others before me. Dazed, I stepped off the stage to sit with Amalie, who patted my hand and mercifully ignored the few tears that escaped my perfectly crafted mask as team member after team member was added to my team.

I could not even move myself to curiosity when Zima Angelov was announced as my fifth teammate. The young man who was a legend in Spec Ops and a hero to hopefuls throughout the academy. No, I let the name slip silently past me as I grieved half of my childhood dream which had been lost.

Chapter Seven

After Amalie left with my parents – with many a tearful hug and promise to continue to write – I scanned the crowd for my new team. My disappointment was palpable, but I quashed it immediately and made my way to meet my teammates. So what if Talia was not on my team? She was still in Spec Ops. We would be in the same housing complex, at the very least.

And we would still be able to see each other outside of that too. I had mourned enough. I should not have allowed myself to hope for her and me to be on the same team anyway, as unlikely as it was to happen.

While I was tied up with Amalie some of the other members of my team had already gathered and were exchanging pleasantries. Jax Aldridge, Kajikawa Himawari, and Félix Guerrero. I couldn't believe I had two people on my team I had expressed interest in, but not Talia.

I stood on the fringes of the circle, unsure of how to insert myself into the conversation and feeling much too self-conscious to do anything. Defeat welled up in my chest, but I decided to try and make the best of it. Before I had the chance to speak a tall, dark-haired young man walked up to our small group.

"Team Deveraux?" he asked, though I thought it was quite obvious.

The four of us made eye contact with one another

before turning back to him. Jax nodded at the newcomer with a smile.

"I believe so," Jax said, holding his hand out in greeting. "I'm Jax Aldridge, this is Kajikawa Himawari and Félix Guerrero."

The dark-haired boy took Jax's hand and shook it with a smile, but it did not reach his eyes. I noticed then, that his eyes were the iciest blue I had ever seen.

"I am Zima Angelov," he said as he released Jax's hand.

I stifled a gasp. *He* was Zima Angelov... I had never seen a picture of him before. None of the Spec Ops hopefuls had, for security reasons. But he looked exactly as I had imagined him. Tall, even taller than Jax, with skin so pale it was nearly translucent his eyes radiated the same cold feeling as a frozen wasteland. He was lean, but muscular beneath black tactical armor similar to Talia's. The only thing that was different from how I imagined him was the three brightly dyed streaks in his swept-back hair – teal, violet, and gold.

The three of them nodded, smiling – though Félix was notably more reserved than the other two – and turned toward me. I gulped reflexively but pushed down my shyness.

"And you?" Zima demanded, gruffly but not unkind. Mostly indifferent.

"I am Daux Deveraux." I replied, forcing the nervousness out of my voice, and offered my hand.

"Ah," he said and shook it. "You were top of your class in several pro courses during your time at the Academy, were you not?"

I nodded my affirmation.

"Since you were named leader of this squad because of your accomplishments," Zima began, tone taking on the same frozen quality as his eyes. "You should have taken the initiative to introduce yourselves and your teammates, as would be your responsibility in the future."

Color flooded my face. I was hardly a few minutes into my leadership position and had already shown signs of inability. Not to mention Zima's criticism, though justified, stung. I had let my anxiety and shyness get the better of me, resulting in a poor presentation to my new team.

"You're right," I sighed, head bowing slightly. "I will make a better effort in the future."

Zima merely nodded and walked back into the crowd, presumably to find the shuttle that would take us all to our new living space. Thankfully, the dormitory caretakers had our belongings in order and shipped them to the teams' flats during the ceremony. In my case, they shipped Amalie's luggage back to my parent's hotel.

With a pang, I realized just how much I would miss her. Having Amalie with me for the past few days had been wonderful. I thought, again, that I would have to find a way to keep her with me eventually.

The sharp, tingling feeling of being watched came over me and I looked up to see my other three teammates gazing at me with curious expressions. What I hoped was a reassuring expression crossed my features and I nodded toward them.

"Sorry about that," I managed. "I guess I was just nervous."

Jax grinned back at me and held out his hand. He had deep brown skin and a blindingly white smile. His dark hair curled neatly and prettily down his back, giving him an almost angelic look.

"It's no big deal," he said as I shook his hand. "I've heard some screwed-up stuff about that guy anyway."

"Like what?" I asked.

"That he's run off every team they've tried to assign him to. And that he's completely ruined others." Jax grimaced and rubbed the back of his neck. "Though, I'm sure the last one is just bullshit."

It was true that just one member of a team that was incompatible with the rest could ruin it, but not totally beyond repair. Usually, the incompatible member was removed and relocated to another division or squad. So, I had no reason to be concerned about Zima ruining our team.

But is there? The thought nagged at the back of my mind.

There always was the possibility of failing so terribly that your team could be disbanded; though, it was incredibly rare.

No, I shook my head slightly, as if to clear it. *Zima has a perfect record, there is no way he would purposefully fail to get a team disbanded.*

"Shall we go?" Himawari asked, gesturing to the exit.

She was gorgeous. Her long, inky black hair was bound in a braid, accentuating her delicate features. Her eyes were so brown they were nearly black and were framed with dark, curling lashes that swept against her high cheekbones when she blinked.

Himawari had a responsible air about her, that was backed by a steely toughness in her dark eyes which I could not ignore. Instead of armor, she wore an outfit of deep violet, black, and gray. A violet cape-like garment was attached to her top at the neck and sleeves and flowed down her back, stopping barely above the floor. She wore thick, black leather leggings underneath her long tunic top which were tucked into high, lace-up combat-friendly boots.

The weapon she carried resembled a fighting staff – a bō – but I was sure from its design it was much more. Her gear was much more reminiscent of a shadowmancer, who typically used wand-like objects for their weapons and magical conduits. That, along with her clothing, made her abilities obvious.

Jax grinned down at Himawari. A smile crept across my face involuntarily. It seemed he was already smitten with her, and I could not blame him. She seemed a formidable girl, and beautiful.

"Yes," I said, clearing my throat. "We should get going."

Heading the group, I lead the way to the shuttle port with Himawari and Jax behind me. Félix brought up the rear, fiddling with a small object repetitively. He seemed uncomfortable with the crowd and was very uninterested in conversing with us. I hoped it was only nerves or shyness rather than disinterest in us as his teammates. Zima would be enough to deal with.

The shuttle itself was nothing grand. It was large with many seats to transport newly formed teams to their flats. Anxiety began to bubble up in my chest again as I stepped onto the shuttle. From now on, these people were the ones I would be closest to professionally and domestically. I was afraid I had already made a bad impression.

Zima had already been on the shuttle and seated before we even left the building. He was near the back of the vehicle, pointedly ignoring the clamor of excited teammates finding space to sit together. Thankfully, those looking for a seat avoided him, so we got two benches to ourselves.

Despite this pleasing development, my other teammates had already claimed seats in the row directly in front of Zima, leaving me the open space next to him. My bones turned to lead as I made my way to my seat. Hopefully, he would just ignore me like he was doing to practically everyone else.

But my hopes were for naught. As soon as I sat down, he turned his eyes on me, and my insides felt like they were frozen over.

"Hello," I stammered, forcing a smile onto my face.

Zima just glared at me and the icy feeling I had previously turned to hot anger. Why was he being so rude to me? I supposed I had not made the best impression at the Hall, but I was sure I had not done anything to warrant hostility from him. How could I have? We had only just met this afternoon.

"It is nice to have *you* on our team Zima," I said, looking away from him pointedly. "Since you have previous experience. It will be good to have someone who knows what we're heading into."

Zima's cold eyes were still on me as he spoke, "That's exactly why I'm here, Deveraux."

That was news to me. I looked back at him, scrutinizingly.

"Oh?" I asked. "And what do you mean by that?"

"It seems that many who are Placed in Spec Ops are not at all prepared for what they are 'heading into'."

A merciless grin crossed his face and he turned back toward the window, leaving me to gape at him like a fish. Not at his rudeness, but at his blunt description of his placement on our team. Like he expected us to be failures before we even had the chance to try.

Once I had forced myself to close my mouth, I turned to face forward. Zima appeared not to want to speak with me any further, and the others were laughing in the seats in front of us, leaving me to sit in silence, alone with my thoughts.

When the shuttle reached the building that housed the teams' flats, each team piled off and made their way inside. The outside looked very similar to my old dormitory, but the inside was vastly different. The lobby alone contained more tech than I had ever seen in one space beside the Academy. It was as fascinating as it was unsettling.

Once we had all obtained keycodes to our flat, we ascended the large, intimidating lifts to the first floor. Ours was the second to last at the end of a long, plainly decorated hallway.

As the team leader, I unlocked the door but stepped aside for everyone to enter ahead out of politeness. Félix even murmured a "Thank you", to which I responded with a surprised "You're welcome".

The flat entered directly into the shared living space,

which was comfortably furnished and stocked with plenty of reading materials, vids, and games. The spacious kitchen was to the right and a dining area beyond that. Down the hallway at the back of the flat were a set of three bedrooms, and another two were off to the left of the living space.

The silence in the small flat was quite awkward as we all stood in the living area, looking at each other, then looking away. Finally, I broke the uncomfortable silence before Zima could open his mouth to criticize me again.

"Why don't we figure out whose room is whose?" I suggested, plastering a cheery grin on my face.

Jax sent a grateful smile my way – which I appreciated – and the others, save Zima, nodded in agreement. He stormed off down the hallway and into one of the bedrooms down there, which I supposed was his, slamming the door behind him.

Trying to remain unperturbed, I lead the way to the two closest rooms and opened one of the doors, flicking the light on as I did so. The room was a deep purple and decorated simply with elegant nature motifs and low furniture. Small potted plants were strewn about the room.

Himawari moved forward into the room and picked up a small card on the low-set table in the center of the floor.

"It says this room is mine," she announced turning to face us.

"It's lovely," I said sincerely.

Nodding slowly, her eyes moved about the room, taking in every detail. Himawari seemed pleased with it and said so before we moved to the room next to hers, which was a bathroom. Full-sized, complete with a large shower and plenty of storage space.

The other bedroom was quite plain with light gray painted walls and lightly stained wood furniture. In one corner there was a large PC setup. Several shelves were set up around the space filled to the brim with videogames, figurines, and what I would later learn were stim toys. A faded pink pillow sat in the middle of the freshly made bed.

Félix brushed past me quickly into the room and grabbed an identical card to the one in Himawari's room off the PC desk.

"This is mine," he stated, staring at the card as if he were trying to set it aflame with his mind.

This was the first time we had heard Félix speak above a whisper nearly the entire time we had been introduced, I realized. He had a pleasant voice, with a soft and lilting accent. He could not have been more than fifteen I supposed.

Now that we were away from the crowds and Zima wasn't trying to freeze me with his glare, I was finally able to observe Félix. His hair was dark, curling past his ears, and his eyes were a dark brown with honey-colored flecks, lined with thick, sweeping lashes. High cheekbones sloped down into an angular but delicately shaped jaw. His lips were full and slightly chapped as if he chewed on them.

Altogether, Félix was a very pretty boy which was surprising as most teenagers I had known acted as if they knew they were beautiful. But Félix did not. He seemed as if he were walled up inside himself in some way. As if he did not want anyone to be let in.

"Would you like to see everyone else's rooms, or would you like to stay in yours?" I asked him gently.

He did not look up when he replied, "I think I'd like to stay here."

"Of course," I nodded. "I'll shut the door behind us."

And with that, we left, but before I closed the door all the way I could hear the bed creak softly as if Félix were already laying down upon it.

Poor kid... I thought as I made my way to the other side of the flat. The others followed, probably due to the base nature of curiosity more than anything.

I was concerned for Félix. He seemed incredibly shy, and despite the Academy deeming it appropriate to Place him, he did not seem as if he wanted to be here. I resolved to keep an eye on him, for his benefit rather than mine.

The next room we entered was Jax's if the way his face lit up when he saw inside was any indication. It was richly furnished, unlike the other two, and *very* colorful. Which was unsurprising because the armor he wore was so richly dyed with a prism of colors.

He stepped inside and picked up the place card which was on the dresser.

"Surprise, surprise," Jax murmured, smiling brightly. "This one's mine."

It was a nice room. The walls were painted a pale teal color and the floor was a sandy oak. It was reminiscent of a beach. The bed sheets were a bright yellow and the furniture was an eclectic array of stained and painted wood.

Jax seemed pleased with his new accommodations and motioned for us to continue our tour of the flat, following us out of the room.

Next to Jax's room was the other of the two full-sized bathrooms in the flat, and across from that was the bedroom Zima had stormed into and never left, so I assumed the bedroom directly at the end of the hallway was mine.

With apprehension and shaking hands, I twisted the doorknob and pushed open the door. The room… was lovely. A four-poster bed stood against the back wall, with gauze curtains cascading around the intricately carved rosewood columns. A plush, soft pink duvet covered the bed, which was piled with overstuffed pillows. A rosewood vanity was on the wall to my left and two my right was a wall of already-lined bookshelves. An embroidered fainting couch sat in front of them.

I was slightly awed by the attention to detail in each of our rooms, and that some of our belongings had already been unpacked for us. It was quite nice to see the rooms having a bit of personality. Hopefully, it would be as comforting to the others as it was to me.

Behind me, Jax yawned, and I turned to him in

surprise. I had nearly forgotten he and Himawari were there. He just smiled good-naturedly at my shock and waved.

"I think I'm going to turn in," he said, bouncing slightly on the balls of his feet. "'Night."

"'Night..." I gave him a small wave.

Himawari watched him as he left, then turned to me.

"He's nice," was all she said, though it seemed she was holding something back. I nodded, waiting for her to say what was on her mind but she did not. Her face was flushed slightly.

Perhaps Jax is not the only one who is smitten... I thought wryly.

Himawari stared at her toes for a moment longer, then turned on her heel.

"Goodnight, Daux," she said and disappeared down the hall.

Once I was alone, my new bedroom seemed to shrink. Claustrophobia began to engulf me, even with the door open. Fear. I was afraid. Not of my teammates, or even Zima, but of failure. And now that I was all alone it began to eat me alive.

The flat was eerily silent when I found the courage to emerge from my new bedroom, flipping on lights as I passed through the space. The darkness was unnerving here in this unfamiliar flat. I found that my toiletries were all unpacked in the bathroom I would be sharing with whom I assumed was Himawari due to the unfamiliar, but feminine, toiletries.

My hands shook as I attempted to brush my teeth, and kept shaking until I felt the vibrations deep in the hollow of my chest cavity. Instead of placing the cap back onto the toothpaste, I sent the tube clattering to the ground and froze.

Praying the sound didn't wake my likely sleeping teammates, I scooped it up and placed the cap back on with more force than necessary before setting in on my hair. Brushing and braiding the long strands before sleep was usually a soothing ritual, but tonight it was anything but.

The shaking had not ceased. It only worsened to the point I had to settle on the cool tile of the bathroom floor and lower my head between my legs. My breath came in quick, short gasps which left me feeling lightheaded and weak.

Come on, Daux. I chided myself, swaying in place. *It's just a panic attack. It's new and scary. I can do this.*

But could I? I wasn't so sure.

When I had regained enough composure to stand relatively steady on my feet, I splashed my face with some cool water and restarted my braid. And restarted it. Then restarted it again before I could get it right.

Frustration churned within me alongside the anxiety making the cool bathroom feel once again too hot – stuffy even. I ached to jump into the shower and rinse my troubles away with ice-cold water, but I didn't dare. I hadn't lived with others since I left for the Academy at thirteen – and though this was not much different from the dorms – I was too afraid of waking anybody up should they be sleeping.

Finally, I finished up in the bathroom and tiptoed to my new room, jumping at every sound. Laughter and music trickled faintly into the flat from the surrounding neighbors. Others were celebrating their Placements and their new teammates. Others weren't tiptoeing around their own living space, fearing the ire of Zima Angelov. Everyone else – except maybe Talia – was happy.

Even after spending all that time in the bathroom trying to compose myself, I still felt like my new bedroom was closing in on me when I stepped inside. My comfortable cotton nightdress felt scratchy and hot, making me want to rake my nails over my skin; though, I refrained. When I climbed into bed that night, I was sure it would be the longest I had ever lived through.

Short shallow breaths. In and out. In. Out. In. Out.

Chapter Eight

Never was I more grateful for the morning to come. Throughout the night I tossed and turned, afraid to make too much noise and alert the others to my predicament. I was even too nervous to get a glass of water from the kitchen we all shared.

But once my alarm had started to softly go off, I silenced it and leaped from my bed, hurrying to the bathroom. In the newness of the morning, I could see that it was a nice bathroom. Nothing extravagant or large, but big enough to share comfortably.

Quietly, I turned on the shower and waited for the hot water to warm up before stepping inside. It was a comfortably-sized standing shower, which I was grateful for. I always seemed to slip in tub showers.

As tempted as I was to linger in the deliciously warm water, I held off. Others may need a shower too, and I did not want to start as a water hog. Once I had turned off the shower, I was hit in the face with a blast of hot air, and I shrieked a little in surprise.

I had not realized, but the shower had a built-in drying system. My heartbeat began to slow after I took a few breaths, allowing the warm air to dry my hair and skin. The sensation was nice, relaxing even, and after a few minutes shut off.

I toweled myself off in case of any lingering water and

wrapped my bathrobe around myself, knotting it at the waist before exiting the bathroom. All was still quiet in the flat, so I decided to start the coffee pot and tea for everyone, assuming they would all probably appreciate caffeine as they likely had a difficult time sleeping too.

While the coffee steeped and the tea water boiled, I headed back to my room to prepare for the day. We would be touring the building's amenities, the training grounds, and the main Spec Ops branch office today. And in the evening, we all would be attending a gala celebrating our placement which was thrown by the Academy. Virtually everyone who was placed the day before – plus their families – would be in attendance.

Traditionally, it was a grand affair and would need hours of preparation on our part, but we would not have much time at all considering all the things we had to do today. Because of this, I braided back my hair with a red ribbon and dressed in black training gear and tall black boots. It was a simple outfit, easy to change out of, and appropriate for the places we would be touring. It was also extremely comfortable.

Once I finished dressing, I went back into the kitchen and began toasting myself some bread, then poured the hot water over a bag of green tea. When the toast was finished, I slathered it in high-protein almond butter and turned to bring my meal into the dining area but stopped dead.

In the entryway to the living room stood Zima, watching me with his arms crossed. A slight grimace passed over my face before I schooled my expression into one of cool politeness. Zima had been extremely unpleasant to me and the others the day before, and I had not forgotten. Nor had I any idea how to treat him.

Zima was supposed to be a legend, a hero even. He was so looked up to in the circles of people who wished to get into the Spec Ops division. Even Tali was enamored with him to an extent, having sent me a message the night before with bittersweet congratulations and barely concealed excitement about my illustrious team member. But he was acting like a jackass, and I did not know how to deal with it.

"Good morning," I said, continuing my way to the dining room without waiting to see if he would return the greeting.

Placing my food and tea at the head of the table, I sat down and began to tuck in. Surprisingly, Zima followed me and continued to stare. I gave him a pointed look and took a long sip of tea.

"There is coffee and water for tea in the kitchen if you would like some." I waved my hand in that direction.

Zima stared at me for a few seconds longer before Félix appeared at his shoulder, apparently waiting to come through the doorway.

"Good morning Félix," I called cheerfully and gave him a small wave.

Turning around and heading back into the kitchen, Zima finally took his eyes off me, and Félix hurried into the room.

"Is there something wrong?" I asked.

He shook his head and came to stand next to me, his fingers fluttering slightly.

I repeated my question, smiling up at him and adding, "I don't bite"

Félix stared at me for a few seconds before answering. "Where are the coffee mugs?"

I grinned. Here I thought something was wrong. "They're in the cupboard to the left of the sink."

"Thank you," he said with a look of relief on his face, then turned on his heel and left.

I continued with my breakfast until Himawari burst into the dining room, arms filled with various toiletries.

"I can't figure it out!" she exclaimed.

"Can't figure what out?" I asked.

"It's different from my old dorm," she said, seeming

incredibly flustered. "I need to shower."

"Oh, I'll come and help you," I reassured her, standing to my feet. "It took me a minute to figure out too."

I followed her to our bathroom and let her set her things down before I strode over to the shower and slid open the glass panel. It was similar to the smaller showers in the dorm bathrooms at the Academy.

"What is it you're having trouble with?" I asked.

"This is different from my old shower," she explained, frowning. "It's dumb, but I just can't get it to work."

"It's not dumb," I said and showed her how it worked. "There, you need to press the temperature button on this one before you turn it on."

Himawari nodded at me and grinned. "Thank you."

I replied to her thanks and left the bathroom to give her privacy and finish my breakfast. I remembered back to when I first moved into the dorms at the Academy.

The facilities there were completely different from the ones I had at home, and I was too embarrassed to ask anyone for help. Eventually, an older girl came and helped me, which I was grateful for, but too ashamed to thank her later. Being a person sucked sometimes, all the imagined pressures and stipulations on how you should act.

When I returned to the dining room Félix, Jax, and Zima were sitting at the table together. Jax and Zima were engaged in conversation, astonishingly, but from what I had seen of Jax, he seemed like he could get a brick wall to talk; though, Zima was expressionless, which seemed to be a default for him.

Félix, on the other hand, was quietly sipping his coffee and reading something on his holonav. He looked up and waved when I entered the room. I returned the gesture and sat back down to finish my breakfast.

Soon enough, Himawari joined us, sitting to my left with a cup of tea. The table was quiet, but it was a pleasant kind of quiet. Just five people eating together and occasionally engaging in sleepy, morning conversation. It was nice, something I had always enjoyed with Talia when she stayed over at my old dorm.

But our schedule was packed today, and no matter how much I was enjoying the moment we needed to get moving. I cleared my throat and waited for everyone's attention before speaking.

"Everybody, we have a busy day today, and I'm sure you're all aware of the celebration tonight. I think it's time we head off."

It was quiet for a few moments, and I was afraid I had overstepped and maybe upset the three teammates I liked. Nevertheless, I stood up, took my dishes to the sink, and headed for the door. They were close behind me, and Himawari smiled as she fell into step beside me, so I had nothing to worry about from her.

When we made it to the lobby, it was already slightly crowded with other new Spec Ops teams awaiting their tours. As I gazed about the large lobby, I was shocked to find Riannan standing with a group of three other girls. In my haze of disappointment during the Placement ceremony I did not pay much attention to who accepted what and missed Riannan's Placement.

"Do you know her?" Jax asked, seeing my stare, and following it across the room.

"Yeah… We took our exam together," I replied cautiously.

"You should go talk to her."

I frowned. "We should stay together. And besides, it would be impolite."

Apparently Jax thought my response funny and laughed, loudly.

"What?" I asked, chagrined.

"Nothing," he said, still laughing. "It's just, what's impolite about talking to someone you know?"

"But I don't *know* her."

And I did not know Riannan, not really. I knew she was nice and had a memory-related special ability, but that was it. It felt weird to walk up to her as if we were old friends.

"Have you said more than three words to her?" Jax asked.

"Yes…?" I replied.

"Do you know her name?"

"Also, yes."

Jax chuckled a little, "Then you know enough to at least go say hi."

I thought about it for a moment, but Jax must have taken my silence as a decision of inaction and grabbed my arm, dragging me over to Riannan's group.

"Jax," I hissed, "This is rude, we can't just walk up to her!"

He chuckled again and ignored my protests the whole way.

"Hello," Jax said in his soft, smooth voice when we reached Riannan and her team. "I think you may know my team leader, Daux?"

Riannan's eyes lit up when they landed on me.

"Yes," she exclaimed, moving to grab my hand. "I do! How are you doing, Daux?"

"Good," I stammered, timidly gripping her hand in return. "How are you?"

"Just great! Can I introduce you to my team?" she asked, already waving the other three girls over before I could nod.

"This is Hawthorn and Willow Berry, and this is Meera Joshi. Girls, this is Daux Deveraux."

Each of the girls shook my hand in turn, and I introduced Jax to them.

Willow and Hawthorn were sisters – Willow being the eldest of the two – and enrolled at the Academy at the same time, hoping to work in similar fields. Both girls had near-identical pretty faces with olive-toned skin, prominent cheekbones, and button noses. Though, Hawthorn had sandy blonde hair and Willow's was a deep brown.

Meera was a strikingly beautiful girl with eyes so dark one could get lost in them which were framed by thick, dark lashes. Her full lips and deep golden-brown skin made her nearly impossible to look away from. A small scar at the left corner of her mouth did nothing to detract from her striking beauty. Her hair was hidden under a rich blue headscarf, an indicator she belonged to a religion that stayed loyal to the Old Gods after they abandoned Eturnus.

Once the introductions were over, Riannan pulled me into a one-armed hug.

"I didn't think I'd get to see you again!" she exclaimed.

"Me either," I admitted, pointedly keeping my gaze away from Jax's smug face as he talked with the other three girls.

"What floor do you live on?" Riannan asked.

"The first on the end of the hall, and you?"

"Four in the middle. Are you planning on eating in more?"

"We haven't discussed things yet."

That seemed to surprise her, but Riannan was a bubbly, social person and I was not.

"We stayed up half the night hammering things out and getting to know each other!" she said, shocked.

"Some of my team..." I paused, looking over in their direction. "Aren't very receptive to me..."

Riannan's gaze followed mine and observed Félix, Himawari, and Zima. Himawari was untangling a pair of earbuds and Félix was squeezing a small ball as they spoke quietly to each other. Zima was off to the side, glowering and not talking with anyone.

"That's right, you got stuck with Zima Angelov." Her tone of voice was decidedly more unkind than I had thought her capable.

"Yeah..."

"I heard he never sticks with a team for long. I don't think you have anything to worry about. Just do your best."

I smiled. Riannan was nice. Too nice, almost. I was glad she had made it to Spec Ops, nonetheless. While Tali and her team were also here, somewhere, our duties could make it so that we may not be able to see one another as frequently as we would like. It made it nice to have another extremely friendly face around.

"Well," Riannan said, sounding disappointed. "It looks like my team's tour guide is here."

I looked up to see a smartly dressed man beckoning her and her teammates over with a kind smile.

"Oh… Okay. Have a nice time," I said, moving to return to my group.

"Don't sound so glum," Riannan grinned and hugged me. "We'll see each other tonight at the party and you can introduce me to the rest of your teammates. Maybe we can do dinners together sometimes?"

"That sounds wonderful," I agreed, and she hurried off after her already-leaving team with a vigorous wave.

I watched them leave, a little happier than I had been when I woke up that morning.

"Was that so difficult?" Jax asked, standing next to me with his hands in his pants pockets.

"Yes," I replied simply and turned my nose up at him, spinning on my heel and marching toward the rest of the team. He and his laughter followed.

When we reached the others, I noticed Félix was now wearing the earbuds and squeezing his stress ball to a beat. Himawari gave Jax an admiring look as she moved to stand next to me.

"He said it was a little loud," she explained.

"Whatever makes him more comfortable," I replied. If Félix needed something to assist him in uncomfortable situations, and it was not harmful, then I did not care. He deserved to feel secure.

I understood – to an extent – anyway. It *was* loud and crowded in the lobby this morning and interacting with people was difficult for me too. As I looked over at Félix again, Jax was showing him something on his holonav, and they were both giggling like children. Good. They continued messing about on Jax's holonav while Himawari and I chatted as we waited for our tour of the building and grounds to start. Zima stood off to the side and kept to himself.

Soon, a chipper, blonde woman walked up to us and introduced herself.

"Hello, you all must be team Deveraux, I'm Cherry, and I will be your tour guide for the day. It is wonderful to meet you all!"

We each said our hellos, and Cherry started us off on our tour. First, we made our way down a large corridor leading to the multiple indoor facilities the Spec Ops complex had to offer.

"Here is the pool room," she trilled, gesturing to the room with an enormous pool in it. There were sections for swimming laps, water aerobics, and multiple other functions.

"The pool even has a terrain function to change the depth or add current. When these functions are used, they are all controlled by heavily regulated monitors so it's perfectly safe," Cherry said, her peppy smile in place.

Next, she led us to another large room, this one with mirrored walls and exercise equipment of all shapes and sizes.

"The exercise and physical training area," she announced as we entered. I was in awe at just how large the place was and how many different types of machines and training equipment it contained. And from the other's faces, they were too. Except for Zima.

"There is a sparring ring as well as a stretching and dance studio in the back," Cherry stated merrily, already leading us in that direction. "They are also quite spacious."

I was beginning to think Cherry's parents should have named her "Cheery" instead. She chattered incessantly with her chipper voice and saccharine smile as she led us through the three connected rooms, explaining the disinfectant measures the complex implemented. Nobody is that happy to be talking about bodily fluids. Nobody.

While she was describing – in great detail – an incident I do not wish to ever be reminded of, I caught a glimpse of Zima, and he was grinning. My eyes nearly bulged from their sockets, turning away before he could notice I saw him. As I did, I thought I heard a soft laugh.

I pursed my lips as I tried to keep from laughing as well.

Finally, Cherry led us through all the indoor amenities – explaining everything in great detail the whole way – which took up the whole morning, and we still had the training grounds to tour. Though she was only doing her job, Cheery Cherry was beginning to grate on my nerves.

"And here are the outdoor training grounds."

We had finally arrived.

It was a large and expansive place with flat grounds which could be manipulated to create different terrain. Near the entrance to the training grounds was a section of consoles that would control the terraforming floor and augmented reality settings.

"The training grounds are an extra space where teams can do trust-building exercises as well as simulated training procedures," Cherry explained. "There are, of course, other places simulated training is offered for teams, such as the Special Operations headquarters. But these are closer to home and offer nearly the same quality of operations."

We all gave impressed and thankful responses to her explanation as she walked us through one of the simulations, then quickly said goodbye and hurried on our way to an awaiting shuttle, ready to whisk us on our way to Spec Ops headquarters.

"Man, I thought that would *never* end," Félix groaned as we passed through the lobby.

"She was very longwinded, wasn't she?" Himawari said, attempting not to laugh.

"More so than I would have liked," Zima agreed, also trying to abstain from laughter.

At least he sort of got along with the others.

The shuttle ride to headquarters was fairly short and uneventful. We along with several other teams were greeted by off-duty Spec Ops members to show us around.

Our new guide was tall, and handsome, with dark skin and short, closely cropped curly hair.

"I'm Dev," he introduced himself, extending his hand to each of us to shake. "I'll be your guide today."

He briskly led us off the shuttle and up to the front doors of the building where he flashed a badge in front of a magic sensor, then pressed a few buttons on his holonav. The doors flashed open, and our guide escorted us inside.

"This is the Special Operations headquarters." The new tour guide, Dev stated as we stepped up to the building.

Inside the building was exactly like the pictures on the site. It was white floor-to-ceiling with Corinthian columns lining the walls. Teams, scientists, and magic users bustled up and down the halls. Instead of appearing high-tech like the flat complex, Spec Ops headquarters seemed more magical in both appearance and overall atmosphere.

"This is the reception and lobby area," Dev said with a bland smile, stating the obvious.

"Rather obvious, don't you think?" Jax whispered to me, a mischievous look on his face as he echoed my thoughts.

I stifled a laugh but nodded my head discreetly in agreement.

Up and down the halls we roamed, Dev explaining the numerous departments on each floor in brisk detail. I did prefer his quick, easy descriptions to Cherry's much longer, rambling ones.

Our last stop was the top floor, where the Overseer's office resided. The Overseer was exactly as one would expect: the overseer over all of Spec Ops. Every team and department reported to her and her team of assistants.

Several other teams were there ahead of us, shuffling in and out of the room, taking a quick peek. We had been informed previously that the Overseer would be attending important meetings all day, so our introduction would be made at a later date. Dev, ever the efficient guide, hardly let us have a look around the assistants' office before ushering us out for the next group. We did not even get to look inside the Overseer's office.

All things considered, we were in and out of headquarters in under an hour, thanks to Dev's well-organized tour plan.

"Thank you for showing us around, Dev," I said as we were leaving.

"You're welcome," he replied, holding out his hand to give mine a businesslike shake. "Though it was merely a formality for your team. Zima could have shown you around."

"True," I surmised. "But thank you all the same. It will be a pleasure to work with you."

Dev grinned at me in response and went about shaking the hands of the rest of my team – fist bumping Félix – as we herded onto the shuttle and set off for home.

The next few hours after we entered the flat were a flurry of magic and activity. Himawari and I were using a variety of spells and beauty tech to help us get ready faster, while the boys were rushing in and out of their bathroom and Zima was trying to get Félix to stand still long enough for him to get Félix's tie straightened properly.

The spells were relatively easy for anyone possessing the ability to use elemental magic. It was mostly the manipulation of a device – a set of hair curlers for example – one would secure in their hair, then use the simple manipulation of fire to react to the sensors in the curlers. Within minutes, one's hair would be set and ready to style.

Or with makeup, the use of wind magic to manipulate the cosmetics which were made specifically for ease of magical use. They took some practice, but once I had gotten a handle on them, they were easier to use than hand-held makeup products.

In the comfortably sized bathroom, it was very easy for me and Himawari to get ready together. It was much more awkward than when I was on my own in the dorm bathroom, or when Talia was with me. But I didn't hate sharing. After a while, it was nice to sit with another person and talk about makeup and hair. Talia didn't care for anything other than mascara or nail polish.

Himawari, who was now dressed in a stunning floor-length gown of purple velvet so dark it was nearly black, and her inky black hair piled on top of her head intricately, was ready before me and trying to make sure Félix had an extra pair of headphones and a stim toy in his pockets. She and Zima shared an exasperated look as Félix escaped them yet again and attempted to restyle his hair for the umpteenth time.

Himawari grabbed him and said a few impolite words as she wrestled him back out into the living area where Zima waited with a cool expression on his face.

Jax peaked his head out of the bathroom at them, straightening his tie, which was patterned decoratively with golds, teals, and rich blues. His suit was a deep blue damask, accented with gold. He wore a teal velvet waistcoat and a gold-colored shirt underneath. He had somehow managed to style his hair into multiple twists in a short amount of time – probably with magic – which swept over his shoulder dramatically.

"Need any help?" he called over to them.

"Please," Zima implored and Himawari nodded emphatically.

Jax grinned and brought his comb with him.

"Listen Félix, I'll do your hair for you. Just let Zima fix your tie."

Félix pouted, but allowed the other boys to attend to him, then rushed to his bathroom to see the result. Which was when he nearly collided with me as I was emerging from my room.

"Watch it, Félix," I said, laughing.

"I look *awesome!*" he crowed from the bathroom.

He did look very nice in his navy-blue suit, I had to admit; though it nearly took an army to get him there.

Himawari and Jax sighed and shrugged at me in affectionate exasperation. In such a short amount of time, being around Félix felt like having a younger brother. It was kind of nice.

"You look great," Jax commented, taking in my appearance fully since Félix barreled by me.

"As do you," I replied, returning the compliment.

"She looks gorgeous, Jax." Himawari huffed at this unintentional slight and strode over to me, straitening one of the straps on my gown. "I think that color red is fabulous on you."

I grinned. Himawari, though somber in magic, was quite the expressive person. And I did agree with her; I loved the way I looked in that particular shade of red.

The dress itself was a rich, rose-red taffeta embroidered with a floral pattern from top to bottom. A slightly squared neckline and boning gave a corseted effect, which tapered into a full, A-line skirt slit up to mid-thigh on the right side. I had worn the same shade of lipstick Amalie had gushed over the morning of my Placement to match the dress.

"Do most people you know attend parties with daggers strapped to their thighs?" Himawari asked, perplexed.

"No…" I mused, twisting to look at the small, decorative dagger in its equally decorative leather sheath I had trapped there. "I do not suppose they do."

"It makes you look dangerous," Félix commented on his way out of the bathroom.

"Well, I suppose that was the look I was going for," I said demurely.

"It works," Zima said from behind my group of admirers.

My eyes flashed to him, already feeling the ice in his eyes freezing my insides. He was dressed in a suit of all black which only served to make his eyes and skin paler. The only color on his person was the three richly dyed streaks of teal, violet, and gold in his hair.

Instead of staring, I brushed past my teammates and headed towards the door.

"We have a gala to attend."

As previous years of students foretold, the party was a lavish one. As soon as we walked in, we were greeted with extravagant sights and smells. The guests were dressed in their utter best, magic and tech glittering around each person. The banquet tables were laden with delicious-looking food from many different countries and gorgeous sprays of flowers and magically frozen ice sculptures.

I handed the announcer our invitation and waited patiently for him to call out our team and names.

"Team Deveraux has arrived," he called, holding the invitation up to read off our names. "Leader: Daux Deveraux. And her Teammates: Félix Guerrero, Kajikawa Himawari, Jax Aldridge, and Zima Angelov."

A few people stared as we descended the grand

staircase – attempting to get a better look at Zima no doubt – but we were hardly the guests of honor and did not require attention from the crowd. All the better for it because Félix was already beginning to show discomfort.

Out of the corner of my eye, I saw him slip his earbuds into his ears, turning on his music as he did so. Jax also noticed and slid an arm around Félix's shoulders, squeezing him, and whispered something to him before moving on to greet his family.

Since the gathering was mainly a celebration of the Placement of this year's group of graduates, there were not a huge number of people. Testers and their families did not always attend, but I saw several from my Placement there that evening. Though, it was mostly Academy students and their immediate family members that I recognized.

That was when I noticed I was alone. Jax, Himawari, and Félix had all found their way into the arms of their families and had begun celebrating. My eyes swept the room, searching for Tali – who had been messaging me off and on all day with pictures of her outfit and adventures – and her teammates, but I only saw my parents.

Disappointment flooded through me; Amalie was not there, and probably would not be attending anyway. My parents never took us to functions like this when I was a child, and I should not have expected them to start now.

Riannan, who was across the room from me, caught my eye and waved energetically. Waving back, I started to cross the room toward her. But my father, catching sight of me, ushered my mother away from her group of gaggling government spouses and over to where I stood. I shot Riannan an apologetic look and turned to face my parents.

"Daux, how lovely to see you," he said with the false warmth he always used in public.

"Hello, Father." I nodded, then looked to his left. "Mother."

"Hello, dear," she said pleasantly.

Then things turned awkward, as they inevitably would, and I began to fidget under their scrutiny.

"Daux, darling." My mother's sharp, warning tone sent a tremble of displeasure down my spine. "Stand up straight, what will people say? I do not want them thinking you were raised with cattle."

"Is that a dagger under your dress?" my father tutted disapprovingly. "I suppose it's expected since you've joined that barbaric organization. You could have at least accepted a military position as an alternate Placement."

"Or even requested to be an aid to your father!" Mother trilled, fidgeting with one of the straps on my gown that must have slid down off my shoulder too far for her liking.

"Well, I was best suited to this position." I hated that my voice trembled as I spoke, but it was nearly impossible to repress.

"Obviously," Father rolled his eyes, swirling a glass of sparkling wine in its glass. "You always were such a ruffian. Playing with fire like your grandmother, using that ridiculous ability to play silly games. Magic isn't a blessing, Daux. It is a curse, and you know it."

Chagrined and angry, I bit back the furious words building in the back of my throat so I would not cause a scene. Though, after several more moments of insults and critiques from my parents I could take it no longer. I wanted to scream his Neo-Traditionalist views to everyone in the room. That my father hated magic. How little he thought of women. I wanted to shout about how he was using his position to enact laws that were designed to oppress, disguised to seem harmless and insignificant.

That would have him lynched without a doubt.

Could I do that to my mother? Possibly. But could I do that to Amalie? She wouldn't understand. And then... then *I* could be called into question. I could lose my position at Spec Ops. They monitored the Neo-Traditionalists heavily. Father couldn't be but a blip on their radar, he was too crafty.

But if I were to say something now, I would be ruining myself.

But that didn't mean I had to let him dress me down in public any longer.

I stood to my full height and looked my father in the eye, about to let him know in front of everyone what I thought of him when a body wreathed in black interjected itself across my vision.

"Zima Angelov," he said, holding out his hand to my father.

"Ah, Angelov," my father exclaimed, garnering some attention from the people around us, which was likely what he wanted. He always loved to be seen as a paragon of society – a real people's man. "I had seen you were on my daughter's team. A great accomplishment. Her mother and I are very proud."

A thin smile crossed Zima's face at my father's posturing. He seemed to sense it was insincere too.

"Yes, I'm sure," he said moving to my side and slipping an arm around my waist. "At the risk of being rude, I'm afraid I have to steal Daux for a dance."

My jaw nearly dropped, almost exposing whatever plan Zima had, but I was able to keep my expression to one of polite surprise as I looked up at him. He dared to wink at me.

"Oh, *please*," my mother gushed, reaching for my father's arm. "Don't let us keep you!"

The thought of being alone with Zima was nearly enough for me to call out to my parents as they walked away from us. Nearly.

"Thank you," I said, attempting to step away.

"Don't mention it," he replied, continuing to lead me to the dance floor.

"You were serious?"

"As the grave."

Again, I was shocked. But it was reasonable; if my

parents had happened to look over and see us not dancing it would mean more time spent with them or an embarrassing scene.

I let Zima sweep me into his arms and followed his lead as carefully as I could. Gratitude for the elective dance lessons I took at the Academy welled up. I had taken them on a whim when I had a free period in my schedule, and I was never happier that I did so than at this moment. I did not think I could have stood the mortification of being unable to dance properly at a time like this. Any other, maybe. But not now.

Zima's behavior from yesterday – and this morning – was still fresh in my mind and my mental barriers rose. I was unwilling to let him have another reason to dislike or belittle me. Steeling my spine, I stepped in time with the music, keeping pace with Zima through the choreographed sequence.

"I can see why you're anxious all the time," Zima spoke after a while.

"What do you mean?" I focused on his face instead of my feet.

"Your parents," he smirked, lifting me off my feet for a moment and leaving me nearly breathless by the lack of effort it took on his part. "They're insufferable."

"Oh, that."

Zima laughed – actually laughed – and spun me around, sending my dress twirling in a large circle around me.

"Yes, that. How do you put up with it?"

"I don't typically," I admitted, struggling to force down the blush that so desperately wanted to make an appearance. "We do not make a habit of interacting with one another."

"That explains a lot."

I frowned. "What is that supposed to mean?"

"Why you're abrasive but lack confidence," he

explained.

"Well, one reason could be because someone – whom I had just met, mind you – decided it would be a wonderful idea to inform me I was already horrid at my job."

That same smirk from before lifted the corner of Zima's full lips as he attempted not to laugh again.

"Well, it is a part of my job to guide you."

"Be that as it may, you were incredibly callous."

"Why do you think they call me 'Zima'? It means *cold.*"

The way he spoke of his actions – and moniker – was so matter of fact it took me by surprise. Like he was resigned to the name and had little to no remorse for upsetting me.

"I mean no offense, but that seems ridiculous," I remarked as he lifted into the air again.

"Let's not discuss this right now," Zima murmured into my ear, pulling me in close as he set me back onto my feet. "We're supposed to be celebrating."

The blush I had been fighting for so long during the dance blossomed across my cheeks, up my ears, and down my neck. I could not speak. I could barely breathe. Dancing with him was too much. My initial dislike of Zima, though still there, was becoming muddled in a way I could not comprehend.

His hands on my waist, his breath on my ear, the daring rescue from my parents. The behavior Zima was displaying tonight was so different from our first meeting. It was jarring. It was… frightening.

But I conceded to his plea that we keep the discussion lighthearted as we danced one dance after the other. We pointed out Jax and Himawari who were attempting to do the same, and Félix who was speaking enthusiastically with his family.

Riannan and her team were chatting and taking sneaky glances our way. She even held up her thumb in approval and I flashed a grin at her. Even Talia swept past me dressed in all black with an elated grin in the arms of her new teammate, Gwyn Heir. I ignored my confusion, my apprehension, and the way my heart was beating in favor of lighthearted banter that was sure to disappear as soon as the clock struck midnight.

Though, some questions were never far from my mind. What was going on? What was Zima playing at?

And why was I tempted to play along?

Chapter Nine

This morning was like the last several. I awoke from a restless sleep and set about making coffee and tea for my teammates then tiptoed to the bathroom for a shower.

A rush of affection and pride when I remembered Himawari asking for help the first morning in our flat. It felt nice to be helpful in some small capacity. When I finished my shower, I dressed and went to make myself some breakfast.

Perhaps we should come up with a chore system. I thought as I made my food. *It might be nice, and it would certainly be helpful.*

I made a face as I saw the dirty dishes in the sink from several days of rushing around. Yes, a chore system would be helpful.

After I sat down at the table, I opened my holonav and began creating a page for the chore list. Once everyone was awake, I'd ask them all to come to the table, so we could make the list together. I did not want to be authoritarian and wanted everyone's input on the list. Hopefully, that would make it fair and even better for those who disliked doing certain household chores.

We also need groceries… I mused. We had basics, but I wanted everyone to have something they enjoyed in the house. Even if it was something small. So, once everyone came to breakfast that morning, I brought it up.

"I was thinking," I began when everyone was seated. "That we could write up a list of foodstuffs we want to keep in the flat. And a chore chart."

They all looked at me expectantly, so I continued feeling slightly more confident.

"We could easily be called upon at any moment for a mission. It's possibly in our best interest to set up a delivery, that way everyone can get what they want, and we can put it into our allocated funds. I've started a list on our account if anyone wants to add anything."

"That's a good idea," Jax offered encouragingly.

"What about the chores?" Félix asked, picking at his toast. "I like doing dishes."

"Well…" I said, observing each one of their faces. "I was thinking we could rotate chores so it would be fair."

The others were quick to agree, though Félix insisted on being in charge of dish duty on nights it wasn't his turn to cook. He said the repetition of doing the chore was soothing for him and would ground him in a routine for the times we would have to interrupt it on missions. The others found that acceptable but were willing to rotate everything else.

The whole time we discussed the chore list, the groceries, and if anyone had any allergies. I expected Zima to interject with some critique or another. It surprised me that he did not. He sat there, engaged in the conversation – well, as much as he normally was which was not a lot – and let me speak without so much as a glare.

Once everything was finalized, I tapped the input screen a few times and the chart was sent to each of them through our team's dialogue box. There. Done and done. That went a lot easier than I expected, especially due to Zima's cooperation, which I had not at all anticipated. Perhaps our interaction the night before had changed something.

"This all sounds good to me," Jax said, rising from the table.

Himawari and Zima agreed, and they left the room together.

"That went surprisingly well," I commented, feeling a little dazed.

"Yep," Félix concurred, finishing off his toast.

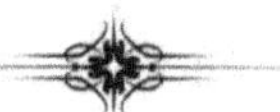

"How do you want to go about this?" Jax asked as we made our way to the outdoor training grounds.

"We should spend the morning getting to know everyone's magical abilities and fighting styles. We have already done weight training and stretch training together. I think it's time to move on," I replied, keeping my eyes away from Zima. I desperately wanted to understand his shift in behavior from that night, but I also did not want to seem approval-seeking either.

"Will we be doing a simulation or just team exercises?" Himawari inquired.

"I thought a team exercise would be best for now," I explained, pulling my hair back away from my face, and securing it with a ribbon. "We need to understand one another before we work on larger scenarios."

Once on the grounds, everyone lined up with their weapons. Jax used a variety of knives that conducted electricity. Himawari had her staff which transformed into a double-ended spear when she pressed a small button. Félix's weapons were a pair of knuckle blades which, he explained, helped him conduct his explosions on impact. Zima used a sword, like me, but his transformed differently than mine.

Next, we reviewed each other's magic. We all were proficient in the basic and elemental styles of magic; however, we needed to know and understand our partners' special abilities and weaknesses. I was already familiar with

Jax's magic to an extent, having shared a class with him. Félix and Himawari were easy to understand as well, having seen berserkers and shadowmancers during training sims at the Academy. Zima's ability was also common knowledge, but I had yet to see it in action.

Everyone had their styles and strengths. We each had our limits. I for instance could not count on my elemental magic if I overused foresight. My energy would be too depleted.

That was similar for everyone who had a special ability. We needed to be careful and conserve our energy, so we were not caught in a tough spot without our magic. Though, as Spec Ops operatives, we were in a much better spot than the average magic user.

That's why this training session was so important. If I knew everyone's strengths and weaknesses, then I could accommodate missions around them and their abilities. I could pair us up in ways that would balance the team out evenly.

Jax went first.

"So," he began, bouncing on the balls of his feet, his hair fluttering about him as if it were charged with electricity. "I specialize in electricity and light magic. The first is volatile at times, which is a fallback. Water is also a danger around it, and metals. Unless I can use them as conduits."

He demonstrated his meaning with his blades, conducting the electricity through them as he threw a few at the targets set up around the parameter. Upon impact, each target was fried. Then, before our eyes, Jax disappeared. A second later, he reappeared, holding the knives he had thrown.

"That was so *cool!*" Félix exclaimed, fluttering his hands at his sides.

"Thanks…" Jax said sheepishly.

"How did you do that?" Zima asked in a much more

subdued tone, though it was obvious that he too, was impressed.

"I manipulated the light to create a sort of invisibility cloak while using it to move at heightened speeds," Jax replied.

"Impressive," was all Zima said before turning away, to which I exchanged a knowing look with Jax.

Light magic was as volatile as it was rare. It would have been unsurprising that Jax was Placed in Spec Ops for his magic alone, though he was proficient in offense and defensive maneuvers. I was still surprised by his willingness to work with the team considering his gentle nature.

Next, I encouraged Himawari to step forward. "Show us what you can do."

Himawari moved with languid grace, holding her staff as if it were an extension of herself.

"I, as you know by now, specialize in shadow manipulation," she said, flicking her staff open to reveal a thick, black fabric so dark it seemed to negate the light around us. "This is a magical fabric that expels light. I can use it as a cloaking mechanism like Jax's light cloaking technique, but can shroud others in shadow for a short period without it."

She whipped the staff closed and shifted to a defensive posture.

"The shadows of inanimate objects are the easiest, but I can also manipulate living shadows."

Before our eyes, each of our shadows lifted from beneath us and took corporeal form in front of Himawari. Everyone – myself included – shifted, trying to see if we still cast a shadow. We did not.

All at once, our shadows converged on Himawari, attacking her as if they were our doubles. She defended against them passably, considering it was a five-against-one fight, and she had to exert energy to manipulate the shadows. But she had room for improvement.

Shadowmancy was an ability that quickly drained a person's energy, causing them to have to rely on their combative skills. And Himawari's needed improvement. She was good enough to pass the Placement Exam, but for us to rely on her on missions, we would need to help her improve.

Félix went next, explaining his magic and weapons with rapturous excitement.

"I'm a berserker!" he exclaimed, knocking his knuckles together, creating sparks. "Which means I can concentrate all my magical energy into a huge explosion of power, or smaller ones if I want."

To demonstrate, Félix stuffed his knuckle blades into his training jacket and pressed his palms together. Sparks began to fly from his hands, then up his arms, then his whole body. Félix seemed to vibrate with magical energy – hair and clothes flying wildly – and then, he exploded. Dirt and fire rained down on us from above, obscuring Félix and our vision.

With a flick of his wrist, Zima sent a large gust of wind flying past us and toward Félix. It quickly cleared the training grounds of the shroud of dirt and flame with its biting chill. Our teammate stood in the middle of a large crater, slightly scorched, smoking, and grinning from ear to ear.

"That," Zima said incredulously, gazing at Félix with wide eyes. "is a powerful ability."

"I know, right?" Félix exclaimed, fluttering his fingers.

He climbed out of the small crater to join us again, slipping his knuckle blades back onto his hands, and brushed himself off.

"That's what happens when I don't use a conduit," he explained, cheeky grin still in place. "I need something to focus the magic with, or it gets out of control."

"Berserker magic is often connected to emotion, isn't it?" Jax asked.

There was a pause as Félix's grin faded and he looked to the ground. "Yeah…" he said finally, his fingers fluttering the way they did when he was nervous or excited. "Sometimes when it gets too loud… or whatever… like, too much? I don't know. Or when something goes wrong… It's hard for me to explain."

"It's okay. No one is rushing you," I said, shooting a look at Jax who mouthed 'sorry' back at me.

"When I get overwhelmed," Félix said finally. "When I get overwhelmed, my magic kinda gets away from me."

He looked at us with fear written on his face. I had read him wrong previously. Félix wanted to be here with us, but he was afraid. He was afraid of us rejecting him out of fear because of his magic, because of who he was.

Berserkers were often cited as the Neo-Traditionalist argument against magic in society. Their magic was dangerous and incredibly explosive when left untrained and unchecked. Also, as Félix stated, was heavily influenced by emotion. Strong emotions in particular. All magic was affected by emotion to a degree, but the more volatile ones proved the most easily influenced.

Most berserkers opted to take temporary blockers on the off chance their emotions cause a devastating event, and Félix was no exception. But that did not erase the stigma – or the abuse from any Neo-Traditionalist hecklers should they find out if someone was a berserker.

"We're a team," I said, moving toward him. "You were assigned with us for a reason, and you have nothing to fear from us. We will do what we can to assist you, and you will do what you can to help us. That's what being a team is: relying on one another."

Holding my hand out to Félix for him to take, I looked over my shoulder at the others. They had followed me over to where he stood, careful not to crowd him.

"We're with you man," Jax said and Himawari agreed.

"Daux is correct," Zima concurred, surprising not only

me but everyone else. "As long as you're on a team, you can rely on them for anything."

Félix smiled and let go of my hand, satisfied with our answers to his unspoken question.

"Do we get to see what you and Zima's magical abilities are?" he asked, excited again.

I looked to Zima for confirmation, as I had thought it may be a good note to end the training session on, but he nodded his head, showing his approval.

"Well," I hedged, smiling nervously. "Why don't we spar and show them? My ability isn't all that flashy like everyone else's."

"That's an excellent idea," Zima agreed, a fierce light in his eye.

Our three teammates made themselves scarce on the fringes of the training ground as Zima and I took up our positions. One breath in, one breath out. I focused my magical energy on my eyes, activating my ability.

Zima on the other hand stood across from me, motionless, observing.

I gestured for him to make the first move with a grim smile.

He did so, unsheathing his sword, as he stalked toward me. His expression mirrored mine, a cool, bleak smile, and intense focus.

I could see *everything*. Foresight was an intense skill, but an overwhelming one. It was not a habit of mine to use it more than necessary because of the energy it expended, and it was always a shock to my system when I first activated it.

Zima's pace was quickening. Jax's fists were tightening. Himawari's expression tensed. Félix was trying to hold himself still.

Insects were buzzing all around, each one an iridescent kaleidoscope of color. Birds sang in the trees, their feathers an even more riotous display. The clouds in the sky were rushing past; I could nearly see the wind.

And then Zima was upon me, brandishing his sword, left hand raised and beginning to sparkle with magic. All the while I had not moved a muscle.

His grim expression shifted into a brutal grin, icy eyes flashing with triumph.

My sword swung upward to meet his, an awful crash of metal upon metal. Zima's eyes belied his confident expression. I had surprised him.

He jumped back, attempting to put distance between us, but I followed. A swing of my sword sent him back again. My own eyes locked onto his movements, reading them almost before he had a chance to decide in his mind.

A jab, a parry, arched swings. All the loud clangs of metal meeting metal. My ears began to ring.

Still, I persisted.

Then Zima unleashed his magic.

Ice began to envelop the ground. Even with foresight I barely saw it coming.

With the click of a well-placed button, my sword transformed, taking the shape of a compound bow. Flame ignited my fingers, and I sent an arrow of fire straight toward Zima.

He sent up a wall of ice to block it, the fire melting the ice slowly before fizzling out into nothing.

A flurry of flame arrows shot from my bow as Zima sent wave after wave of ice toward me until we were surrounded by puddles of freezing water.

"Do you concede?" I asked, aiming another arrow at him as he panted.

A wicked grin broke out across his face. "Never."

I returned his grin – a rush of exhilaration surging through my chest – and readied my arrow, but a shout from Himawari stopped me.

Next to her was Dev, the Spec Ops agent who showed us around our first morning here.

Returning my weapon to its original form, I jerked my head at Zima to follow me to the rest of our team.

"You've been requested for a mission," Dev announced gravely.

Chapter Ten

The drive to HQ was filled with nervous anticipation. Félix's hands fluttered continuously until he remembered the stress ball in his jacket pocket. Jax's leg bounced up and down, his whole body lined with nervous energy. Himawari picked at her fingernails, and I nervously handled the pommel of my rapier.

Out of the five of us, Zima was the only one who was calm, sitting with his back resting against the shuttle seat as though this were another day at the office. Well, it was. For him at least. For us, this was to be our evaluation – to see if our field performance backed up our Placement scores.

I was dreading it.

Sure, the team building was going well – at least with everyone but Zima – but I didn't think we were ready at all. Perhaps we had been selected *because* Zima was on our team. That would make some sense… But we had hardly trained together yet, and Zima did not like me. We had only been together for a handful of days.

Dev led us up to the Overseer's office for the second time this week, and yet again she was not there. Instead, one of her many assistants awaited us by the secretary's desk with a holofile, which she quickly transferred to our holonavs wordlessly.

When I tapped the holograph's screen to open the file it immediately jumped to a set of coordinates and a sparsely detailed mission summary. A quick in-and-out sabotage objective. We were to travel to a neighboring country – Accordancia – and take out a small Coalition base that had set up between our borders. We were to bring back the modest crew of soldiers as prisoners.

Before I could thank Dev or the assistant, Zima was already storming from the room. My teammates blinked wordlessly at me. I hurriedly gave my thanks – though the assistant didn't look up from her holonav again – and rushed from the room after him.

Thankfully he wasn't walking too quickly, and the rest of us were able to catch up. Wordlessly, we made our way to HQ's hangar where they kept several armored autos and mini-jets for quick drops – like the one we would be doing.

It was moderately sized as far as hangars went, holding just around sixty aircrafts as well as stations for repairs and armored autos. The building was constructed of durable metals and concrete, all imbibed with wards to prevent damage from magic or physical attack. Inside was grey and dark, lit only by magic lights to conserve energy in case of an attack. Despite Spec Ops being a separate entity from the military, this space had a very military feel to it.

"Team Deveraux?" a pilot asked, looking up from her flight log as we approached.

"Yes," I answered as Zima opened his mouth to presumably do the same.

I had to bite back a smirk at the annoyed look that crossed his face.

"She's been fueled up and looked over thrice," the pilot said, patting the hull of her mini-jet. "We're ready to go when you are."

I looked back at my three other teammates who gave me nervous gestures of agreement before I answered. "We're ready."

"Then climb in."

Inside looked like any typical tactical jet. Dark, durable

materials for the seats and safety straps. Sleek and practical were the lines inside and out; everything about the aircraft was streamlined. There were no weapons onboard. We wouldn't need them as we had our own.

The border was a few hours away by flight, and with our coordinates, we would get there by nightfall. Spending hours in an enclosed space with Zima was not something I looked forward to, but there was nothing to be done. The engines started, quietly for a jet, but with enough sound that many people in the hangar covered their ears.

I quickly strapped myself in and steeled my mind for the long ride ahead.

Thankfully the hours had passed quickly. Félix sat next to me and chattered about video games and coding – something which was next to a foreign language to me – but his conversation allowed me to focus on something other than the slowly ticking seconds and Zima's freezing gaze.

The few times our eyes met I refused to show weakness and look away first, though that only made the cold feeling inside me spread every second that passed. It felt like swimming in tundra-level waters – the air-snatching cold that left you breathless and tingling in pain.

Still, I didn't back down. Even if it was as something as immature as staring. That may have said more about me than I cared to admit, but I couldn't let him see anything other than strength or the disrespect would continue.

The openness we shared at the gala had not resurfaced – even during our sparring match, which was a whole different sort of vulnerability – and after the way he continued to treat me… I wasn't sure I wanted it to. But that small percentage of my mind – my heart – that did, I shunned completely, writing it off as the need to please I inherited from my mother.

It was something that shamed and angered me simultaneously.

The time between being plagued by Zima's judgmental gaze, and Félix's friendly chatter, I decided to look into my teammates' files. They had been shared to our holonavs after our Placement. I had glanced briefly at them in the days before to gauge their abilities and personalities, but that was about it.

It was obvious during our group training session that the others had not done much looking into each other's files either. I couldn't blame them; we hadn't expected to be called in so soon. I expected that it was due to Zima being our teammate that we were being sent out on such short notice.

The first file I went through was, predictably, Zima's. The basics were there: his Placement scores, history with Spec Ops – that which wasn't classified at least – family history, and his personality profile. It was jarring to me how so much of a person's personal history could be condensed into such small amounts of data to be viewed and shared by others.

He scored high in the physical and magical ability portion of the exam, which I was unsurprised by. His records were all clean and he had excellent records in all his past missions, at least those I could access. There was one, though, that was blacked out. The one that shared the date on which his former teammates died.

For a second I glanced up at Zima from across the jet, sure he could tell what I was doing, but he had his head tilted back against his seat. The tricolored streaks in his hair fell over his eyes, obscuring them. But from the steady rise and fall of his chest, I knew he had fallen asleep – at least for now.

Having given up on his Spec Ops records, I returned to his Placement exam scores. The Simulation portion was surprising, to say the least. High altruism, selflessness, and a strong sense of justice were perhaps not so shocking… But the other aspects of his personality that the exam recorded were. Cheerful, adventurous, friendly, outgoing. Happy family life. All of this was either opposite or dulled down in the young man across from me.

What had happened on the day his teammates died to change him so?

Other than their deaths of course. That was stupid of me. If the people around me here died today even, I wouldn't return home the same. How could I be so insensitive?

Frustrated with myself, I swiped to the next file. Félix's.

Berserker magic was often tied to emotions, and Félix admitted that autism made regulating his emotions more difficult. The notes in his file indicated that this caused Félix to withdraw from his peers out of fear, though his family encouraged him and helped him use blockers regularly.

I peeked up at him out of the corner of my eye. He had his noise-canceling earbuds in, stress ball in hand, with his eyes transfixed on the screen of his holonav. A small smile toyed at the edges of his mouth.

If I hadn't decided that I liked him already, this was the moment when I would have resolved he had a place in my heart. Félix may have been withdrawn with his emotions and social interactions, but his scores were impeccable and he had already proved to be a kind person. There was no doubt in my mind he would be an invaluable teammate and friend.

Next, I scrolled through Himawari's file.

She came from a long line of shadowmancers, dating back to long before the war. There were some notes on her mother and grandmother, particularly. They were prolific shadowmancers who worked with the NAF's frightfully undersized covert intelligence military. Himawari was the first of her family not to work in an exclusively intelligence military position.

Her name, ironically, meant "sunflower". I would have

to ask her if she knew the story behind her name.

Jax's file came last, but certainly not least.

Something that jumped out at me that I hadn't noticed before was his nonaggression. I had noticed in my class with him that he was always quick to diffuse a volatile situation peacefully, but I hadn't noticed his aversion to violence to the extent in his file. In all of his simulations he chose the peaceful option first, only using violence as a last resort. The simulation also recorded intense feelings of guilt after the fact, and that he had been violently ill inside the simulations. While it was a *very* good thing to be as peaceful as Jax's files claimed, it could prove dangerous on a mission. Especially if we were required to be on the offensive.

I could understand pacifism. An aversion to violence was not something I dealt with; it wasn't my first response either. That being said, I was also quick to jump in with my fists, weapon, or magic when the need arose.

Jax… it seemed as though he would fight in his defense or the defense of others, but only if he was pushed to do so. That is commendable, but in a combat-oriented job such as the one he'd been placed into – and accepted – it was something that concerned me. I resolved to discuss it with him in private.

Soon, but not soon enough for me, the jet landed in a covert station where it would be refueled and waiting upon our return. Hopefully without complication. It was only a small base. What could go wrong?

Everything. Apparently, everything could go wrong.

Almost as soon as we touched down in Accordancia, Zima started barking orders.

"Zima," I snapped, interrupting his instructions. "I appreciate your input and experience, but I would appreciate it if you would *share* it with me, not command me and the rest of the team. That is *my* job as you've reminded me often enough."

He glanced me up and down, a sneer forming on his lips, before turning on his heel and storming away with a gesture for the rest of us to follow.

This was going to go swimmingly.

We climbed into the awaiting stealth auto – which was smaller and sleeker than its armored counterpart, equipped with cloaking technology – that was to take us to the drop point. The ride was short, but after being in the jet for as long as we were I was becoming antsy.

From the drop point, we trekked through the dense forest until we happened upon the temporary base the Coalition soldiers had set up. It was a small, domed building made of fiberglass and nylon, centered in the middle of a man-made clearing. These temporary buildings were often used as shelters for exploration groups or archeologists. It seemed that in this instance, the Coalition was set up here to wait for a larger group to move in. They had a lot of weather-sealed crates littered about the clearing.

Only one guard was stationed on the outside of the building.

Before I could even give the order, Zima directed Himawari out of cover to apprehend the guard. She did so without difficulty, taking him down with a swift maneuver of shadow and physical force. I had to admit that I was impressed even though I was put out at Zima's consistent undermining of my authority.

When I emerged from cover, Himawari had already locked the soldier in a pair of magic-blocking cuffs which we were required to carry with us despite the Coalition's lack of willing magic users in its ranks. It was impossible to know when they would have brainwashed magic users fighting on their side.

The Coalitions scientists – mad and sadistic people who created the plague of mutated flora and fauna that threatened the healthy populations – often tortured them with physical and psychological torments to break them and make them explosive suicide soldiers.

It was either that or enslavement, and neither was a choice.

With a hand over her nose, Himawari unlatched a vial and held it under the soldier's nose. Instantly, his eyes rolled back in his head, showing the whites rendering him unconscious. Quickly, before the fumes reached any of us, she latched it back and stowed it in her robes.

"Nightsbane," she said, standing gracefully. "My grandmother brews it."

Nightsbane had many different names and could be made in countless ways, but in its gaseous form, it was the most potent. This version was typically crafted by shadowmancers, using poisonous plants and shadow magic to create a toxic fume that rendered its victim unconscious. If ingested, or too much of the gas was administered, it could lead to a very slow and painful death.

"Nice work," I commented, pleased with her quick thinking. Almost pleased enough to forget Zima's slight on my authority. Almost.

I turned to face him as he was coming up behind me with Jax and Félix. "I do not want to remind you again, that *I* am in charge. I appreciate input and feedback – if you have any, I would gladly hear it – but please leave making calls and judgments to me."

Himawari looked between him and me, crestfallen, as though she was the one being chastened. But before he could open his mouth to reply, or I could reassure Himawari that she was not the one to blame, a spray of bullets flashed through the tree line.

"Get down!" I shouted, yanking Himawari low to the ground with me.

I pulled her close to the temporary building, behind a rations crate, while activating my foresight. At once everything was sharper and more defined. I could see movement in the trees, circling the clearing.

I cursed.

Zima, Jax, and Félix were all sheltered behind crates, readying their weapons. Jax's hands were shaking, and I could see a sheen of sweat breaking out beneath his crown of braids. A sinking feeling settled in my gut. Somehow, I felt that this wasn't going to go as smoothly as I hoped.

Before I could stop her, Himawari charged from our cover with a shout. Shadows of various objects streamed behind her like demons howling in the wind. While she did draw the attention of the gunmen, all she ended up doing was making a target of herself. She could not see where the soldiers were. *I* could barely see where the soldiers were even with my foresight. Only a glimpse of their silhouettes through the trees as they darted around, looking for a target.

And she'd just given them one.

Bullets tore through the clearing and Himawari's shadows swirled around her, shielding her from the barrage. Though not completely. A cry of pain over the deafening sound of rapid gunfire reached my ears.

"Himawari!" I cried, pressing the button on my wrist that would release my helmet from its binds. "Get back in cover!"

I could feel the cool metal forming over my head, leaving very little visibility. On the upside, the material used was virtually bulletproof.

Charging from my shelter, I could hear the pinging of bullet casings grazing against my body. The impact was softened somewhat by my armor, but it still hurt like hell. Unsheathing my rapier, I raised it over my body and pressed the pommel, transforming it into a shield. Its third – and final – transformation.

But before I could reach her Himawari screamed, releasing the swirling sphere of shadow in a shockwave of dark matter. My shield was no match for the impact, and I was flung back into the temporary shelter with such force that my head spun, and the breath was snatched from my lungs.

I lay there, dazed, while the world above me spun in nauseating circles. If not for my helmet, my skull would possibly be shattered on the hard fiberglass. This was not going to plan at all.

And selfishly, all I could think of was how Zima was going to berate me later. If we survived that is.

When I was finally able to right myself, I saw that Himawari had knocked down an entire chunk of the trees lining the clearing, and one soldier – a young woman – was pinned beneath a fallen trunk. The other soldier, a man who appeared to be in his late twenties, lay prone on the ground.

I prayed they weren't dead as I stumbled over to them.

Himawari was sitting with her head in her hands as I passed, I couldn't bother to check if she was okay. We were supposed to take these soldiers back as prisoners. All of them. If these two were dead, we were screwed.

Zima had reached the man before I did, a flash of pale skin and black battle clothes, kneeling at the fallen soldier's side to check for his breath and pulse.

Though he was annoyed, he had the grace to inform me of the man's condition. "He's breathing. We need to extract him immediately."

"See to it," I responded, ignoring the pain threatening to split my head open.

He heeded my command immediately, cuffing the soldier, then hauled him over his shoulders. He was already signaling the auto before I reached the final soldier.

The young woman was another story completely. As soon as I got close to her, she began to scream.

I jumped back in shock. She had been so still and quiet before this; her reaction took me by surprise. Her face was covered in bloody scrapes and debris from Himawari's attack and underneath the tree trunk I knew her legs – and possibly her spine – were fractured.

But her screams were not of pain but of rage. Her black eyes bugged out of her head, bloodshot and wild. Sparks formed at the tips of her fingers and I noticed with horror that she wore similar knuckle conductors to Félix.

A foul curse flew past my lips as I ran once again for cover, air rushing in my ears through the barrier of my helmet. I ducked behind cover just in time for her explosion to release, sending dirt, broken bits of trees, and destroyed storage crates raining down around me.

This was exactly what I was worried about. A suicide soldier.

In and out. I reminded myself, realizing my breath had become unsteady. In and out. In and out, in and out, in and out.

I risked a peek around the storage crate I'd taken cover behind to see the young woman crawling on her forearms toward our direction – the tree pinning her to the earth having been destroyed by the blast of energy she sent out.

Zima had taken his hostage soldier a good distance away, and Himawari had followed with the one she had cuffed. From what I could see, Zima looked entirely unimpressed. I fought the urge to roll my eyes.

Jax rushed to the soldier's side, conducting knives at the ready, but his movements were slow, hesitant. Like he wasn't sure if he should – or could – attack her. Standing over her, hesitating. Panic was written all over his face, running through every line of his body.

Sparks of flame began to run up the length of the soldier's body.

"Jax!" I screamed, but it was too late.

The explosion threw him through the air, and the crate I was hiding behind flew into me with such force that I was crushed beneath it. I barely heard the sickening crack Jax's body made when he landed.

Another explosion shook the ground with deafening

force.

Concentrating magic into my hand, I took hold of the fire and smashed my fist into the crate, sending it flying. As soon as I was free, I launched myself to my feet to see Félix standing above the soldier in the middle of a smoldering crater. The suicide soldier lay beneath him, unconscious.

He shot me a sheepish grin, and I noticed one of his eyebrows had been singed straight off. One of his knuckle conduits was missing. That would explain the huge hole in the ground he was standing in. It resembled the larger one he had caused earlier in the day.

Sighing as I observed the horrendous state we'd left the small camp in, I pulled my cuffs from my belt and slid into the crater to snap them around the unconscious woman's wrists. Then I hauled her over my shoulder and climbed back out, straining under the dead weight.

While we were supposed to have destroyed the supplies and shelter for the soldiers who were supposedly on their way to construct a more permanent base, we were not supposed to have caused destruction of this magnitude. I could almost hear Zima now, lecturing us on the importance of "working together".

He was the one who disregarded the chain of command and didn't give me a chance to assess the situation. Was my performance less than stellar? Yes. I could admit to that. I froze and perhaps did not act as quickly as I should have, but had I been given a moment to assess what was going on… perhaps this would not have turned out so messy.

Shaking my head, I dropped the woman to the ground at Zima's feet and hurried to Jax's side. Himawari had beaten me there, cradling his head in her lap. His long braids spilled across her legs and onto the ground in a dark wave, having been knocked loose from the explosion.

Tears glittered on Himawari's lashes as she looked up at me from the ground. "I'm sorry, Daux…"

Her tone was pleading, as though this whole situation

was her fault. As if it alone could be one person's fault. Even though I wished I could blame it on Zima – or myself – I couldn't. It was a culmination of underprepared agents with no field training entering into a situation they were horribly underprepared for.

Zima was not enough to get us through a mission perfectly, but it wasn't up to us to refuse an assignment when we were called in. And even if it was poorly executed, the mission was still successful. Just barely.

We still had to bring the soldiers in for questioning. Had to get back safely. *I* had to make it a few more hours without murdering Zima. Or berating myself for botching my first mission.

"Later," I sighed to Himawari. I couldn't deal with apologies at the moment. Getting back home was the main focus.

Pulling an emergency kit from my sword belt, I knelt to the ground and placed a stim-tab into Jax's mouth – a small tablet made with magical properties to help promote healing and wake someone from unconsciousness. Soon enough, his eyelids began to flutter. Then he groaned in pain as he tried to sit up.

"Are you awake?" I asked him, straitening up.

"I-I think so," he replied as Himawari helped him sit upright.

"Good, then let's go." I spun towards Zima – ignoring his glare – and pulled the dead weight of the injured soldier over my shoulders. "Félix, grab a prisoner and follow Zima. Himawari, you help Jax walk."

With that, we set off. I ignored the aching in my feet and back until we got to the awaiting auto when I dumped the woman into a seat and promptly fell into one next to her. She wouldn't be waking for quite a while, and if she did, I'd put her back under with some of Himawari's Nightsbane.

Despite the on-paper success of this mission, I knew we'd botched it. Félix… whatever he did, caused way more obvious destruction than we needed. Himawari throwing herself in harm's way – being overeager – nearly cost us the mission. Not to mention Jax had almost gotten both of us killed. And Zima just watched. He barely lifted a finger other than to apprehend one of the already incapacitated enemies or to try and do *my* job. Which, yes, I had done very poorly.

I could probably write a book on all of my contributing failures to this mission. But as we boarded the jet, I knew the Overseer would care to hear little of it. My induction into Spec Ops had gone much worse than I had believed.

It had been a disaster.

Chapter Eleven

When we touched down, I dumped our prisoners into the hands of the awaiting interrogation team with a shudder. That was something I never wanted any part of. What they did to people in those interrogation rooms was a secret to the public, but we all knew the gist of what went down. All Spec Ops agents did. I had made sure to read all the files I had access to the moment they were released to me.

People were given the option to give their answers voluntarily, and if they didn't the interrogators would hook them up to a machine with tech similar to the simulation pods used in the Placement Exam. This would allow the interrogators to delve into the person's mind and see their thoughts, memories, and whatever else they had stored in there.

It was an experience that left the most disciplined soldiers hollow and broken afterward. Especially if one lasted for weeks on end.

I shuddered again at the thought of what I'd handed those people off to, even though they had tried to kill me. Had tried to kill my teammates.

Zima glowered and stomped off in the direction of the Overseer's office. After a few minutes with Félix, repeatedly squeezing his hand until we both could breathe properly, I followed Zima, sensing the shitstorm that was to ensue.

I had barely raised my hand to knock at the door when I heard the Overseer speak.

"You're sure about this, Angelov?" she asked in a deep, rich alto.

Zima nodded, and though I could not see his face, I knew he was wearing that cold, impenetrable expression he had.

"Deveraux is incompetent and a danger to the squad. Her orders were often correct but executed poorly. And to make matters worse, she has no control over her team, who are nearly as incompetent as her."

Disbelief rushed through me. I could not believe what I was hearing. Normally I would look down on eavesdropping, but I could not bring myself to move away from the door. A sharp pang of hurt like a knife buried in my chest as I listened to the harsh criticisms Zima was doling out on us to our superior.

Admittedly, some of his critiques were true. We had just started working together and were bound to make some mistakes, mostly due to being practically strangers. But Zima's words were harsh. Too harsh in my opinion. Especially towards others.

According to Zima: I, as the team leader, was inept at working with others. I was headstrong, willful, and arrogant. These traits made me ineffective as a team leader and incapable of heading missions. Critiques of myself I could handle well enough, but the way he was speaking of the others hurt the most.

Félix struggled with loud noises and bright lights. It was something he could not help, though we were trying different countermeasures to combat his sensitivity. Himawari was very mistrustful and independent, though she was trying to make improvements to work with us as a teammate. And Jax... Jax was rather inexperienced in combat. His pacifistic nature made such a thing difficult for him to undertake.

These were not necessarily problems – or faults even – but Zima was explaining it in such a way that made my teammates seem completely inept and underserving of their positions. That, I could not stand for.

I crept from the door and to the stairs. I would not allow Zima to tear apart our team, that much was for certain.

I found Jax in his room later that evening. We had all decided on simple convenience meals that evening, and no one ate at the table. All of us we nursing our injured bodies and bruised egos. Especially Jax at this moment.

I knocked softly on his door and quietly waited for an answer before opening it, carefully as I was balancing two bowls of ice cream in my left arm.

"Hi," I murmured, closing the door behind me.

"Hey," Jax responded.

He was stretched out on his bed, arm flung over his eyes. His braids spilled out over the sheets and off the side of the bed like a dark waterfall. Not for the first time, was I struck at how pretty Jax was. I wondered why my face wasn't flushed and why my heart wasn't beating like the girls in the fantasy stories I read.

I had never really reacted that way to anyone… Well, anyone except—NO! I was *not* going to go there. Nope, nope, nope.

"I brought you some ice cream." I sat the bowl on the bed next to him, before settling myself on the rug.

"What flavor," he asked, lifting his arm to look at me.

I took a bite of my own, savoring the cool mint-chocolate taste before answering him. "I got you strawberry. Mine's mint chocolate chip."

A smirk appeared at the corner of his lips at my answer and he sat up, picking up his bowl and tucking in. I chose not to ask what that was about. We sat like that for a bit, allowing ourselves to acclimate to the quiet. It was easy to sit here with him. I *liked* Jax. I wish I had allowed myself the confidence of getting to know him at the Academy.

Better late than never. I thought to myself. Talia would have said the same. She always let these things roll off her back.

"Jax," I asked when I found my voice to do so. "Why did you join the Academy? With your ability, it would be pretty obvious they would put you on track to be Placed in Spec Ops. I can tell even without reading your file that you dislike combat."

Jax sighed, staring into the soft pink of his ice cream. I could see the conflict warring on his face plain as day. It hurt my heart to see him like this, and I hoped he didn't think I blamed him for our disastrous mission.

"I'm the first person to manifest this ability in my family since the war," Jax finally admitted, eyes on his bowl. "My dad was in the police force, but he retired early because my mom and Dad wanted to take care of my brothers. I knew that if I enrolled in the Academy that I would at least be on track for a well-paying job to help support them.

"But you don't like fighting, why go into any sort of position where you would have to compromise your integrity?" I asked, my ice cream melting from the heat of my hands.

His throat bobbed as he swallowed back against tears. Guilt flooded through me. Perhaps this conversation could have waited until he was in a less vulnerable state.

I moved to stand – to apologize and leave – but he held up a hand to stop me.

"My youngest brother manifested this ability too," Jax said finally, his breathing shaky and uneven. "And he killed my mother. It was an accident, but we were fighting. It was over something stupid – can't even remember what – and she got in between us. She was dead before help arrived."

I wanted to offer a word of sympathy, anything but my

traitorous mouth wouldn't work. Instead, I moved to sit on his bed and slipped my arm around his waist with my ice cream in my lap. Talia used to do that for me when I first came to the Academy. Just sit and hold me while I talked about what was bothering me or cried.

He leaned into the touch, the vibrant smell of his hair – and what I suspected was his magic – assailing my senses.

"So, you don't like violence because of what happened to your mom… but that lead you to the Academy and Spec Ops anyway?" I repeated to make sure I understood. "How does your dad feel about that? Your brothers?"

"My dad is prouder than anything. I've never seen him so happy," Jax said, a hint of pride in his voice. "My one brother takes blockers now and is in therapy once a week… But both of them are proud of me too."

"And you? Are you proud of yourself? Are you happy?"

This was much deeper than the normal pacifistic answer I had anticipated, but I needed to understand him. I needed to know if we could work around his misgivings. And I needed to know if Jax was going to be okay.

I was slowly beginning to realize that Jax was my friend. Friends talk about these sorts of issues with each other. They help each other move past difficult moments and encourage them to keep going.

"You know what, Daux," he said in a voice trembling with emotion. "I am. I am proud of myself. I worked hard to be here. I hate what I have to do and what I am going to have to do, but I have a purpose and I have a team."

"You didn't answer my other question," I reminded him. "Are you happy?"

"Right now? No. But I will be. It'll pass, and I've got you and the rest of the team to help me through that."

An emotion I could not describe struck me at that moment. Jax considered me a friend too. All of us – maybe even Zima. He *trusted* us to help him get through his difficult times. Even this aversion to the violence that we would certainly be exposed to in our line of work.

We sat like that for a long time, the condensation of our bowls soaking into our laps. But neither of us made any motion to change position. It was calm and quiet; Jax would share little anecdotes about his mother, father, and brothers.

He would list other reasons for his pacifism – accidentally hurting a puppy when he was a kid and having a panic attack over it, or watching the violence in the world around us and coming to the conclusion that there had to be a better way. It didn't change what he had decided to do. He didn't have to *like* what he was doing, he just had to believe he was protecting something better.

I was about to say something – anything – to acknowledge his last confession and hug him tighter when a knock sounded at his door. Whatever ice cream I had left over was now melted, unfortunately. So, I drank it down like an unsatisfactory milkshake and stood to answer Jax's door.

Zima's cold glare appeared on the other side, causing my heart to stop and then stutter back to life. What could he want with Jax? Was he here to dole out his brand of discipline that he hoped I would not notice?

"We need to talk," he said with thinly disguised annoyance, answering my unspoken question.

He was here for me. How did he know where to find me?

"What about?" I asked.

"It's a team matter."

"Jax is a part of the team."

Zima huffed, not bothering to hide his annoyance any longer.

"I would like to speak to you about this privately, please," he hissed.

"Just go, Daux," Jax interjected from his bed. He sounded tired. "I'll be okay."

I nodded once at him, then gestured for Zima to get out

of my way, and stalked down the hall when he did so. Whatever he wanted, it would have to be good. Jax needed me, and Zima interrupted the support I was giving Jax as team leader – as his *friend*. He better hope it was good enough to warrant an interruption, for his sake.

Chapter Twelve

What?" I snapped, rounding on Zima after placing my bowl in the sink.

Though he was several feet away from me in the kitchen doorway, the space between us felt much too close. Like there were mere inches between us. I felt stifled, choked by the animosity radiating off him in waves. Pulling me away from Jax during a vulnerable moment was one matter, it was another altogether to try and intimidate me. To make me feel afraid.

After overhearing Zima's conversation with the Overseer, I made a point to try to improve myself – and aid the rest of the team – in every capacity. But it was proving to be difficult when I kept getting interrupted at my very first attempt.

"What?" I repeated, placing my hands on my hips.

Zima's eyes roved over my face with what felt like suspicion, though that could have been my conscience for eavesdropping.

"With what happened on the last mission it's important that we are making sure Félix isn't constantly ready to explode," he said finally, crossing his arms over his chest.

"What do you mean 'we'?" I sneered. "You are just worried about yourself. Besides, he takes his blockers when we are not doing training or going on a mission."

"That's not what I mean and you know it," Zima

scoffed.

"Do I? Please, enlighten me on what I know – according to you."

He rolled his eyes, running a hand through his hair – the colored streaks trickling through his fingers like silk. Suddenly I was back in his arms at the gala, those colors shining brilliantly in the bright lights. I felt warm, almost giddy, as he lifted me into the air. My worries were only an afterthought.

Why did he have to go and ruin everything? I should not have expected his behavior that night to preface our future together as teammates – his daring rescue on my behalf notwithstanding. But I had hoped it would. At least a little. Why couldn't our situation have been improved that night?

Because he was a stubborn ass, that's why.

I shook my head, banishing the thoughts from my mind. Zima wanted to talk to me for a reason. I might as well hear him out, because no matter my feelings toward him, he was a brilliant tactician when we worked together.

"In the field, when he's not on his blockers, Félix could prove to be volatile," Zima explained calmly, despite my antagonism. I had to give him a few respect points for that, albeit begrudgingly. "Berserker magic is incredibly dangerous. It's up to us – as his teammates – to help him de-escalate his emotions during those possible scenarios. That, and Jax and Himawari also seem to need to learn how to do so as well. The former hesitates and the latter is too impulsive."

That… That was actually a sound idea. And I hated to admit it. A hot bubbling rage flashed up inside me, making my hands ball into fists and my jaw clench so hard I nearly cracked a tooth. I tasted smoke at the back of my throat. I hated that he was being sensible, actually offering a reasonable suggestion as though he were concerned about Félix – about any of us.

That Zima had the nerve to refer to himself as our teammate when he had been anything but.

How dare he?

Instead of voicing my anger, I swallowed it back as I always did, physically willing myself to relax before voicing my thoughts. "Thank you for your suggestion, Zima. I appreciate the concern. I will bring up the topic with the team and ask for their input."

Without lingering for a response, I turned on my heel and headed back to the rest of the team where they went through simple three-person maneuvers while they waited. There, I managed to finish training without so much as another glance at Zima.

Breathe, just breathe. I told myself. In and out. In and out. In, out. In. Out.

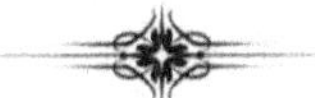

I could not explain my anger, except for the fact that Zima's concern about the others was more likely on his behalf than any real feeling for our teammates. Was it judgmental? Absolutely. Had Zima given me any other reason to trust him? Other than saving me from my parents on the night of the gala, no, he had not. And I barely counted *that* as it was.

Nevertheless, I spoke with the others about Zima's suggestion and – surprisingly – they were receptive to the idea. Surprising, because it was Zima who brought it to my attention. Had it been Jax or Himawari – or even Félix himself – I would have been less taken aback. After the last fiasco of a mission, my other three teammates had expressed disdain for anything Zima had to say, much the same as myself.

But this *was* a good suggestion, and it made me even angrier that I had not thought of it myself. Another one of my obvious shortcomings as a leader. I was more preoccupied with the problem that was Zima Angelov than taking care of the needs of my other team members.

Later that night, while I was lying in bed reading a book, a soft knock sounded at my door. It was so light I barely registered it, but when it came again, I grumbled my way to the bedroom door to see who it was.

I opened the door to reveal Félix, who was fidgeting nervously with his fingers. I pulled the door open wider to allow him to step in. When he did, I peeked around the doorjamb to see if anyone else was in the hall – a slight activation of foresight allowed me to see the absence of anyone in the dark hallway.

"What do you need, Félix?" I asked, closing the door behind me.

"I've been talking to Jax," he stated, looking about my room. At all the books lining the walls and the antique furnishings.

"And?"

"We want you to teach everyone that breathing technique you do."

Breathing technique? What breathing technique?

"I just… breathe like everyone else," I explained, chuckling nervously.

"No, you don't," he countered, fingers fluttering. "You do it a special way, and you've even helped me a few times with it."

The sudden memory of my maternal grandmother flashed in my mind's eye. It was before my father had banned them from seeing or contacting me and Amalie. I was crying, hyperventilating. No matter hard I tried, I could not stop my breath from coming in short bursts. I was not getting enough *air!*

My knee was hurt – it was bleeding. I had fallen off the swing set. And it hurt! Oh, it hurt. There were little pieces of dirt and gravel embedded into my skin, and I could not breathe!

Then Grandmother was there, holding a wet handkerchief to the evidence of the tumble I took, soothing me.

"Come, my little deer, breathe in," she paused, waiting for me to try. "Then hold it a second. Now breathe out. Let's try it again: in, out. In, out."

I did so for a few moments, my breath coming in shaky sobs, but soon I was breathing normally again. My knee still burned and throbbed, but I was not hyperventilating. Tears were no longer blurring my vision. The main problem was not fixed, but somehow it did not seem half as bad as it did at first.

Grandmother reminded me to keep breathing while she cleaned and bandaged my knee and had given me a piece of candy after for being a good girl. I had not done anything except breathe, but I had carried that with me from the time I was small, utilizing it every time I was upset or in pain.

"I guess—I guess I have," I conceded to Félix's earlier statement when I came back to myself.

"So, will you help me teach the rest of the team how to do it?" he asked, hope shining in his eyes.

"It's nothing special… I'm sure if any of you have had counseling then you would have learned it." Félix was asking with such hopefulness, but I did not feel qualified. Team leader I may be, but I was certain of my failings and nothing else.

"Well, I know a bit about breathing exercises," he admitted. "My mom taught me some to help with meltdowns, but I want the others to benefit from it too. And if they notice me getting upset, then they know to remind me to do it because I could forget."

That may be true, but infantilizing Félix was the last thing I wanted to do. He was autistic, not a baby, and I would be a very bad team leader if I or the others made him feel that way.

"I don't want to treat you like a child, Félix…"

"Well, I kinda am," he laughed. "I'm only fifteen. But I'm asking you to help the others because we need to rely on each other. The breathing exercise will help all of us, not just me."

That was a very astute observation on his part. I had been spinning the whole thing negatively, that it could be an embarrassment for Félix or an inconvenience. He was not only thinking of the well-being of the team as a whole but also their individual interests. It was a maturity I expected from a much older boy than merely fifteen.

So, I agreed to teach him and the others, even if I did not think it was anything special. From the look on his face, I could tell it was very important to him, and really, who could say "no" to Félix's puppy-dog eyes?

"Okay," I called, clapping my hands together to get everyone's attention. "This is pretty simple, so I'm going to demonstrate then we will all practice together."

We had gathered in the indoor training facility for this exercise, inside a private room to keep distractions to a minimum. Félix was practically bursting with excitement, fingers fluttering and bouncing in place. At least one of us was happy about this.

I hated having to be the "teacher" in this sort of situation. Being a team leader, I supposed that was something I would have to get over, but I would get over it later. Now, I had a breathing technique to teach.

"Okay," I repeated, feeling much less sure of myself than I had before. "I'll admit something right now… I'm very nervous. I've given presentations before at the Academy, but this is more intimate than a class of twenty-five plus students listening to a report on the quantum theory of magic."

That earned me a few chuckles from everyone except

Zima, which I was unsurprised by. He merely glowered off to the side with his arms crossed over his chest – like he thought this was a waste of time.

This was *your idea, arsehole.* I thought angrily.

Straightening my already rigid posture, I began my demonstration.

"You can do this in almost any position," I explained, placing my right hand on my diaphragm and the left, over my heart. "Just make sure you can feel your abdomen expanding and contracting with each full breath in and out."

Closing my eyes, I allowed myself to sink into my breath. The air filled my lungs – my abdominal cavity – and left it slowly through my nose. Each inhale was like a balm over frayed nerves, each exhale leaving me feeling lighter.

When I reopened my eyes I felt better, not completely, but Zima's glowers no longer seemed so irritating, and my teammates' watchful eyes no longer seemed as daunting. My feelings of anxiety seemed a bit less insistent, and it felt as though my breath was coming easier.

"Now, I'll come around to each of you and make sure you're doing it 'properly,'" I said, forming my fingers into air quotes.

Himawari and Félix caught on immediately – the latter having learned breathing exercises previously. I only had to show Himawari where to position her hands so she could feel how the air was flowing into her body, explaining her inhales and exhales only had to be as long as a count of four. Félix needed no such guidance, breathing steadily in and out with a pleased smile on his face.

But Jax and Zima seemed to be having a hard time. Just my luck. I was happy to help Jax, but Zima's icy glower wasn't making me any keener to get within a few feet of him. What I could not understand was that this was *his* idea. Why didn't he want to be a part of it? Was it me?

It was probably me.

Jax had his hands in the right place, but his count was

off. There wasn't a right way to breathe, but he wasn't keeping his inhales and exhales in time. That was what was going to help him calm – deep, even breaths.

The closeness we had garnered the night of our first mission warmed me. I was pleased he was willing to continue with the team. That he was part of orchestrating this little class. Mostly I was pleased Jax believed in me.

As I helped him, quietly counting aloud for him until he got the hang of it, I could see that Zima looked as though he were ready to storm out of the room. Before he could, I left Jax to his own devices and hurried over.

"This was your idea, you are not leaving until you do this with the rest of us," I hissed quietly so the others couldn't hear, my eyes flashing fire.

The frost in his eyes met the blaze in mine, but it did not diminish it. I did not cow before him. I refused to let him get the better of me again. I refused to let him brush this off.

So, I glared at him until his posture relaxed somewhat and grabbed his wrists to show him where to place his hands. I nearly dropped them, shocked that his skin could be so warm when he was such a frigid bastard. Instead, I placed his left hand over his heart and his right over his stomach with jerky movements, keeping my hands over his so he could not move them away.

I had not so much as brushed passed Zima in the time elapsed since the gala. Now I was holding his hands. Now I was centimeters from touching his chest. His stomach. I could smell the scent of ozone and mint – ice magic – on him.

Suddenly, I was very grateful that I had instructed the others to close their eyes during this exercise. Otherwise, I would be hearing distinct snickering coming from directly behind me. The lack of mocking laughter did nothing to dispel the heat that rushed into my cheeks as I stared up into those cold angry eyes. Those three colored streaks in his jet-black hair.

"Breathe with me," I commanded in a whisper, ignoring the crimson staining my cheeks. Ignoring the beating of my heart and the way his own was racing beneath our hands.

He complied, eyes never leaving mine. And we breathed together, our inhales and exhales mingling in tandem, steady and even until my hands began to shake. The ice in his gaze never once melted by the flame in mine – hardening, but never wavering.

Our teammates melted into the background until there was nothing but us and the heated glare we shared. That's when I finally released him and took a step back. My heart had never slowed and my feelings had not calmed. My thoughts still spun with the speed and force of an unimpeded whirlwind. I needed to be alone.

"There," I said, my voice clawing up my throat in an embarrassing rasp. "That's how you do it."

Zima only nodded his response and I stormed from the room, hyperaware of everyone's eyes on my back. I did not stop until I was sure no one was following me, then I leaned up against the plain beige wall next to me and sank to the ground.

What *was* that?

What had just happened?

This whole affair had been Zima's idea. This was all his fault. My oncoming panic attack was his *damn* fault. Just like everything else that had gone wrong since I had been Placed.

Heeding my own advice, I screwed my eyes shut and forced myself to breathe. Forced the air into and out of my lungs until I could think of nothing else but the sensation. In and out. In and out. In. out.

But that glare was never far from the back of my mind.

Chapter Thirteen

Zima's door loomed before me, dark and menacing. It was the same color and height as my own – as every door in the flat in fact – but that did nothing to dispel the fear in my heart as my knuckles reached up to rap against the hardwood.

I jumped when it wrenched open before I could even pull my hand away, revealing Zima's familiar glower.

We had barely spoken two words to each other in the days following his proposed experiment. I had definitely not touched him. Even if I had wanted to, I doubt I could have brought myself to do so. The thought of his burning skin beneath my palms sent a strange sort of shiver up my spine that I found incredibly unpleasant.

It wasn't until he shifted his arm above his head to rest against the doorjamb did, I realize we were staring at each other. Glaring, staring… A little of both if I were being honest.

"What?" he snapped.

"We have a new mission in a few days," I hissed back, turning on my heel and escaping the few feet across the hall to my room.

The door slammed behind me pointedly, and I leaned against it in relief. Just what was it about him that got me so worked up? The desire to fight with him – to force him to respect me – grappled with the desire to run away. Each time, it seemed, running won out.

Coward.

Coward, coward, coward. I thought hatefully, scrubbing at my face with my hands. Trying to dispel the prickling sensation of tears in my eyes.

What was it about Zima that allowed him to get under my skin so easily? It was as if he knew all the chinks in my armor and could slither through them, and wreak havoc on my insides. Tear away at my confidence until there was nothing left but a tiny ember. It was as if he *wanted* to tear me apart from the inside out.

A deep angry breath filled my lungs.

I was not going to let him destroy me.

The newest mission was going to be even less covert than our first. We were to retrieve a holodrive with classified information and destroy the building we find it in. A bit like the last mission; however, there were to be no prisoners this time. Unlike the last mission, there were not supposed to be any soldiers at the location. But I had commented that I was unsure about killing Coalition soldiers. Zima – ever the ray of positivity and sunshine – snorted.

"You're going to need to change that attitude and fast, Deveraux," he had said, a sneer upon his sculpted face. "Those soldiers have been born and bred to kill people like us. They will not think twice about killing, or capturing to enslave."

At the time, his words made me angry, furious even. But I could not deny the truth in them. No Coalition soldier in their right mind would waste the opportunity to kill or enslave a Spec Ops agent. We were supposed to wield the strongest magics and have better combat skills than the regular military. Should they take one of us... it would not only be bad for which one of us was taken prisoner, but it would also be disastrous for the NAF.

We were also privy to national secrets that the regular soldier was not. Our magic would be a deadly asset; our compliance would be deadlier. So, if there were soldiers at the house searching for the info…

Hopefully, I would not have to kill anyone directly. Despite the truth of Zima's words, I was not ready for that sort of responsibility on my hands – someone's life.

More evidence that I was unfit to lead this team.

I knew if I was keeping tabs, Zima would be too.

The thought made me bristle as we headed out to train on the outdoor training grounds. After our last disaster of a mission, I knew we needed to go through some maneuvers and plans before we departed in a few days. So, I uploaded the info we had on the location and any soldiers there and allowed the simulator to work its magic.

The simulator was large, desk-like in shape, and sleek. Only the download slot and touch screen were visible and were protected from the elements and stray magic by a combination of weatherproofing and magic-repelling spells that were recast every month. Soon enough, the machine began to work its magic. Interactive simulations were nothing new in our society, but the tech was still incredible to see with my own eyes.

I watched in rapt fascination as the simulator created a life-sized interactive replica of the building we were set to besiege, down to the trees outside blowing in the wind. The lace curtains in the windows. The porch swing rocked back and forth.

It was a house.

A farmhouse to be exact. Two stories painted white with green shutters and a roof made even more welcoming by a magnificent wraparound porch. Lace curtains fluttered in the windows, and I could almost smell the scent of freshly baked loaves of bread and pies wafting through the open panes of glass.

I had known it *looked* like a house, but seeing it there made my stomach knot up around a ball of lead. It only looked like a house, somewhere far in the countryside of a neighboring Coalition country – Eidolon. Though, despite the building's seemingly charming exterior, it was not a house. Inside was empty, save for a staircase that led to an underground bunker that housed defecting NAF citizens. People who thought magic should be criminalized and eradicated. People like my father, but with a bit more guts to leave.

There was not supposed to be anyone hiding out at this place currently, but the last defector – a ranked military officer and her wife by the surname Mason. They had fled with some important information regarding our military defenses, Spec Ops, and census results.

But when the Masons were captured by a Spec Ops team a few weeks ago when they attempted to flee Eidolon from NAF pursuit teams, they claimed to have left the holodrive at the safe house.

Recon teams that were shuttled into Coalition territories on reconnaissance had reported back that the intel had not made it into Coalition hands. And now they were sending *us* to retrieve it.

And blow up their safe-house in retaliation.

After the fourth time running the simulation, I would have thought it would be easier. But every time it reassembled itself nausea hit my stomach like a tidal wave. I knew when we went to complete our mission that it would not be a real house waiting for us. But the image of a *home* – constructed so similar to the one my grandparents had lived in when I was a child – made each lick of flame, each explosion, harder to bear.

As the simulated flames rose higher and higher into the air, as the skeleton of the building groaned under its weight, exhaustion began to wash over me in waves. Gods, it seemed like days had passed since we began.

Was it really only this morning? I thought, looking up at the large digital clock on the simulation board.

Now, it was afternoon, and I was aching and tired. My stomach growled involuntarily. I had not eaten since I woke up in a rush to come down here and train. The thought crossed my mind to suggest taking a rest when Zima caught my eye. Jax noticed and signaled for Félix and Himawari to continue the drill.

A huff of annoyance blew from my nostrils, but I jerked my head towards the privacy of the simulator, and he followed close behind. So close I could feel the vibrations of his movement in the air and the scent of his magic assailed my senses, sharp and cold.

"Yes?" I asked when we were too far away to be overheard.

"Why are you hesitating?" Zima asked, crossing his arms over his chest.

The fabric of his black tactical armor creaked with movement, drawing my eyes to the pale skin of his hands. How the sleeves of his armor tapered to his wrists. The blue tinge to his fingers where his ice magic had escaped past the barrier of his skin.

It was strangely beautiful.

Then I remembered those cold pale hands lifting me into the air and spinning me effortlessly, as though I was not something hard and muscled. Something cynical most people were too afraid to touch.

"Deveraux?" Zima said, brows furrowing.

"It looks like a house," I blurted.

"And?"

I bristled but took a deep breath before answering him. The sound of a small explosion – most likely caused by Félix – thundered in the background. A small shower of dirt rained down around us, and I ignored the muted "Sorry!" that rang out behind me.

"I don't need you to lecture me," I countered with

finality.

My feelings were none of his business. My fears were mine to deal with. It was almost satisfying to see the shadows of his face darken in anger. I had to fight back the smirk that threatened to grace my lips in response.

I got under his skin too. Good.

"From what I've seen here," he said, posture tightening. "I think you do need lecturing."

"I didn't ask," I responded, sucking my teeth.

The air around us grew cold, the frigid temperature permeating my tactical gear. Zima's lips were turning slightly blue. Almost in automatic response, I let a small ember dance over my fingers – the hot temperature meeting with the cool air.

Small clouds began to form around our heads – the atmospheric reaction to our magics mingling. I could feel it, smell it. Ozone, mint, smoke. Crackling in the air around us at our stalemate.

"What about it looking like a house has you so bothered?" Zima pressed, jaw muscled jumping.

"Why do you care?" I snapped.

The temperature of my magic flared with my temper.

"Because I need to be able to trust my team one hundred percent when going out on a mission."

"Funny," I retorted, tossing a few stray hairs that escaped from my braid – now damp from the clouds – out of my eyes. "I need the same thing. I wonder why that's been so difficult?"

"Deveraux," he warned.

"Angelov," I sniffed.

How could I tell him that it was difficult for me to destroy something that represented happiness – safety – even though I knew in my mind that it was merely an illusion? I could barely have that conversation with myself, let alone with the person who had been a near-constant thorn in my side since I had met him.

Someone who seemed determined to ruin my career and what remained of my self-esteem.

"Let's run it again with a few more variables before taking a break," I said, ignoring the growling of my belly and the light mist that was sprinkling around us. "I'm not confident we're ready for every plausible scenario. And after we take a break, we'll run them again."

With my head held high, I strode back to the other members of our team, not bothering to hide the stormy look on my face. Jax only rolled his eyes good-naturedly and elbowed Félix, which I ignored and commended them to get into formation. I was going to do this my way, and I was going to do it right. Zima was not going to get to me. I refused to let him.

Chapter Fourteen

Breathing wasn't helping this time.

Nothing was helping.

My mind was racing, my heart was beating a tattoo inside my chest, and my lungs could not grasp purchase on oxygen. It was too hot. Sweat slicked my skin - I could smell the scent of smoke rising from it.

I bolted from my bed; afraid I would set it aflame. Staring at the hardwood frame in the dark I soon began to shiver standing there in just my nightgown. Rarely did my emotions manifest through magic, unless I was particularly stressed or frightened. Then it expressed itself in fire magic.

All I wanted was to sleep.

It did not look as though that was going to happen. And since it wasn't going to happen, I figured I might as well go fix myself a glass of water.

With shaking limbs, I exited my bedroom and tiptoed my way through the darkened flat and into the kitchen where I flicked on the light above the sink. It wasn't too bright but prevented me from stumbling around in total darkness, helping to avoid a stubbed toe or bruised knee, which I was prone to in the dark.

I had not spent much time in this space other than doing my own cooking and cleaning chores, but it was a nice space. Sleek, decorated in shades of white and grey. State-of-the-art appliances and equipment. An easy, accessible kitchen…

And I was grateful I had it to myself.

After the incident in my bedroom – almost setting my bed on fire with me in it – I figured it was best not to activate my foresight in the case of an emotional surge taking over my magic. I liked this kitchen; I would hate to burn it down.

As I sipped the cool water – condensation already forming on the glass due to my abnormally high body temperature – my breath finally began to slow. Large, but steady, gulps of air filled my aching lungs, cooling me; soothing my thundering pulse.

Finally, I was able to face the thoughts that had plagued me in my fitful slumber.

We had received the wrong coordinates for our mission, I had dreamed, leading us to a similar looking home still in the country of Eidolon. I had burst into the building, Zima and Himawari at my flank, leaving Jax and Félix to use their electric magic and explosive berserker magic to set the house up to be destroyed.

But to my horror, there was a family inside. A father, a mother, and their two small children. They were sitting down to a meal – meager as it was on Coalition rations. Only those who were up high on the social and political spectrum were able to have good food. These people were very clearly not.

I had been more confused by the presence of actual furniture and working electricity in the house than by the family. In the simulation we had trained in nothing of the sort had shown up, and it was supposed to have been an exact replica. So why was there furniture and working electricity? And why was the family above ground for that matter?

Then a seismic boom shook the house, sending furniture and dishes crashing to the floor.

I quickly tackled Himawari to the ground, shielding her with my armored body.

One of the children's shrill screams rang in my ears over the sound of the explosion. Then the acrid smell of smoke – of burning insulation, weather-treated wood, and siding – choked my senses, leaving me even more disoriented than I already was. Jax and Félix had set fire to the building too soon.

No. They hadn't merely set fire to it.

They had blown it in half.

It was a miracle we were still alive.

As I gazed up at the gaping, blazing hole in the house we'd burst into, all I could hear was the crackling of flames and the single cry of a child. Begging, pleading with her parents to wake up. I could not hear the other child.

And when I had finally looked toward them, the family whose lives we had just ruined, all I could make out were the icy blue irises that plagued my waking moments. Blazing with judgmental rage and hatred.

The very same eyes that were now staring down at me in a dimly lit room.

My water glass slid from my fingers in what I told myself was exhaustion, and because the glass was slick from condensation. But if I were being honest with myself, it was fear.

Zima caught it before it could shatter to the ground, gently setting it on the countertop without spilling a single molecule.

Stupid show-off.

"Deveraux," he said, voice rough with sleep.

"Zima," I responded, grasping my arms around myself.

He stared down at me groggily for a few moments before running a hand through his hair, sighing as he did so. It was like an eternity waiting for him to speak, to berate me again. Everything that came out of his mouth was usually along the same lines – do better, be better, or give up.

But what he said next surprised me.

"Are you okay?"

I blinked at him in surprise and shivered against the cool air.

It wasn't until he repeated his question did I answer

him.

"No," I said, wrapping my arms around myself if only to maintain my dignity.

In my haste to escape my bedroom, I had neglected to grab a robe and my nightgown – while not immodest by any means – showed more skin than I cared to share with this particular person in a darkened kitchen in the middle of the night.

What surprised me more than his question, was my honest answer. Why was I being truthful with him? Why didn't I just brush him off?

"You should try and rest," he suggested.

"I can't," I whispered, cursing my honesty again.

"Why?"

I stared up at him, not bothering to hide my incredulous expression. And he stared down at me, totally and completely unreadable.

Why did he care?

What was his angle?

"I don't have to tell you," I whispered.

"No, you don't," he agreed, shrugging. "But if we're going off on a mission tomorrow you need to be at your best. You're the team leader."

There it was. His answer to everything. Be better, you're a team leader. Like he was throwing it in my face. If he thought he could do a better job, then he could have it, because I was just about finished with him.

The anger in my chest ignited, nearly engulfing me again. I had never had any issues with my magic behaving like this… why now? Was it Zima? The stress I was under?

Flame broke out over my fingertips, gently running up my arms like a candle's wick catching fire. Shame filled me, which only heightened my anger, leading to the flame burning hotter. But I could not run. I would extinguish my magic. I would show Zima I had control.

Then cool hands rested on my shoulders, brushing their

way downwards until all that was left was wet, reddened skin. When Zima drew back, his expression was still unreadable, but his hands were pink from the reaction of his ice magic against my fire.

"Wh-why…?" I asked, shivering once again. But not because of the prickling, numb feeling that now ran up and down my arms.

Zima didn't answer me, instead turning on his heel and storming from the room. Relieved or disappointed, I fell back against the sink, refusing to let my gathering tears fall. He was not going to have power over me. He wasn't.

But he did.

In some small way, Zima's opinion mattered to me for reasons I could not express or even begin to understand. And I wasn't about to start trying.

Just as I was about to shove off the sink and rush back to my room, Zima appeared in the doorway with a small syringe in his hand. Instantly, I knew what it was.

"No," I protested, shaking my head vigorously.

"Deveraux," he said softly, calmly – like he was trying not to spook me. "This is just a temporary blocker; it only lasts a few hours. It'll be out of your system way before we get to the drop point."

That didn't matter.

I had taken blockers when I was a child. My father forced them on me because he hated having a daughter with magic. I was a disgrace, an embarrassment to him and my mother. A black mark on their spotless reputation with all of their bigoted friends.

But Zima didn't know that. How could he? He never let me get close enough to open up. And I could hardly believe he cared. He was only concerned about me because of his safety, which I supposed was fair – to a degree. I felt the same way about him.

"Deveraux," he whispered, taking a careful step towards me. "The blocker will help you sleep. You can't go back to your room with your magic reacting like this."

Zima was right, and I hated that. I hated *him.*

Why did he have to make me feel so small and inadequate? Like a child dressing up in their parent's clothing, pretending to be so grown up and important.

The muscles in my jaw jumped with the tension I was placing on them as I ground my teeth together to keep from shouting vile, hateful things at him. Words born from the fear of that syringe he held in his pale fingers and the feelings of frustration and anger I held against him.

Watching me with wary eyes, Zima continued towards me with careful even steps. As though I were some sort of wild animal – meant to be feared, and approached only with the utmost caution.

I resisted the urge to bare my teeth at him.

When he was toe-to-toe with me once again, I realized I was shaking. I cursed myself internally, willing my body to stop trembling, but it did not. Gripping the countertop behind me, I clenched my jaw even harder, demanding the fear leave my body. Demanding that I calm down.

But the feeling of my magic flickering out when my parents forced the blockers on me as a child sent a wave of nausea crashing over me that nearly knocked me to my knees. My fingers slipped from the countertop and spots danced before my eyes.

Instead of cold tile, I was met with a t-shirt-clad chest and strong arms. The cold metal of the syringe bit into the exposed skin of my back, causing me to flinch further into the arms that held me.

Zima had caught me before I had fallen. I was never going to live this down. But… he smelled of sleep and the lingering scent of magic, and for some reason that began to soothe me.

"D-Deveraux?" Zima asked, pulling me upright.

"I'm fine," I ground out, my fingers finding purchase on his shirt.

He did not look convinced, detaching my hands from his clothing and lifting me onto the countertop with such ease that it would have taken my breath away had he not already stolen it from me.

In and out. I reminded myself, allowing the air to pass through my nostrils, down the trachea, and into my lungs – filling up until my diaphragm strained with the pressure. Then back out through my trembling lips.

In and out. In and out. In and out.

All my hard work was nearly undone when I realized Zima was maintaining eye contact – breathing along with me, mirroring my breaths. He was silent, encouraging me to continue, breathing with me until the shaking stopped.

"Do you want me to do this for you?" he asked once I was calm, lifting the syringe between us. "Because I won't do it without your consent, and you're in no state to do it yourself."

If there was judgment in his words, he hid it well. I could only detect concern in his tone, in his expression. Why was he helping me now? This was a moment I was baring my inadequacies to him in a way no one but Talia had seen, and he was not belittling me.

It was too much.

"Just do it," I hissed, clenching my fingers into my nightgown.

Zima's lips mashed together into a thin line, but he nodded and knelt before me on the cold kitchen floor. Then he placed his hand over mine which was fisted into my nightgown, dragging it up my thigh. My eyes never left his face as he helped me push the fabric up to expose the flesh of my thigh.

He was stoic throughout, as each centimeter revealed more of my pale skin – a sharp contrast to the tan on the rest of my body. Not a flicker of emotion as he flicked the cap off the needle and lined it perpendicularly to my skin. And when he began to count, even his voice was steady.

Even so, I was not prepared for how much the injection was going to hurt.

It burned up my thigh, scorching through the muscle until it was quickly replaced with the icy feeling I remembered from so long ago. It moved slowly through my body, quenching the flame that burned through me until only a small ember remained. Temporary blockers never extinguished magic like a three-month – or longer – injection, but the dulling effect I felt was much the same.

I barely even noticed that Zima had removed the needle and that his fingers were now carefully massaging the injection site, but when I did my face burned despite the icy chill coursing throughout my body.

If my mother could see me now. I thought ruefully.

I, in my nightgown, seated on a countertop with my legs bared to a young man who was kneeling before me in a darkened kitchen. It was the sort of thing that would have had her head spinning. And I would likely have been on the receiving end of the worst dressing down of the century.

When Zima met my gaze from his place on the ground before me, I could have sworn I felt the crackling of his magic – the scent of it – but the blocker had dulled my senses, confusing me to the point that I was unsure of anything.

Abruptly, he stood and lifted me from my spot on the counter, then stormed away without another word – tossing the syringe into the hazardous waste receptacle as he went. I blinked after him in a daze. I could still feel his hand on mine, his cold fingers on my thigh. A tremble ran through me, but I was no longer sure if it was from anxiety.

The walk back to my room was long and arduous, but I eventually reached the doorway. Before entering, I paused, straining to hear if Zima was still awake – and as keyed up – as I was. But with the blocker still freshly in my system, I could not activate my foresight – meaning I could hear nothing.

When I fell back into bed, the image of his icy blue eyes boring into mine as he knelt before me on the floor haunted me past the point of wakefulness. Past the point of lucidity. It followed me into my dreams, leaving me further troubled than I already was.

Eidolon was a beautiful country filled with rolling highlands and would be dotted with sheep and other grazing animals had the Coalition government allowed its citizens to farm – or live on anything but their allotted rations. Any farming done in Coalition-controlled countries was strictly controlled by the government; people couldn't even forage to sustain themselves.

It was either: joining the military, working in factories, or working in industrial farming for rations. There was no art, no music, and no books. Nothing for enjoyment or pleasure. Nothing to make life worth living. Just survival day after day. Even to this day, most Coalition-controlled countries were still as poverty-stricken as they were during the Great War. Disease and famine ran rampant through their territories, and their government did little to help.

It was a factor of their totalitarianism that I never understood. Especially when people defected from the NAF only to live in poverty. Unless they were considered important enough to garner favor with the militaristic government's leaders, then they were lavished with the best the Coalition had to offer from their hordes of wealth. At least, that was what I garnered from the reports I had read.

I met Zima's eye as he exited the auto after me, and the magic in me surged in response. Quickly, I tamped it down and looked away. The blocker had worn off by the time we made it to the hangar in the morning for the first half of the transport. And despite the inability of magic to roast me alive in my bed, I still slept fitfully thanks to a certain someone.

We had stopped at the edge of a copse of trees and would make the rest of the way to the safehouse on foot, using Jax's magic to bend the light around us – rendering us invisible to the naked eye. As far as Spec Ops knowledge went – the Coalition forces had no way of detecting through such a disguise, unless they had enslaved someone with similar abilities to mine or had magic disruptors engaged, and intel noted they did not. Infrared tech couldn't even penetrate through the life-blocking signals we each had in our armors.

Each of us was equipped with a sensor so that we would be able to see one another, even when glamoured or rendered invisible. So, there was no chance of losing one another.

We were set.

And yet, I still felt apprehensive.

The dream I had before Zima administered the blocker continued to haunt me, though I knew it was practically impossible for such an outcome to present itself.

Shaking my head, I gestured for Jax to begin disguising us, then stepped through the tree line. The sun beat down heavily over my head and beads of sweat quickly began forming along my hairline, streaming uncomfortably down my neck.

All my senses that the blocker had dulled were back with a riot of color and sound so vibrant and loud I began to feel dizzy.

In and out. I reminded myself. *In and out.*

My head spun and my vision swam as we continued our way across the open field. My ribs began to feel constricted by my armor. I couldn't breathe.

Yes, I can, I am getting enough air. I hissed internally, irritated by my inner turmoil.

We pressed on, eventually coming to the large house with the wrap-around porch and lace curtains. There were no civilian or armored autos parked in the drive, and no indication of life. But the yard was unkempt and the house looked as though it had received a fresh coat of paint within the past few months.

Suspicious.

But not an indication that there was anyone here now.

Once we made our way into the unfenced yard, I allowed my foresight to search for any non-obvious signs of life. Sound, smell, and vision all exploded into my sensory network, leaving me temporarily dazed. After a few seconds, my mind began to process all of this feedback, translating it into something I could understand.

And to my immense relief, I saw nothing.

Just to be on the safe side I kept foresight activated as Félix and I disabled the security system on the building. It was a simple procedure, just shorting out any electrical connection the house contained. There were no reports of any magical barriers and my foresight did not detect any either, so we were able to enter without issue.

Me, Zima, and Himawari made our way up the porch steps as Jax relinquished our disguises. My heart thundered in my chest as a wave of nausea crashed over me.

I'll be okay, I have to be okay. I attempted to reassure myself.

Shaking my head, I rammed my shoulder into the door, face flaming with embarrassment when it didn't budge. Jaw tight, I stepped back and kicked my leg out. The door swung open with a bang at the impact of my booted foot.

Inside was all dark. And mercifully empty.

No family was sitting around a dinner table, no children to die in an explosion, and no innocent lives were needlessly taken. Relief washed over me, but I could not bask in it. We needed to hurry. Once the Coalition forces realized this safe house's security system was offline, they would send *at least* a group of five people to investigate the problem.

Motioning for the other two to follow me, I entered the

house. It was just like it was in the simulation, which was such a relief. We didn't have to look hard for the bunker. It too, was exactly as it had been in the simulation – behind a hollow panel in the wall.

I would have liked to smash through it, just because I was feeling keyed up, but I pressed the panel in and to the side like the good little Spec Ops agent I was even though we were going to destroy the house as soon as we got the holodrive – and ourselves – out of there.

Down the dark staircase we went, holding our breath until we came to the door at the bottom. This one we would have to demolish. It was supposed to be made of a durable metal alloy, around six inches thick, and activated by a specific code that was set to change at specific intervals.

Since the power was shut off and we did not have the code, I stepped to the side and allowed Zima to work his magic.

"You're up," I whispered.

"You need to calm down," he commented and stepped forward.

That remark alone nearly set me over the edge, but I didn't allow it. Instead, I focused on the ice crystals forming on the door as Zima pressed his palm flat against the metal. It blossomed outward like an old god of winter blew its glacial breath over the door's surface. It was gorgeous.

Then he removed a spike from his belt and thrust it into the door, shattering it instantly. A wave of biting air crashed into us, shocking my system. It was exactly what I needed to jolt my system out of whatever dysregulation it held onto.

"Okay," I said, pushing past Zima and into the bunker. "Let's find this holodrive and get out of here. I'm sick of this place."

I didn't wait for any sound of agreement, beginning my search without any source of light. With foresight, I could easily see in the darkest of places, and this room was hardly that. Especially with Zima and Himawari switching on the headlamps on their sensors. Himawari being a shadowmancer could "see" in the dark better than most, being able to sense nearly anything in shadow, but her eyes were still limited.

It took us all of five minutes to find the holodrive. As the defectors had said, they had just left it lying around when they fled the safe house. Specifically, they had left it lying on a small table. Important NAF information – classified information – just lying there for anyone to take or see.

Anger at the two women who had betrayed my country – the entire government – flared within me. I tamped it down, refusing to let my emotions affect my magic the way they had last night. Not in front of Zima. I could not do that again, especially on a mission. No doubt he was holding last night against me. He probably kept a little mental notebook of all the times I messed up, filing it all away to use against me.

Gods above, I was paranoid.

"Time to go," I snapped, my tone harsher than I meant, grabbing the holodrive and slipping it into my hip-pouch.

Stepping out of the safe house was like a breath of fresh air. The heat, the sunshine, and the humidity washed away the echoes of my nightmare the night before. This was a nice place. Too bad Eidolon was a Coalition territory. I would have liked to visit again.

Maybe one day it wouldn't be, but that was unlikely to happen in my lifetime.

As soon as we stepped onto the lush grass Jax cast his magic over us, rendering us invisible yet again. I signaled the awaiting auto that we were making our way back towards them as I headed away from that nightmarish house, the others on my flank. Only when we were about thirty meters away was Félix able to detonate the explosive magic he cast on the building.

Debris and flame rained down around us, and I raised my shield over my head to deflect the falling wreckage. Himawari tucked herself up under my arm with a cheeky grin, which I returned. But instead of the satisfaction I thought I would feel at the destruction of the safe house, I could only feel exhaustion creeping over me.

A restless night combined with Zima's strange behavior, the mission, and the drain my magic was putting on my body all amalgamated into the most bone-crushing enervation I had ever experienced. I could only pray the auto would be ready when we reached the extraction point.

And it was, thankfully. After everyone climbed in and I cast one more glance around the perimeter, I allowed myself to fall into a tired heap in my seat. Jax quickly relinquished his magic, revealing himself to be nearly as bone-weary as I was. I couldn't even bring myself to give my teammates a word of congratulation or an encouraging smile.

With the holodrive tucked carefully into my hip-pouch and the safehouse destroyed, exhaustion finally overtook me. Heavy lids and bleary eyes turned into even breathing which eventually turned into the sweet escape of unconsciousness. When we crossed the border into our own country, I was already sound asleep.

Chapter Fifteen

The tension between Zima and I did not dissipate. He was ever the shadow of disapproval. Several times he had taken me aside privately and criticized my decisions during training and the missions. The energy between us in those moments I could not describe. I could feel the magic crackling around us, raw and powerful. Zima's eyes – cold as ice – would bore through me, freezing my insides.

I refused to back down and show weakness. Zima may have been intimidating, but I had lived with an intimidating man most of my natural life, and I was not about to let another make me afraid. If he had a problem with me, he needed to speak with me to fix it. Same with the others. I would not stand for his bullying.

And I refused to acknowledge anything that happened between us in the middle of the night. I would ignore the ghost of his cool fingers on my skin and the overwhelming scent of his magic that refused to leave my senses. It was of no consequence. I disliked him.

Hated him in fact.

The others were concerned about the tension between Zima and me. When pressed by them, I had to reveal why things were so heated between us. That Zima had been critiquing my actions faster than I could improve; though, I did not reveal to my team what Zima had said about them. Nor did I divulge what happened the night before we left for Eidolon.

Himawari suggested treating Zima more gently. Félix believed that we should request he change teams. And Jax, dear, dear Jax. I could still feel the migraine that came on when I heard his suggestion.

"Just kiss him," he had said, grinning his devilishly charming grin. "Ease the tension." Perhaps Jax had been joking, but I paled until my knuckles were white as bone.

The thought of even being in such proximity to Zima again, enough to kiss him, made my stomach flip and my heart pound. Kissing *him* was the furthest thing from my mind, and I had never kissed anyone to begin with. Despite Zima being one of the prettiest people I had ever met, I was not sure I wanted to kiss him. Nor did I think it would solve the situation.

The sight of him kneeling before me on the floor, strong hands on my thighs, flashed in my mind's eye, and my pallid skin immediately erupted in a bloom of scarlet red.

Nope.

No, no, no.

I was *not* going to think about *that*. Thank you very much.

The others seemed to think Jax's suggestion was hilarious; Félix laughed until his cheeks turned purple, and Himawari forced him to drink a whole glass of water so he could try and breathe. I declined to join them in their merriment.

Even Talia, the very person I thought would understand my ire, agreed with Jax during one of our infrequent messaging sessions. She thought a "steamy make-out session" as she put it would break the tension, and we would all live happily ever after. Or at least she would get a good laugh out of it, and I would be a human popsicle.

She got the hint I was angry after I refused to respond

to the three following messages she sent and showed up at my flat with my favorite chocolate bar as an apology.

"I can't stay," she had said, pressing the candy into my hands. "We're on our way to the hangar and takeoff is in like, twenty minutes."

I just glared at her, and she winked before I could slam the door in her face. I later sent her a picture of me eating the candy as proof I accepted her apology. The next day she called me on her flight home from her mission, only to reiterate that she thought Zima's attitude toward me was based on more than dislike. I ignored her comments and changed the subject. We hung up with the promise to get together sometime soon.

Despite my team's encouragement, matters did not improve between me and Zima. I had tried Himawari's suggestion of patience and kindness, which was met with cool disdain. The thought of a squad change request *had* crossed my mind a few times if I were to be completely honest, but I ultimately decided against that resolution. I doubted the higher-ups would even accept it seeing as Zima's reputation had preceded him as a hard-ass and rumors pegged him as a team-breaker.

I did not even entertain Jax's suggestion. Not even a little bit. Not even when Zima and I were toe-to-toe in a shouting match during a horrendous team training sim, his beautiful blue eyes staring wrathfully down into mine.

"It was a bad call, *Deveraux*," he snapped, eyes blazing.

"It would not have been, had you executed it like we've been trying to do for the past hour!" I hissed back.

Again, I could feel the crackle of magic in the air surrounding us. Those same clouds of condensation, the reactions of our magics to each other, began forming around us once again as the argument became more heated.

Jax, Himawari, and Félix stood a few feet from us, just watching warily. They learned very quickly that once Zima wanted to lay into me there was not much they could do, save getting their asses handed to them as well. I did not blame them for choosing to stay out of it.

"You need to be able to think on your feet," Zima seethed, eyes studying my face. I was positive he was able to detect the slightest change in my features.

"I *can* think on my feet," I argued, placing my hands on my hips. "What we are doing right now is *practicing* maneuvers, not our ability to switch between them."

"The team is all over the place, Deveraux!"

"Only because you refuse to work with us!"

"Guys…" Jax called, panic rising in his voice.

Before I could react, I was swept off my feet and into the air. The giant mech suit – piloted by a simulated Coalition soldier – we had been battling in the simulation had launched me into the air at a deadly speed. Blood was rushing in my ears so loudly I could hardly hear my screams or the shouts of my teammates.

"Daux!" A shout sounded below me, louder than the others. If I had not known any better, I would have thought it was a roar.

Swiftly, I flipped myself in mid-air, turning myself towards the direction of the shout. I had no time to feel it, but shock flooded through me. Zima's face was white as he rushed for me, and the others were fighting the simulation.

Jax and Himawari were busy with the mech, cornering it as Félix rushed it with his berserker magic – I could practically see it running through his veins.

Sprinting toward me at a frightening speed, Zima launched himself into the air. Involuntarily, I reached my arms out toward him and he collided with me, nearly knocking the breath from my lungs. His arms wrapped tightly around me, crushing me to his chest as we fell.

Over Zima's shoulder, I could see a wave of shadow flashing toward us. He seemed to be expecting it and curled himself around me as the shadow hit us. It enveloped us, lowering us gently downwards. Waiting for us on the ground were our teammates, Himawari using her staff to bind the shadows around us.

They rushed me when Zima's feet were firmly planted on the ground, but nearly knocked him over with their affection. With my friends' arms around me, I finally allowed myself to calm down. I hardly remembered my arms were wrapped around Zima's neck.

Gently, he set me to my feet and reached up to remove my stranglehold on him. My eyes flashed to his face in embarrassment; half waiting for him to start tearing into me again. But he did not. His eyes blazed with blue fire, but it was different from the iciness of his wrath which he so often turned upon me. That fire reminded me of that blazing look that night in the kitchen not too long ago.

My body warmed all over, an indiscernible emotion flooding through me, and I let my arms drop to my sides. We stood there for what felt like hours, staring into each other's faces, until a soft cough to the left of us jerked us out of our trances.

With a jerk, I turned toward my teammates, who had backed off a few steps, allowing Zima to set me down. They surged toward me again, Félix grabbing me by the hand. When I turned back to Zima to thank him, he was already stalking away, toward our building as the failed simulation shut down.

"That was awful," Jax commented as we, without Zima, all sat in the living room icing our various injuries.

I nodded absently in agreement. My mind was still on Zima and our argument during the simulation training. Not on the way he gently cradled me in his arms. Definitely not the way he looked at me while he held my hands in his. Never that.

"Daux," Himawari called, breaking me from my stupor.

"Yes?" I asked, looking up at her.

"We are…" She hesitated, her brow furrowing. "We're concerned about you and Zima. Things clearly aren't good between you. Or with the rest of us."

She cut me off as I opened my mouth to protest. "He has a problem with us too, you can't deny that."

My eyes lowered, not really in shame, but I did feel bad for keeping some of the truth from them. To my discredit, though, I thought I could handle it myself.

"I know I should have spoken with you all about it, especially where it concerns you." I sighed, gripping my elbows in my hands. "It's not that I did not trust you, it's just that I wanted to be able to deal with the situation on my own. I see now it was a mistake."

It was difficult to let my insecurities show. Jax, Himawari, and Félix were quickly becoming my friends. I knew, if I let them in, they could be as close to me as Talia; still, it was something that would be incredibly difficult.

Seeing the looks on their faces when they realized I had kept Zima's words from them tugged at my heartstrings. I had not meant to hurt them – of course I had not – but it happened regardless.

"From now on," I began, drawing myself up to full height and looking each of my teammates in the eye. "I will be more transparent. I want us to work well together and be friends."

Félix grinned and gave me a thumbs up. Jax and Himawari converged upon me to envelop me in a huge hug, which Félix joined, patting my back. In their embrace, I felt a warmth blossom in my chest. One that I had only begun to feel with Riannan. One I truly had with Talia.

Despite that warmth… Despite the budding friendship between us, I felt a deep, growing resentment. Zima would not tear this away from me. I would work with him. I could do that. For my new friends, it would be easy. But I would not allow this to be taken away. I wouldn't.

173

Chapter Sixteen

The Overseer's assistant's face was grim as they relayed the news to us that morning. During a solo investigation into an untouched area on the Coalition-controlled Floral Islands, one of Spec Ops' top agents – Dr. Javier Moreno had gone holo-silent and they had not heard from him in over forty-eight hours. This was incredibly unusual for him. They had reason to believe he was kidnapped by a small band of Coalition soldiers they believed to have set up a base in proximity to his last location.

The untouched area was one of the many places Coalition experiments had not invaded into the local flora and fauna. These experiments started during the war and continued even now. They caused horrific genetic mutations in all life forms – excluding humans – leading to shortened life spans, deformities, and leaving the plants and animals completely inedible for human consumption. Non-magical humans at least.

Zima, always looking for an instance to undermine me, explained it would merely be a routine mission that would help our standing in Spec Ops since we had already been doing so poorly. He had already spoken with the Overseer's assistant without me. My skin bristled at the slight, but I did not wish to let my personal feelings toward Zima jeopardize this "routine rescue" as he and the assistant had called it.

While we were still working out the kinks in our strategies and maneuvers, I believed we could complete this mission successfully, even if we could not do it to the standard of more experienced teams. After receiving our orders, I lead my team down to the awaiting auto. I would make sure this rescue was a success if only to command Zima's respect.

"Gotta be careful out here," the guide, Jakob, said, his white teeth flashing against his dark brown skin. "The natural fauna is just itching to rip your face off."

"I'm sorry," Himawari interjected. "Rip our what's off?"

"Faces," Jakob reiterated jovially, gesturing to his face which bore a prominent scar running from his hairline to his jaw. I had been wondering how he acquired that.

"You don't want to tangle with a 'roo," he said ominously, his joviality suddenly replaced with a severity I was surprised he possessed.

"A what?" Jax echoed.

"A kangaroo," Félix whispered behind his hand.

"Ah," replied Jax.

"Just a regular kangaroo?" Himawari stammered.

The guide nodded.

"Ain't none of those fancy half-breeds or mutants where we're goin'," he said.

I tried to catch Zima's eye, but he had maneuvered himself to face the road. Untouched areas – places where magically mutated animals had been unable to encroach – were rare and almost more dangerous because of the ferocity at which the native fauna protected its habitat. If we were headed there, then our "routine mission" was much more important than Zima let on.

Presumably, it was not "routine" at all. If the Coalition

was privy to a full-fledged Spec Ops team headed to an untouched area, then it would be a cause for them to secretly dispatch a unit there. Luckily, sending a newly formed team such as ours would barely be a blip on their radar.

But where exactly were we headed? And what for? Zima owed the rest of the team an explanation.

While he and the guide had their eyes on the road I signaled to the rest of the group with my hand. When I had their attention, I sent a message to our team chat, excluding Zima, to explain my theory and to be on guard. The three pinged back their affirmatives and that was that. Now we would wait to reach our destination.

Once we were close enough to our coordinates, Jakob stopped the vehicle and let us out with a cheeky grin and a wave before driving off back toward the air-drop point. He would get about halfway and hide the auto to wait for our signal. Then he would meet us back at our current coordinates.

"So, he's not dropping us off at the exact location?" Jax asked somewhat nervously.

Zima merely shook his head, stormy as ever.

"The unmutated creatures are more likely to detect a non-living object than a living being," I explained. "Our visual appearance and scent will of course be unfamiliar, but we will be able to pass with less detection than an armored auto."

"And," Himawari interjected. "The Coalition soldiers at the base won't be able to detect us as easily either."

"Exactly," I concurred.

Jax nodded, still wary, and we made our way into the untouched rainforest.

The other members of Dr. Moreno's team had given me one of his spare pairs of glasses, so I could familiarize myself with his magical signature and track him. Considering the density of this untouched area, all the help I could get was well appreciated.

At the first activation of my foresight Dr. Moreno's gold-colored magical signature wafted all over the place, flitting from tree to brush at random. It seemed that anything and everything caught his eye. Until the signature solidified into a rope of energy, distinctly mapping out his movements as though he had drawn them out on a map for me.

Gesturing for the rest to follow, I noticed immediately how silent the area was. Insects were buzzing and birds singing, but something was off. We neither saw nor heard any small, non-threatening mammals running about. Nor did we see any large ones. Just bugs and birds.

I signaled my discomfort to Zima as we traversed through the dense foliage and he, again, nodded. But this time he spoke.

"I noticed too," he whispered so as not to alert the others.

"What could be the problem?" I asked, lowering my voice to match his pitch.

Zima shrugged one shoulder, eyeing our surroundings while making sure the other three stayed ignorant of our conversation.

"I'm not sure," he murmured finally. "If predators and other large animals are wary, then prey animals and insects should be afraid too."

I was silent for a moment, then it hit me.

"They couldn't be that stupid!" I exclaimed softly.

"What?" Zima asked, now on high alert and expecting the worst.

"They must have activated some sort of field."

A field was a type of repelling energy that was discovered in the early stages of the War. People on all sides used it as a means of protection from rapidly mutating animals, plants, and normal apex predators. If it were strong enough, the field could even repel humans.

However, the energy that type of field needed to produce it was hardly worth the protection it offered because the energy pods needed would be easily spotted and then destroyed from a distance; although, it was possible the pods could have their sort of protection.

In this case, it did not appear this field repelled humans, only animals. These types of fields often went undetected, but those with trained eyes and ears could spot the disruption in nature almost instantly, like Zima and I had.

A mistake on their part.

"If that's the case, it does not appear as if they suspected anyone coming to retrieve the target," Zima said, grinning. It was slightly malicious and cold, indicating a deep hatred for the Coalition I had not seen surface before now. It almost reminded me of the grin Zima had on his face during our sparing match all those weeks ago.

I suppressed a shudder at the sight and pushed forward. The field's reach would prevent any agitated predators or any other animals, but the minute we disabled or destroyed it, they would all come rushing back, and we would be at their mercy. Hopefully, we would be able to enter the base without destroying it.

Because of that possibility, we silently agreed to keep the other three ignorant of our observations to keep them from panicking. Félix had already demonstrated difficulty keeping his magic in check during high-pressure situations, which was natural due to his berserker magic. Himawari was entirely too jumpy, and Jax was incredibly anxious on missions where combat was a possibility. All aspects were something to work on, but we needed this mission to go smoothly, so Zima and I stayed quiet.

As we headed deeper into the rainforest the more unsettling the silence became. Even the others began to pick up on it, Félix staying closer to Zima and me while Jax and Himawari stuck close to each other. It was quite clear to everyone now that there was something afoot.

Too soon Dr. Moreno's magical signature led us to a derelict-looking building in the middle of this rainforest.

According to the Spec Ops database, it wasn't unusual to find old buildings such as this in Coalition-controlled areas. But those buildings were typically used for purposes the Coalition deemed as heretical – like safe houses for people with magic or resistance gathering places.

This building didn't look like either of those and the more I concentrated on it the more the edges began to blur. No Coalition squadron would take a skilled Spec Ops agent to a derelict building in the middle of the rainforest. Soon enough, the true form of the structure began to take shape. It took all of my effort, and Dr. Moreno's signature began to blur and disappear the more the base began to define itself.

Sweat began pouring down my face and neck beneath my helmet because of the strain – and the terrible humidity. Once I had completely cut through whatever disguise mechanism the Coalition soldiers had used to disguise their base, and saw that it was indeed a Coalition base, I relinquished my concentration from it, and Dr. Moreno's magical signature began to form again.

"It's a disguise," I hissed at Zima, reaching for his arm. I snatched the elbow of his sleeve and pointed at the once again crumbling structure.

"Do you think it's a transmitter or magic?" he whispered back, not bothering to shake me off.

"A transmitter, it has to be a transmitter." Dispelling a magic-based disguise would have been difficult enough. This one had to be a transmitter because I had to use all of my focus to dispel it, and even then, once my focus was relinquished the image went back to the way it was. So, the transmitter would have to be destroyed.

Transmitters were delicate and prone to malfunction and explosion when overheated, but the disguise they provided was nearly as good as any glamour. It could change the interior and exterior of any building, even hiding any potential threats from the naked eye. Or anyone who didn't have an ability like foresight.

Zima nodded, still looking at the roof of the building where the transmitter and the field seemed to be emanating from.

I signaled to Jax and Himawari and they rushed over to us. Félix, who was already with us – and who overheard – filled them in.

"I could take out the transmitter with a shadow," Himawari suggested, already gripping her staff.

I nodded my consent, pointedly ignoring Zima and whether or not he approved. With my direction of her shadow, Himawari and I made quick work of the transmitter, and the base's original structure was in full view. I resisted the urge to rip off my helmet because of the sweat, humidity, and quickly forming strain migraine and marched forward.

Perhaps it was a gamble to take out the transmitter so soon, but since transmitters were prone to malfunction, it wasn't an uncommon occurrence. I just hoped that the soldiers would be distracted trying to repair it, allowing us to slip in with less of a chance of detection.

Thankfully, that was exactly what happened. Several engineers appeared on the roof, along with several armed guards for protection in case the malfunction was not as humdrum as it appeared. We took this opportunity to apply camouflaging glamours with the help of Jax and Himawari's magics and slip into an unmanned supply door, unnoticed.

Once inside, I whispered for Zima to scout ahead while we waited for his signal, which came not long after. I motioned for the others to fall in line behind me and we set off after him.

He was waiting on us at the end of a long corridor, which felt vaguely familiar. Himawari, carefully using her shadows, was able to take out any detection devices. Jax and Félix kept an eye on our flanks for an ambush. All in all, I was pleased with how things were going.

There had been no disruptions and the enemy had not figured out that the transmitter had been sabotaged rather than simply shutting down on its own. So far, we were doing well and staying safe.

"Dr. Moreno's signature is leading me this way," I whispered to Zima, pointing to the left and up a flight of stairs.

Zima nodded, his expression was tight and his movements were jerky. From his body language alone, I could tell he bristled at not taking point on this operation, but I was not going to let him ruin another one.

"So, if we follow you and things keep going smoothly then we should make it to him and get out with no problems," he said tersely.

I nodded, stepping carefully up the stairs. "We can't guarantee that things *will* continue to go smoothly. We could be discovered at any moment, and the whole operation could be compromised."

Zima pursed his lips in annoyance but nodded, which was surprising.

"I know that Deveraux," he bit out, hurrying his pace. "But you don't have to make your faithlessness in your team so apparent."

Before he had even finished his sentence, I was rolling my eyes. Himawari, who was next to me, sniggered quietly but kept her focus on shielding us with her shadows. Our glamours should keep us from being detected by sight or cameras – unless they had glamour detection software – which Himawari would then shield us from sight with a strong shadow or disrupt the camera feed. With Zima and I in front while Jax and Félix brought up the rear, we were impenetrable and would be able to take on much of what the enemy could throw at us.

We had run this in a similar sim several times before Zima even said we were acceptable enough to try for the real thing, as the only one of us who had done any sort of mission like this successfully. Which made his comment even that much more irritating. It was not a lack of faith in my team that had me nervous. There were too many variables; it was impossible to calculate a one-hundred-percent desirable outcome. Completely impossible.

Faith in your team was imperative. Without it, there would be no completing anything with true success. But *blind* faith in your teammates alone would get you killed, or worse. There were things you just could not put on your team, or your friends, and doing so was not only stupid but deadly.

I trusted all my teammates with my life, including Zima; however, I did not trust the unpredictable variables to be on our side. Zima's harsh judgment was unfounded and just another way to try and get under my skin. *He* was the one who had so little faith in us.

Once we got through the door, Dr. Moreno was already on his feet, pressed up against the wall as if that would somehow save him from an imminent attack. Luckily for him, we were not there to do him harm.

"Who are you, what do you want?" Dr. Moreno cried in a hoarse whisper.

"Calm down," I soothed, holding up my hands in a placating gesture. "We are with Spec Ops; my team and I are here to rescue you."

"You'll have to show me some identification…" he said, visibly forcing himself away from the wall to move closer to us.

I placatingly held out my holonav, reassuring him gently that we were who I said we were. He held his holonav up to mine to verify the information. While the target examined my Spec Ops ID, and Zima's, I checked his to make sure he was not a Coalition plant.

Holonavs are heavily encrypted and difficult to distinguish from a regular wristwatch until it was activated and it displayed the interactive holoscreen – which explained why Dr. Moreno's hadn't been confiscated. It would be incredibly difficult for a small band of Coalition soldiers to try and gain access to our target's holonav to lay a trap. The only way to gain information from another person's holonav would be for them to share it willingly or they would have to be an expert hacker. It was unlikely they had one in such a small base.

As such, the target's ID popped up, showing his name, job description, team, and clearance level. Dr. Javier Moreno, Biologist and Zoologist, team: Axel, clearance level: 2.

"Pleased to meet you, Dr. Moreno," I said with a voice I would have used to soothe my sister or a small animal.

"I'm sorry," he apologized, his worry lines heavily pronounced.

"No need," I responded quickly, removing the magic-blocking cuffs on his wrists.

Félix was quickly tapping away signal scramblers on his holonav from the doorway. Hopefully, they would be able to keep the Coalition soldiers from noticing our entry into the room.

"You've been through a lot. There is nothing to apologize for," I reassured him, still smiling as Zima and I made our way back out of the room and motioned for the doctor to follow.

Exiting the room was easy enough, but as we rounded the corner three armed guards were waiting for us. Shocked, I sprang into action, knocking one of the guard's weapons from his hands and sending him sprawling toward the ground. The next rushed past me toward the target but was blocked by Zima and swiftly rendered unconscious with the hilt of his blade. He quickly froze the third where he stood and plucked the gun from his hands, tossing it across the room, and froze the other two guards as well.

Now on high alert, Zima and I gripped Dr. Moreno's arms tightly in our hands, keeping him in between us as we all marched toward the unguarded door we entered through, glamoured and shadowed. We made it to our exit in a matter of minutes, and soon the humidity outside was seeping through my armor again.

Thanks to Jax and Himawari, we were able to escape the facility unscathed. Outside, however, was another problem. The soldiers had been unable to repair their transmitter… but in doing so they must have caused an energy surge to the field that repelled the nonmutated animals. The scene that lay before us would render me nauseous for weeks after.

There were two large male kangaroos and a small pack of jackals tearing into the Coalition soldiers on the ground. Hawks and other large birds of prey were launching themselves onto the soldiers on the roof. Vultures and crows circled overhead, indicating the outcome.

The Coalition soldiers at this base were already small in number, and the animals were having no problems ripping them to pieces with their claws and teeth.

"What do we do?" Jax asked, looking positively green.

"We let them be," I replied gravely, observing the grisly scene as I willed myself not to be sick. "Our mission is to rescue Dr. Moreno, and we must get him to safety."

"Okay," Jax snapped shakily, keeping up his cloaking magic.

All we could do was hope that the animals in the area would be drawn to the sounds of gunfire and the Coalition soldier's screams instead of our scent. I prayed to any of the Gods still listening that our glamours and shadows would still be enough.

Zima and I, each gripping Dr. Moreno tightly by the arms, ran through the dense underbrush as carefully as possible. Neither of us wanted to harm the doctor, nor did we want to attract any undue attention from animals, but we had to run. It was either that or the animals at the base would track and descend upon us before we could safely extract the scientist.

Creatures of all shapes and sizes rushed past us, crazed

looks in their eyes. Each time they got too close we froze, refusing to even make a sound. It was undoubtedly one of the most stressed I had ever been, having to pause and remain silent, knowing it would mean certain injury or death for everyone if I made one slight error. We all collectively let out a sigh of relief when we broke through the trees and undergrowth.

But it was not over. We still needed to make our way back to the rendezvous point and the animals were still prowling, waiting for something – or someone – to encroach upon their territory. It was still more running from there, and I was winded. All of my senses were on overload and the burning in my lungs and legs with each step wasn't helping. I knew the others were feeling it too. Especially the doctor.

Zima and I kept our grasp on Dr. Moreno, refusing to let him slow his pace. Then, finally – thank the *Gods* – we made it to the rendezvous point where Jakob and the auto awaited us. I nearly cried with joy but refused when I saw Zima's cool, collected face.

Himawari, Jax, and Félix on the other hand, collapsed immediately and wailed their relief, along with Dr. Moreno.

Once we had gotten settled and were on our way from that hellhole, I was able to reflect upon the mission we had been given. A "routine mission" Zima and the assistant had said. Of course, the tense air in the Overseer's office this morning had conveyed otherwise, but I had assumed it was due to Zima's poor reports on our team thus far.

Zima's lack of trust in me – in his teammates – inadvertently caused us all to be implicit in the deaths of several Coalition soldiers. I did not want to join Spec Ops to become a murderer. I wanted to protect, that included those who were brainwashed by the Coalition. That would weigh heavily on me for a long time to come. Not only could we have potentially prevented the deaths had we known the true nature of the mission, but we could have been better prepared to protect Dr. Moreno.

But this mission was *not* routine. Dr. Moreno's ID and credentials attested to that. He was nearly as high a ranking as the Overseer as far as clearance and was hardly captured for trespassing too close to the Coalition base. No. There was more to this so-called "routine mission", and I intended to find out what.

Chapter Seventeen

Once Dr. Moreno was in good hands, me and the team made our way to the Overseer's office to report on our mission. I wanted answers. And since Zima had not been forthcoming on our ride over, I would seek them elsewhere.

The Overseer's secretary showed us into her office to wait, with offerings of tea and coffee. We declined, and he left shortly after, closing the door behind him. The assistant Zima had spoken to was nowhere in sight.

The office was exactly as I remembered it, devoid of the intimidating presence of the Overseer. Without her there I was able to observe the room without seeming nosy or disrespectful. It was plain, with white walls and beige flooring accented with dark furniture. The most opulent piece in the room was a large, plush-looking leather chair that sat behind the plain wooden desk.

All in all, it was an incredibly unassuming office space, which was the direct opposite of my father's office in the NAF governors' offices. He had decorated it lavishly, like his home. I had only seen it a few times in my life, but it left me with the impression that most officials' offices were that way. But that appeared not to be the case.

After only a few minutes, the Overseer stepped into her office and made her way around her desk to sit down. She was a tall, powerful woman with dark skin and eyes so dark they seemed to be black holes, sucking in all the light around them. Her hair was woven into numerous minuscule braids and coiled tightly around her head. She looked as imposing as her reputation, which was a bit of a marvel to her subordinates.

We all stood to attention when she entered the room and the others only sat when she signaled for them to do so. She waved Zima and me up to her desk for us to report.

"Ma'am," I began, clasping my hands behind my back respectfully. "I was unaware that this was a mission of great import, as was the rest of my team."

She raised an eyebrow at this, turning to look at Zima, who surprisingly avoided meeting her eyes.

"I think it was incredibly dangerous for us, as inexperienced as we are now, to head into an untouched area unfamiliar to us and be expected to be responsible for another human being's life, especially one such as Dr. Moreno. Though we were made to practice in a similarly constructed sim, we could have put his life in peril because we were kept in the dark."

While I was unfinished – I had *much* more to say – the Overseer politely held up a hand to stop me.

"You're telling me, Deveraux, that you and your teammates were not informed of the nature of this mission?" she asked, eyes still trained on Zima.

"Well…" I started, looking toward Zima as well before turning back to the Overseer. "Zima appeared to be well-informed on the nature of the mission. When pressed, he would give neither me nor my teammates any information. One of your assistants appeared to be in on the details, though."

The Overseer grimaced and folded her hands over the top of her desk. "It was not my decision, nor my intent, to have you all believe this mission was a routine rescue mission. Zima did not agree and went behind my back – with my assistant no less – to tell you so."

Our eyes remained on the Overseer, but hers were fixated on Zima, who sat stiffly in his chair next to me.

"Dr. Moreno is one of Spec Ops' top scientists. His magical abilities allow him to catalog and categorize flora and fauna as easily as if he were in a lab. This is helpful in our endeavors to reverse the damage done to our world by the Coalition scientists. Dr. Moreno is indispensable, and his rescue should have been seen as a top-priority mission. Certainly not as mundane as a *routine rescue.*"

"If I may," Zima spoke up but was immediately silenced by those deep, dark eyes.

"You may not, Zima Angelov," she growled, leaning slightly over her desk. "You *may* count yourself grateful, due to the success of your mission, that I do not suspend you indefinitely and mark this on your record as insubordination as well as obstructing information for a top priority mission."

Fierce, like a lioness. That was the only way I could describe the Overseer. She was beautiful and deadly at that moment. The way she looked at Zima with those dark eyes of hers… I would not have been surprised had she chosen to leap over her desk and rip his throat out with her bare hands.

"Your opinions on your teammates have been made and noted," she hissed, baring her very sharp-looking teeth. "Despite that, they have done exceptionally well and have executed a top-priority mission with virtually no flaws. Whatever your reasoning may have been, it was poor judgment on your part and could have jeopardized your team as well as Dr. Moreno. I am disappointed in you."

Then those terrifying eyes turned upon me.

"As for you, Daux Deveraux," the Overseer began, leaning back in her plush leather chair. "You and the rest of your team may go. I must speak further with Zima. I expect a report on my desk first thing tomorrow morning."

Motioning for the others, I stood and nodded my head. "Yes ma'am."

Silence followed us out the door and into the hall. It

followed us all the way down to the main floor as if all the people here knew the Overseer was angry. As if they thought she would explode at the slightest of noises. That silence followed us all the way back home.

"Why don't you, I don't know, message her?" Jax asked, hanging upside down off Félix's bed and staring at me with his braided hair spilling onto the floor.

I was typing up my report on our mission, and only half contributed to the conversation. We were sitting in Félix's room, having all had dinner, and wanting to hang out. Félix, who wanted to play a video game while he ate, suggested we all sit in his room.

"What?" I asked, finally looking up at him.

He rolled his eyes and gestured to Himawari for help. She merely shrugged her shoulders and smiled.

"Talia, your best friend? The one you haven't stopped sighing about since we moved in?" he said, tone slightly snide but good-natured.

"I have not done that," I argued, frowning.

"Oh, I wish I would have gotten the chance to speak with Tali at the party!" Félix sighed in a falsetto voice from his spot at his gaming setup.

I made a face at his back.

"I wish I could have spoken longer to Talia the other day when I passed her in the lobby!" Jax said, in his breathy imitation of my voice.

"This is becoming tedious," I snipped.

"Oh, Talia, I miss you, my dear sweet Talia!" Himawari whined, throwing herself to the ground next to me.

I shoved her away petulantly. "I do not sound like that."

"You do," my teammates said in unison. Félix even

turned away from his game to look at me.

"You are all incredibly uncouth," I huffed, turning my attention back to my holonav.

"And you are insecure and dumb," Jax said, grinning.

"Mature."

"More so than *someone* who insists on pouting and waiting for her friend to message her first."

I gestured rudely at him, sending them all into fits of giggles. Perhaps I had been moping around about Talia

"What?" I snapped, eyes flashing.

"You've never done anything like that before!" Himawari cried, clutching her sides as if she were in pain.

I blinked. "Done what?"

"Flipped someone off," Félix said, wiping his eyes. "At least, you've not done that in front of *us* before."

"And here we thought you were so prim and proper," Jax teased as he rolled off Félix's bed.

It was silent for a few moments, just the tapping and clicking of Félix's pad when he returned to his game. Then I repeated the gesture, grinning this time.

"Gods, Daux, where did you even learn that?" Himawari asked, playfully pretending to be affronted.

In response, I merely held up my second hand.

"Now stop that," Jax admonished, also feigning offense. "We can't have everyone thinking our esteemed team leader is a scoundrel!"

Pretending to ignore them, I stood and began to observe my hands, as though they were foreign objects. I made sure to hold them close to my friends' faces.

Jax and Himawari met each other's gazes and got to their feet, coming to stand on either side of me.

"Well, Himawari, I do believe our errant Daux needs to be taught a lesson," Jax said, grinning wickedly. Himawari nodded in agreement, her expression disturbingly mirroring his.

In a flash, Jax had his arms around my middle,

clamping my arms to my sides. Himawari paced slowly back in forth in front of us as I struggled, giggling.

"Whatever shall we do with her?" she asked, fighting to hold back her laughter.

"Tickle her," Félix suggested without turning around.

"Great idea, Félix," Himawari agreed, eyes glittering with mischief and amusement.

Jax loosened his grip on me, just enough for Himawari to move her slender fingers against my sides.

I laughed, not because it tickled, but because they were so intent on messing with me. I allowed this to go on for a few more moments before calling things to a halt.

"I'm not ticklish," I told them, still giggling.

"But you were laughing," Jax argued with slight indignation.

"Because this is funny."

"Then how are we supposed to mess with you?"

"That's for me to know and you to figure out."

Félix chuckled from his place at his computer.

"What?" Himawari snapped at him.

"I could have told you she wasn't ticklish," he said snidely.

"But you suggested it!" Jax cried in frustration.

"I know," Félix chuckled, turning to face us again.

"Well," Jax mused, his wicked grin returning. "I suppose we should mess with you instead."

Félix stopped laughing and his mirthful expression vanished.

"I'm good," he stammered.

"No," Jax said, twisting back his long braids. "I don't think you are."

As Himawari and Jax advanced on the helpless Félix, I grinned and shook my head.

"Daux!" he cried. "Help me!"

"Sorry Félix, you're on your own for this one," I laughed.

He cursed and tried to flee, but Jax grabbed him as he had done to me, and Himawari attacked, refusing to stop until Félix was a giggling mess on the floor. I sat and watched, feeling a bit of my heart swell. Love was beginning to grow there, and I was not afraid of it. I embraced it, watching the three of them. We stayed like that, in Félix's room, late into the night, hardly noticing when Zima came home well past midnight.

Chapter Eighteen

Daux," The Overseer said as I stepped into her office. "I'm glad you're here."

I nodded my head respectfully but thought: *You did summon me here.*

"It seems we need your team again."

"Yes ma'am, I gathered as much."

"Did you now? Well, that's good. I'm afraid you will be a member short, though."

"Oh?"

"Yes, I've sent Zima off on another mission."

Interesting. Zima had not spoken a word to us since his dressing down, and hardly interacted with us at all during training sessions and exercises.

"If I may, ma'am," I said hesitantly.

The Overseer looked up at me from the holofiles on her desk, and I flinched internally. There was no unkindness in her expression, though.

"Yes, Daux?" she prompted.

"Why will he not be joining us?" I asked.

The Overseer's gaze lingered on me for a moment before she spoke. "I thought he needed a bit of punishment for the actions he took the other day. They were unfair to your team, in addition to the insubordination. I do not take either of those things lightly."

I nodded my understanding. Zima had been coming

and going at odd hours. The Overseer likely had him doing many different missions for her, as a punishment.

He deserves it. I thought, smiling on the inside.

"Now, Daux," the Overseer continued, sweeping away the holofiles on her desk. "I've called you in here instead of sending you a brief because I wanted to talk to you personally."

"Yes, ma'am."

Her brows furrowed in concern before resuming. "We have received some disturbing reports that the Coalition has infiltrated our government by targeting officials who feel 'marginalized' in our society, as well as installing sleeper agents around our capitol. I need you and your team to gain access to a specific base of theirs to obtain information on the sleeper agents as well as those who may support them."

"Are you referring to the neo-traditionalist movement? The ones who wish to rejoin the Coalition?" I asked, shifting my weight. The group my father had secret sympathies towards.

"So, you're aware. That makes things easier."

"Yes, ma'am."

If only she knew how aware I was.

The Overseer deflated a little and for the first time since I had joined Spec Ops, she looked weary.

"There are those who would have them silenced, those officials. But they already feel as if our government is repressing them and their rights. I'm afraid if we take such measures against them, other than monitoring – as we do with all extreme groups, as I'm sure you know – they will do something drastic."

"What do you mean, ma'am?"

"Their activity has heightened lately. They believe the government is chafing at them and their backward ideals. There is no pleasing them, nor is there anything we can do to calm the situation."

I swallowed. There was no way my team was qualified

for such an important task, much less a teammate short.

"You are sure we should do this without Zima? He's an excellent strategist, and I rely on his input."

She nodded. "Zima is already on his way to complete his assignment, and I need your team to leave as soon as our meeting is over." Her expression turned quizzical. "Have I not asked you to sit?" she asked.

"No, ma'am,"

"You may as well," she waved a slender hand. "We have more to discuss, and this will take a while."

As we sat in the auto, on our way to the navpoint, I relayed the Overseer's instructions.

"So, she wants us to break into this max security, top secret Coalition base, steal this information, and bring it back without getting caught?" Jax asked.

"Yes…" I sighed, rubbing my hands over my face. "If we are caught, or kill any of the guards, they will know their information has been compromised and all the sleeper agents – and likely the sympathizers as well – will be notified in some way. They will all go dark."

"That's just great…" Himawari groaned.

"And we have to do all of this *without* Zima," Jax said irritably.

"Exactly," I agreed.

We sat in silence for a few moments, dreading the mission we were set on.

"So," Félix hedged. "What are we going to do?"

I sighed. "We're going to have to do what we always do. Stick to our plans and pray to any Gods still listening that we don't get caught."

Thirty-six hours later we had made it to our destination. This Coalition base was larger than the last one we had been to. The building loomed before us, the moon casting large shadows across the ground in its shape.

It was not tall but it was imposing, nonetheless. It was reminiscent of the old Coalition strongholds we learned about at the Academy, with its flat roofing and unadorned exterior. I would think they would have improved their architectural design in nearly a century since the war ended.

"It's now or never," I said, gazing upwards.

Thanks to those shadows, and Jax's light-manipulating ability, we would be able to sneak in relatively undetected. Underneath the manipulation magic, we tailored our faces and clothes with shifting magic to resemble Coalition soldiers. Even in a tough spot, they would be passible disguises.

The base had magical disruptors, so we would need to discreetly disable them to break in unobserved. It would not be too hard with the hacking capabilities of our holonavs, but it was nerve-wracking nonetheless.

Sneaking along the perimeter of the building, we carefully disabled the disruptors on that side. A few minutes of quiet signaled that all was well. We all collectively released a sigh. Now would come the difficult part: entering the base, extracting the information, and making it out undetected.

Thanks to the surveillance another team had gathered we were able to discern when a change in guards would occur, allowing us to break into the building without much fear of detection.

I lead the way through the door, looking in each direction for potential threats, then waved the others through. Félix, clever kid that he was, was able to create looping videos to feed into the security cameras during our journey over with only the footage given to us by the intelligence team.

Using his holonav, he fed the cameras the false video while we snuck down the hallways, searching for any sign of unusual guard activity. Eventually, we found our way into our required corridor. It was larger than the rest and ended in a large double-door entryway.

The doors had two guards standing on either side of them, and beyond that were state-of-the-art security measures just in case someone was to infiltrate the base undetected. Like us.

The intelligence team who had hacked into their security system to get us this information had run into some problems with the coding on the door. Thankfully, we had a coding and hacking genius on our team: Félix.

Through his favorite pastime of playing video games, he discovered a passion for coding, which led to a talent for hacking. Which was incredibly advantageous for us, especially now.

Signaling to Jax to relinquish his magic, I made sure to lock in my glamour. With an air of confidence that bordered on arrogance, I rounded the corner, holding up my security badge. The face and body I had taken was slender and tall with black hair and eyes. I had modeled him after a Coalition member seen entering the room often, so there would be less suspicion.

Félix – disguised as a tall, older man known only by the name of "Alden" – stood menacingly behind me. He was allegedly a personal guard who stayed on base with the captain whose identity I had stolen. It was a difficult undertaking, impersonating someone, especially under immense pressure such as we were.

A deep breath. In and out. In and out. In. Out.

In.

Out.

I grinned haughtily at the guards on either side of the door, Félix a stone wall at my back. The men stood to attention, saluting with a hand over their hearts and one at their brow.

"Captain Gladwin, sir!" they shouted by way of greeting; their posture stiff. "We were not expecting you until the day after tomorrow, sir!"

"Stand down, boys," I said in my now oily voice. "There was a change of plans."

"Yes sir!" they replied, immediately relaxing their salutes.

"Now..." I purred, placing my hands on my hips. "Since there was a change in plans, I don't want this visit mentioned to anyone. Understand?"

The two guards shared a long look. Fearing for a moment that I had made a mistake my palms began to sweat, but they turned to me, and one said: "Of course sir, we are not to discuss any activity that goes on in this hallway or beyond these doors with anyone except you."

"Good." I smiled placatingly. "I wanted to make sure you remembered your oaths despite any... changes. New soldiers are always impressionable and a bit naive you see."

I waved a hand expressively, faking despair. The intelligence team had done thorough work. It was almost too bad they were called away for another mission. They would have executed this one perfectly.

"Yes, sir. We remember, sir!"

"Excellent."

Félix stepped forward and the guards gulped. I could tell from the tension in their bodies that they feared the man Félix had taken the form of as much as they feared Captain Gladwin. He pointedly ignored them and opened the code panel on the door.

The little door slid open, revealing a screen. The monochromatic display lit up to reveal the four-digit space for the code, along with the numbers one through ten and the twenty-six letters of the alphabet plus punctuation and symbols.

With an ease that surprised even me, Félix typed in the code, stepping back as the large doors slid open. With a nod to the guards – who returned it with a salute – we stepped through the doors and waited for them to slide shut before we moved further into the room.

It was shockingly small. Gray walls melded into the gray tile floors, giving off a depressing air. The only furniture in the room was a chair that sat in front of an incredibly large monitor, which took up most of the back-facing wall. An equally large control panel sat underneath, lit up with a multitude of buttons.

I waved Félix in front of me now that we were out of the guards' sight and allowed him to take over.

Taking the seat in front of the monitor Félix quickly input the security codes. His fingers moved so fast I could barely keep track of them, even with my foresight activated. Once the security was out of the way, Félix held up his holonav to the console, waiting for the data to begin downloading.

After a few minutes, I started to get antsy.

"This is taking too long; can't you make it go any faster?" I demanded, a slight tremor of worry in my voice.

"Da—Captain," he sighed. "I told you on the way over here that this would take a while. Besides, the captain and his goons are always in here for at least ten minutes at a time. We're okay."

I tapped my foot against the tiled floor. "You're right. I'm just—getting impatient."

What I wanted to say was that I was worried about Jax and Himawari, but I refused to slip out of character just in case our conversation could be overheard somehow.

"Don't be," Félix whispered. "They're literally invisible. If they stay put, they'll be okay."

"But what if they don't?"

He turned the full force of his now gray eyes on me. "Shut up, Captain."

"Okay, okay. Shutting up." I held up my hands placatingly.

My eyes flicked back and forth between the monitor and the doorway, expecting the real Captain Gladwin and his guards to burst through at any moment with Jax and Himawari in restraints.

"Cap," Félix admonished, eyes never leaving his holonav. "You're thinking too loud."

"Sorry," I apologized.

"We've trained well."

"I'm trying not to think too loud, Fé—Alden."

A scoff. "You're doing a piss-poor job of it."

I frowned, crossing my arms over my now-muscled chest. The percentages on his holonav showed it was nearly done extracting the data and copying it to the device.

"How can you read my mind anyway? You're not telepathic," I demanded.

"No," Félix sighed disparagingly. "But we've been living together for a while now. You're kinda predictable when you're worried."

"Thanks."

"No problem. We're almost done here."

I began to worry my lip between my teeth, willing my glamour to stay in place for at least a few more minutes. At least until we could get back to Jax and Himawari.

By the time we left that awful, claustrophobic room, I was on the verge of exploding. Neither Himawari nor Jax had contacted us through our communication line. They were supposed to check in with us every so often, messaging their status or if there was an emergency. The lack of contact made me incredibly anxious.

Despite this, I gave the guards outside an arrogant wave and strolled away from the room. Once Félix and I were out of sight and a few hallways away, I began messaging my teammates frantically.

A few moments later, I got a reply from Himawari.

"Jax and I have been separated." It read.

My heart did not just sink, it plummeted to my toes. Félix could tell by my expression alone that something was wrong. Then he checked his holonav.

He paled visibly, and his fists began to clench and unclench, over and over.

"D—Captain," he croaked.

"I know."

And we ran. We ran as fast as we could through the unadorned halls, slowing only when guards made themselves present until we reached the rendezvous point. A short, stocky man waited there for us.

"Finally," he said, sounding panicked. "My partner was recognized by a couple of other guards, and they dragged him off to another part of the building!"

"Soldier," I hissed. "Quiet! You are in *disguise*, remember? Which direction did they go?"

Himawari pointed down a northern-facing corridor. "That way, I followed as far as I could without being noticed. I can take you that far at least."

I sighed and clenched my fists.

"That will have to be enough. I can use my ability to track him the rest of the way."

Waving her forward, Himawari began to lead us in the direction she followed Jax. She led us deeper into the belly of the complex, down a long span of twisting halls and rooms. I could barely keep track, even with my ability activated.

Then we halted.

"This was as far as I could go without being spotted," she said in her new form's raspy voice. "I'm a rank higher than the privates who dragged my partner off, so they didn't question why I was at the rendezvous point, but his disguise wasn't supposed to be here tonight. They took him with them despite my protests. There was nothing I could do without raising alarm."

"You should have contacted me immediately," I snapped in irritation.

"And what would you have done?" she snapped back. "You and your guard still needed to copy the data; leaving early would have drawn suspicion."

"Yes, it would have. But I would not have left, I would have stayed with my guard and finished my part in the mission. And *you* should have contacted me immediately, as per the instruction I gave you; *any* emergency."

Himawari hung her head. The contrite expression on the man's face she wore would have been funny had we not been in a dangerously compromising situation. And had I not been angry she directly disobeyed an order. And had I not been incredibly anxious about Jax.

"Let's just go," I hissed, leading the way now.

I scanned ahead of me while the others brought up the rear, searching for any sign of Jax's magical signature. One of the great things about my foresight ability was that its unique tracking and vision capabilities made finding even a needle in a haystack simple. Jax was just a needle in a very big haystack.

At first, all I could see were small, silvery shimmers of magical signatures from the weak latent magic the guards possessed. Then the very faint glimmer of blue wafted at eye level, solidifying into a soft teal ribbon. I dashed after it, praying it would lead to Jax and he was unharmed.

I barely paid attention to the direction we were going; my only focus was on the strip of teal leading me to my teammate. Again, I only slowed in the presence of other Coalition members, smirking as they saluted me. It was almost disgusting how easy playing this Captain Gladwin was. He felt like a real creep. The way he commanded power, relished in the deference from his subordinates… It felt like I was in the presence of my father.

Once we passed a pair of groveling Coalition soldiers, we found ourselves in a large corridor. Jax's signature stopped abruptly outside a small door, partially closed.

Himawari, Félix, and I stood outside of it, listening. Laughter trickled out of the small crack. It was not Jax's voice, but the laugh held his familiar cadence.

I pushed open the door, schooling my face into an expression of haughty disdain. The soldiers in the room all jumped to attention, saluting my presence. Even Jax. He may not have been sure it was me, but his acting was impeccable regardless.

"Private Hayden," I snapped.

"Sir!" Jax answered.

"Why are you not at your assigned post?"

"I was… Well, sir…"

I fixed him with a long look, then stared at each of the soldiers in turn.

"Can any of you explain to me why Private Hayden is not in the position I assigned to him specifically?" I asked, my tone harsh and cold.

The soldiers' eyes reflected a fear I had not expected. I knew this Captain Gladwin person was cruel and heavy-handed, but I did not anticipate the fear he would render from his men. As deplorable as it might be, I decided to use that to my advantage.

I rounded on the soldier closest to me, turning the full force of my now dark eyes on him.

"Answer me, soldier," I commanded fiercely. "Why was Private Hayden not in his position?"

I could have sworn he was about to piss himself. A wicked grin spread across my face. He may have pissed himself a little.

"W-well sir," he began, trembling. "We didn't know

he was supposed to be there tonight…"

"Did he not think to tell you of my *direct* orders?"

"I tried to, sir," Jax interjected, feigning camaraderie with the soldier for so long must have been tiring.

"And they did not listen?"

"No sir."

"I see."

My gaze fell upon each of the men in the room, including Jax, taking in their dread, their anxiety, and the desire to flee.

"So, you four decided to take Private Hayden with you, despite his protests and change of post, to this room to do what exactly?" I asked, making sure to inject my voice with as much scorn as I could manage.

I had Zima to thank for that inspiration.

I did not have to so much as glance down to see the opened cans of sparkbeer – a wheat-based alcohol imbibed with electricity magic – and other recreational substances. One soldier released a shuddering breath as if he anticipated his impending doom.

"We had plans tonight sir…" another soldier said, shakily. "When we saw Hayden was still at base, we dragged him along, we assumed–"

"You assumed wrongly" I interrupted.

"Yes sir," he replied, eyes downcast.

I let out a longsuffering sigh. I could not truly punish these men, nor did I want to. There was not much time to enforce such things anyhow.

"I will be… *lenient*… I suppose," I said, sneering.

The men nearly sagged with relief, save Jax who held himself stiffly.

"But," I continued. "I don't want this spoken of again, even amongst yourselves. I'm a busy man and don't have the time to deal with you tonight."

"Sir!" they shouted, saluting.

"Private Hayden," I snapped, turning to Jax. "Come

with me. I have things to discuss with you."

Jax saluted and all but ran from the room.

"Again," I hissed over my shoulder. "I don't want to catch wind of this incident."

My face must have betrayed more rage than I intended to convey because the men fell back slightly. In the presence of a superior officer no less. Another sneer and I left the room.

As soon as the door closed and we were further away – Félix and Himawari on our heels – Jax swept me into his arms, spinning me around.

"Ja—Private Hayden!" I hissed. "Put me down at once! What if someone sees?"

He dropped me to my feet, looking quite sheepish.

"Sorry Captain," he said, stepping back. "You were amazing though! I could have sworn you were the real thing."

"I suppose I'll take that as a compliment," I chuckled. "Though, Captain Gladwin does not have a reputation for being the nicest of people."

"Either way, you saved my ass back there."

"That I did." I smiled and Jax returned it with one of his own.

"This is nice and all," Félix groused. "But we should probably get out of here. Sensitive information to deliver and all?"

"Right," I agreed and we set out towards the nearest exit.

A few more feet and we would at least be free of the building. When we reached the door, it did not open. I slammed myself up against it, but it was locked.

My heart began to race, and my blood began to rush in my ears. We were trapped. We were trapped and we were going to be caught and executed. This was all my fault. I should have insisted on passing this mission to someone else.

Félix was tampering with the lock, attempting to

override the code with his holonav. Himawari was doing the same. Jax grabbed my hand in his and squeezed as if he sensed my anxiety. He was trembling too.

Footsteps sounded to the left of me, and my head snapped up to see two guards laughing as they headed toward the door we were standing in front of. Though our glamours were still in place, it would be odd for the four of us to be spotted together at this side exit.

Himawari and Félix quickly shut down their holonavs and disconnected from the lock. I prayed the soldiers did not see signs of their tampering. Jax quickly cloaked our glamoured bodies and I stepped backward, quietly, allowing the soldiers to pass us. So did the others.

They stopped in front of the door, one of them pushing their key card into the card reader. The lock signaled its release, and the guards pushed the door open, giving off no signs they had noticed anything.

As I let out an exhale, I took a few hesitant steps forward. Carefully, we made our way out the door behind the men letting it slide shut after us.

Once we made it out, we ran. Félix relinquished his hold over the security system. Himawari began cloaking us in shadows, and Jax began to manipulate the light of the moon to hide us.

We ran until my lungs threatened to give out. Until we had made it into the shadows deep into the rainforest. Here, in a populated Coalition base, there would be no non-mutated animals; we were in minimal danger now.

Jax forced me to stop running and he and Himawari wrapped me in a tight embrace while Félix held my hand. Heat rushed into my face and my eyes began to burn with unshed tears. I refused to let them fall.

Refused to let them see my fear and panic. I was their team leader. I had to be strong. And I was. Until they held me tighter.

Until Himawari whispered, "It's okay, Daux."

Then the tears spilled over, and I was sobbing.

"I was so scared we were going to get caught," I cried as they held me.

"But we didn't," Jax soothed in strained tones.

"We're okay," Félix whispered, sounding close to tears himself.

Himawari was quiet, but she smoothed the hair from my face, pulling me close to her side.

"Daux," she said finally. "I understand you're upset right now; it was all a bit much, but we *need* to get to the rendezvous point or they'll leave without us."

"Himawari," Jax scolded. "She's distraught."

"No, she's right," I said, wiping my face with the back of my hand. "We have to go."

Félix still clung to my hand as I led them through the trees. The trek to the rendezvous point was incredibly uneventful, punctuated only by a few sniffles of my own which I refused to acknowledge. I ignored the concerned looks my teammates were shooting me.

When we made it to the awaiting auto, I made sure everyone entered before climbing in myself. Once inside I finally relinquished my glamour, and it was such a relief to shed that wicked Captain Gladwin off my body, even if it was a glamour. Soon enough, I was myself again, blonde-haired and green-eyed. No signs of that smarmy Coalition captain.

The others did the same, slowly becoming themselves again.

"No offense, ladies," Jax said, relaxing back into the rather uncomfortable seat of the auto. "But you look much prettier as yourselves."

"But Jax," I teased in a half-hearted attempt at humor. "Himawari looked so handsome in uniform!"

"I thought I looked rather nice too," she agreed, playing along as she crossed her arms over her chest.

"Whatever, refuse the compliment," he laughed

quietly.

"At least none of you had to play an old man," Félix whined.

We all laughed at that, though mine was hollow.

"You weren't an old man," I said, my weary body falling back against my seat.

"Was so."

"He could not have been a day over forty."

"I know I took one for the team, you don't have to butter me up."

"Now you're just being silly."

"Yes, I am."

After that we all fell silent. I was sure I would be too keyed up to rest, but Himawari grabbed my hand and laid her head on my shoulder.

Exhausted and overwhelmed, I closed my eyes and promptly passed out along with her.

Chapter Nineteen

After we made it safely back to Heliorious and handed over the extracted information and mission report Jax, Himawari, and Félix all fell immediately into their beds and passed out. Or, I thought they had. As I was sitting on my bed in a clean nightdress, braiding my wet hair after I had scrubbed and scrubbed the feeling of the glamour off my body, a soft knock sounded on the other side of my bedroom door.

"Come in," I called, tying off my braid.

Himawari's concerned face popped through the door a crack before she entered fully into the room, closing the door behind her. I was surprised by her showing up. In the short time that we had been a team, Félix had been the only one to visit me in my room with little to no trepidation.

"Himawari," I said warmly, patting the bed. "Come in."

Her teeth worried her full lips as she padded barefoot across the carpeted floor until she reached the bed. She seemed worried, scared even. I hoped it wasn't because of me. There had been problems with her listening to my instructions in the past, doing what she thought was best in the moment, but that had done nothing to hinder our relationship with each other. We had become somewhat close in the short time we had known each other. But our time together hadn't been one-on-one as often as either of us would have liked.

"I'm sorry about earlier," she said finally, moving without her usual grace to sit on the plush bedcovers with me.

My brows furrowed. "What do you mean?"

"Well, I didn't contact you at the appointed times," she said, worrying my comforter with her fingers. "And then when you were upset, I rushed you."

My heart went out to her as I finally saw how upset she was. Her lip was cracked and slightly bloodied from how much she had been chewing on it, and her paleness had nothing to do with exhaustion. She must have been worrying herself sick.

"Himawari," I said, pulling her hand away from the comforter and into my own. "You're okay. *We're* okay. I'm not upset with you. Yes, you could and should have contacted us at the appointed times. But Jax was already in that room with the soldiers and even if it would have been vital to know, Félix and me could do nothing to help him until we extracted the data. And as for the second thing, you made the right call."

When she lifted her head to look at me, tears had begun to pool, unshed in her dark eyes. Her hand squeezed mine as her lips mashed together in a thin line. I could see the visceral, raw reaction of her emotions playing out in her body.

We sat for a moment, in silence as I waited for her to speak. She needed time. With how upset she was, I didn't want to push her for a response. So, I held her hand and waited until the sniffles died away and her death grip on my hand became less viselike.

"I always wanted to join Spec Ops," she admitted, her voice thick. "My mom and grandmother are over the moon, thanking the Gods and all that. But they only wanted me to join because they never made it in. They were in the intelligence unit in the military."

That was a surprising admission. Shadowmancers were typically in high demand for Spec Ops with their wide range of abilities. But intelligence is where my mother had been Placed. Of course, there were more active positions than the desk job in decrypting she had before she married my father. Small-scale espionage was one of them. A good position for a shadowmancer.

Himawari explained that her mother wanted more for her. That Mrs. Kajikawa thought intelligence gathering was beneath her. Important work, but she could be more useful elsewhere. Unfortunately, the Placement Exam didn't see it that way.

She had provided a good life for her daughter, something Himawari's father decided he didn't want when he defected to the Coalition. The idea of a powerful, matriarchal shadowmancer family was too much for him, so he left with his tail between his legs shortly after his marriage to Himawari's mother. What he didn't know was that he had left his young bride pregnant. She named her baby "Sunflower" to remind her that behind all the shadows, there were happier days.

Her husband's abandonment led Mrs. Kajikawa to become fiercely protective of her daughter, while at the same time nurturing every opportunity for creativity and ambition. When Himawari's shadowmancy ability manifested itself at eight, her mother hoped and prayed to our absent Gods that Himawari would be eligible for a Spec Ops Placement. Up until the Placement, she prayed this knowing how dangerous the job was. That her only daughter might never return to the soil of Heliorious. That Himawari might never return home to her.

"But I didn't want to be in Spec Ops because of my mother," Himawari said, running her thumb over my hand that she was still holding absentmindedly. "She never pushed me towards it, influenced yes, but never pushed. She wanted it to be my choice. And… I wanted it. The Coalition has been encroaching, turning people against magic even in Heliorious, and I wanted to do something about it. We can't change who we are; the least they can do is let us live peacefully."

"I think she would be even more proud of you for that reason," I said, patting her hand and wondering why my own parents couldn't be as loving or accepting.

"She is," Himawari agreed, looking up at me sheepishly. "I think that's why I am too self-reliant. I'm trying to prove to everyone – even myself – that I am capable of this."

"They wouldn't have Placed you here with us if they didn't think you were capable."

Emotion welled up in her once again, threatening to spill over at any moment. She dropped my hand, and for a moment, I missed its warmth only for her to throw her arms around me and release that torrent of emotion that had been building up inside of her onto my shoulder. I sat there, surprised, patting her back as she sobbed.

What had I said? Did I insult her?

After a beat, her sobs quieted into barely noticeable hiccoughs, and her tears soaked through the flannel of my nightdress. Self-consciously, she clung to me, and I hugged her close until she was ready to speak again. I understood how she felt, though my parents had not been, and never would be, so supportive. The need to prove myself to myself was strong. Almost unattainable.

"You're right, you know," she rasped, face flushed as she pushed herself upright. "It's hard to believe, but they would not have Placed me in Spec Ops if I wasn't capable. I will do better on trusting your judgment too."

"We're a team," I reminded her, pleased that my words had not insulted her, but instead uplifted her. "Trusting judgment goes both ways. I'll do better too."

With a final hug, Himawari left me all to my lonesome again. With her tearfulness, I was positive that she would have no trouble finding sleep. But it didn't come easily to me once again. All of my team members, except myself, had happy home lives. Including Himawari, whose father abandoned her and her mother before she was even born.

I was always too afraid to speak out about my parents, lest they retaliate against me. Now I was even more scared to do so in case I jeopardized my position at Spec Ops, and my standing with my new friends. Besides, I had no proof of my parent's leanings other than spoken words. Who would believe me if I were to say something? And if I did, who would believe I didn't hold the same beliefs?

Chapter Twenty

None of us woke until late afternoon the next day, meeting in the dining room with various forms of caffeine. We hardly noticed Zima was not present.

At least until he strode through the door, yelling.

"Do you know the danger you put your teammates in, leaving your post like that?"

All of us blinked sleepily at him until we realized his ire was directed at Jax. Zima must have read the mission report when he returned from his mission.

"Well, I could hardly tell them I had to stay in one specific place because I was on a secret info retrieval mission and needed to stay where my teammates could find me, now could I?" Jax countered evenly, taking a long sip of his coffee.

"You could have *stayed put.*" Zima hissed, his eyes shining dangerously.

"And done what, exactly?" I asked, pushing back from the table. "Brought more attention to our presence in that base? That would have gotten us all killed, and lost Spec Ops valuable info on the Coalition and their movements."

"He should not have abandoned his post," he argued vehemently.

"What would you have him do?" Himawari interjected.

"Protect his teammates."

That sent me over the edge. I could handle his

disrespect toward me but to listen to him berate Jax for something he could not control was too much.

"He *was* protecting us, you miserable jackass!" I shouted, storming towards him.

"It seems to me that he was protecting himself," Zima said, crossing his arms over his chest.

"You know *nothing* about the mission we were on, and you obviously know nothing about Jax. He would never abandon us to save himself."

"I know plenty. None of you belong here."

I was seething. My vision began to cloud with rage and unshed tears. How dare he? *How dare he?*

"You don't know a *thing* about us, Zima! Not one single thing. If you had bothered to even *try* to get to know us, you would understand Jax's predicament. You would know that Félix's favorite color is pink, that Jax has a scar on his left thigh from a dumb stunt he did as a kid, and why Himawari's mother named her 'sunflower'. You would understand why I *so badly* want us all to be a team. Why we all want this to *work.*"

He regarded my outburst with contempt before turning on his heel and leaving the flat. Without a word to the others, I followed, tracking him outside and onto the training grounds. It was raining and seemed to have been for a while. The grounds were riddled with muddy puddles, caking my shoes.

"What," I shouted, throwing my hands in the air, and sending the rain flying off my skin in droplets, "is your problem?"

Zima merely turned to face me, cocking his head to the side and observing me as if my reaction were expected – as if it annoyed him.

Fury coursed through me, burning my veins and arteries with each angry throb of my heart.

"What do you mean?" He had the gall to ask as if it were not obvious enough.

Ever since we had met, he had been judging and critiquing me, scrutinizing my every move as if it were his personal mission to hate me. To make sure I failed. To make sure our whole *team* failed. I had put up with it for too long and I would not tolerate it any further.

"What do I mean?" I repeated incredulously, my face contorting in anger. "What do I mean? I mean *you!* Your constant critiques and personal attacks! Your blatant disregard and disrespect towards the others!"

Zima's brows knitted together, and he crossed his arms over his chest. Our clothes and hair were plastering to our skin in the downpour, making my anger worse knowing I looked so ridiculous in front of him.

"You think I don't care about them?" he asked.

"You certainly don't act like it!"

"How is care supposed to be shown then, Deveraux?"

There was no snark in the question. No malice. Nothing but a simple question. And I saw *red.* Before I could stop myself, I was already stomping over to Zima, brandishing my index finger like a blade.

"You are a terrible, *horrible* person who does not care about anyone or anything except himself!" I spat, jabbing him squarely in the chest for emphasis.

And Zima began to crack. Slowly, slowly so I could not see it. His mask, his armor, began to shatter beneath my cold wrath and my hand.

"You don't understand," he hissed.

"You bet your ass I don't!" I shouted back, my eyes wildly searching his too-perfect face for answers he was not giving. "I don't understand you, your motives, or your reason for being on this team. If you hate us so much, just *leave!"*

"I– I," Zima started, hands dropping to his sides, eyes on the ground. But I was not finished.

Red flashed before my eyes again and I reached out, shoving my open palms against his chest sending him crashing to the muddy ground. Dirty water and mud splashed where he landed, splattering my shins and shoes.

"Deveraux–!" Zima started again, attempting to right himself. "Can you just–"

"No," I said and kicked out, sending him back toward the muddy earth.

He struggled to rise once more but I leaped at him, refusing to let up. I struggled with him for a few moments more, throwing insult after insult until I no longer had the strength to scream, to fight.

When I stepped away from Zima, he lay spread eagle on his back, covered in mud and grass. The rain had not let up, and we were soaked to the bone. The drops were slowly washing away the mud and debris from our bodies.

My chest heaved as I stared at him. He lay unmoving – still in the mud – rain making tracks in the grime on his face. His lips were moving though I could not hear what he was saying over the pounding of the rain.

"What did you say?" I rasped, expecting him to finally insult me. To tell me off for letting my temper get the better of me, despite his constant goading.

Zima repeated himself, but I was still unable to hear what he said. So, I stepped closer and demanded he repeat himself. He sat up quickly, causing me to jump back expecting an attack.

"They're all dead because of me!" he shouted. Pain was raw and unmistakable in his voice.

"What?" I asked, taking a faltering step forward.

"It's all my fault," Zima sobbed, his head now hanging between his legs.

My brows knitted together in confusion. I took another step forward and asked: "Who is dead? What is all your fault?"

Zima did not immediately respond. His mournful sobs wracked his body, and I did not understand where this came from. A few more moments passed before he answered. It took everything in me not to tackle him back into the mud at that moment. How dare he? How dare he try and use *emotion* to manipulate me?

"My team…" he sobbed, lifting his face so he could meet my eyes. "The day they died; it was all my fault."

It was not rain on his face as I had first assumed, but tears. Tears of pain, of grief.

Oh.

This was no manipulation.

This was pure, unadulterated agony.

Between shuddering sobs, he managed to get out, "I left them, I was supposed to stay with them, but I didn't. My leader sent me away, and they were ambushed. A group of Coalition soldiers caught them in the middle of our mission. My team leader, my best friend, was still alive when I got back. I couldn't do anything to save her, and it was all my fault!"

Confusion flooded through me. I had known Zima had lost his team. I had known the reason. Everyone did. It was common knowledge among Spec Ops operatives and being his team leader gave me access to his files… The files were classified or archived, and nowhere did they state Zima's direct involvement in his teammates' deaths. At all.

"But, Zima," I started but was cut off.

"I know, I've been awful to you, all of you," he stammered, voice shaking. "You, Daux, most of all. It was wrong, unfair, and awful."

"Y-yes," I agreed. "But—"

"I was trying to make sure you didn't make the same mistakes I did, that none of you would have the same guilt weighing you down."

"Zima!"

"No, Daux! No."

"Zima, you can't–"

"I'm sorry, I'm *so sorry.*"

My legs buckled out from under me. The mud and

rainwater splashed both of us as my knees hit the ground. Zima *apologized.* After months of dealing with his terrible attitude, hatefulness, and coldness and he *said 'sorry'.* It was not nearly enough to atone for how he acted, but I began to feel an immeasurable amount of guilt and sorrow for my role in this scene before me.

I did not understand. I could not have. What Zima had experienced was unfathomable; the incomprehensible loss he dealt with. He had not told any of us, his teammates, what he was going through. But I just *had* to push him. Push him until he broke.

How selfish I was, letting my insecurities and inability to understand others bring us here, standing in the pouring rain. My heart rent in two listening to Zima sob out his anger and grief.

I wished I could take it back. I wished I could take everything back. What I said in ignorance, in selfishness, in frustration. What I had thought of the sobbing young man before me. I could not understand his grief. It had been a long time since I had lost anyone… And I had never had the opportunity to grieve that loss.

But I could understand his guilt. I had plenty of that. If only I had paid more attention to Zima, maybe then I could have sensed that he was not looking down on me. Perhaps I could have understood he was trying to keep himself locked away from us, from me. But I did not. We had both made mistakes.

So, I just watched as one of the strongest people I knew sobbed and beat the muddy ground with his fist. His hair was plastered to his head with rainwater. The grief and anger that lined his face only emphasized the dark circles under his eyes. I could hardly tell which was tears or rain that ran down his cheeks.

Zima was utterly defeated, and it was I who destroyed him. I had destroyed him with mere words. But this was not what power felt like. No, I received no gratification in this victory. There was nothing to gloat about. Nothing to be praised for. I just knelt in the mud and watched him sob as we were both soaked by the rain.

I did not know how much time had passed when the rain began to pick up, and I could hardly hear Zima anymore. We were both drenched to the bone and shivering.

Gingerly, I pushed myself to my feet and made my way over to Zima's prone body.

"Zima," I said, nudging him with my foot.

"What?" he rasped.

"We need to go back inside. We're going to get sick."

"You go."

I laughed, it was cold and emotionless, though I had not intended it to be.

"You're coming with me whether you like it or not; I'm team leader," I snapped, pulling him to his feet and sliding his arm around my shoulder. He put up no resistance.

I ignored all the odd looks and stares we received as we walked through the lobby toward the lifts. Ignored Zima. Ignored my thoughts. My mind was too jumbled with emotions to think clearly anyway.

Jax, Himawari, and Félix were nowhere to be seen when I opened the door to our flat, thankfully. I did not want to deal with what happened out on the training grounds just yet, much less try and explain it.

"She was like you, you know," Zima said as I dragged him to his bedroom.

"Who?" I asked, struggling to open the door and balance both our body weights.

"Alina, my friend."

"And how are we alike?"

Zima shifted his weight and pushed the door open, leaning into the doorframe instead of me.

"Bullheaded." The ghost of a smile graced his haggard face.

A flash of anger rose in my chest, but I quickly stamped it out. Zima was not being hateful. He was not belittling me. Zima would not use the memory of his precious friend to do that.

"I'll take that as a compliment then," I replied, hauling him into his room. I had never seen inside before.

It was dark, but not depressing. The furniture was carved cherrywood, and very large. Almost too large for the room. The walls and upholstery were accented with black and silver, adding to the dark atmosphere. But it was cozy. Surprisingly.

Once in his room, Zima pulled away from me, leaving me shivering. I had not noticed how cold I was until he was no longer at my side.

I watched as he stumbled to his bed on unsteady feet. Watched as he looked down at his soaked clothing and sank to the floor in defeat. My heart seized.

"Do you want to take a shower or something?" I asked, moving to help him back up.

He waved me away, leaning against the side of his bed, his hair, and clothes leaving dark splotches on the rug and sheets.

Had he been anyone else, had this been any other situation, I might have thought him handsome. Maybe I would have even blushed, looking upon his sculpted face. Those icy blue eyes were framed by impossibly long, dark lashes, and obscured by his wet hair. His clothes were plastered to his toned body.

But I did not. The man in front of me was tired, looked tired. He was dirty, haggard, and grief-stricken. I felt nothing but remorse and anger. Conflicting emotions which I could not let go of.

My heart leaped into my throat when I realized I was staring. It plunged to my toes when I realized Zima was staring back.

"I loved her," he murmured, refusing to break eye contact with me.

"What?" I rasped, refusing to acknowledge the turmoil in my chest and just *listen*.

"I never told her though. She loved our other teammate, Farah." A wistful smile. "They announced they were together shortly before they died."

My throat constricted and my eyes began to burn. "I'm… I'm sorry…"

"I'm glad I didn't tell her. She and Farah were good together. I was happy for them. I suppose that's weird, to be happy that the person you love isn't with you, but with another of your best friends. But I was. They died holding each other."

"Zima… I…"

"You don't have to say anything, Daux. As much as I want it, I'm not entitled to your forgiveness. I'm not trying to guilt you into it."

He sounded so defeated. So exhausted. But as much sympathy as I felt for him, as much guilt as I had for pushing him, I was not ready to forgive.

All I could offer him was a small nod and a promise of help, should he want it, before leaving, closing his door behind me.

My body felt as if it were on autopilot as I made my way to the bathroom I shared with Himawari. With numb hands, I removed the wet, muddy clothes from my shivering body and entered the shower, letting the warm water run over me.

I sank onto the floor, the water warming my freezing skin, cleansing me of the mud and grime, and letting myself breathe. In and out. In. And out.

In.

Out.

Chapter Twenty-One

Like normal, Jax, Himawari, Félix, and I sat around our table. We were eating, but silence blared into my eardrums. That part was not normal. They had heard what had happened with Zima and me yesterday. As I had promised, I had been forthright with them and explained what went down.

They were all shocked, to say the least. Not at me, but the reason for Zima's coldness. They felt sympathy for him, as I did; however, they also agreed that whatever his reasons, his actions were inexcusable, and he needed to atone for them.

Félix had come up to me after I had told them and squeezed my hand.

"I understand being so frustrated and angry that it all just boils over."

Then he let go and left me staring after him until I decided I needed sleep. He was kind.

The mood this morning, though, was somber. Zima had not left his room until the wee hours of the morning to shower, after which he promptly left and had not returned. I had even checked his room this morning to make sure he was all right. The only sign that showed he had been there was a pile of muddy clothes on the floor.

I was just about to suggest to the others that we try to reach Zima over our holonavs or go searching for him when he burst through the door and stormed into the dining room.

"The Overseer has summoned us," he announced, trying to appear calm, but was panicked and refused to meet my eyes.

"That's not unusual," Félix commented, not glancing up from his cereal.

The rest of us looked at each other in concern. Zima was hardly *ever* flustered, and this 'outburst' was unlikely to be caused by the incident yesterday. The Overseer must want us for something important if he was this concerned.

Without bothering to finish our meals, we readied ourselves and began the descent from our flat. Halfway down, Jax realized that we had forgotten Félix – who had stayed to finish his cereal – and reconfigured the lift so we could go get him. It would have been funny had we all not been so tense.

Once we were all in the auto and headed toward Headquarters, I was able to get a good look at Zima. His eyes were as cold as ever, but they now contained a shadowy, haunted look that had not been there before. Or perhaps it had been, and I had not cared enough to notice. His under eyes had such dark circles underneath that they looked nearly bruised, and his hair was shockingly untidy.

"Zima," I said softly so the others would not hear.

His head snapped toward me so quickly that I thought his neck would crack. I nearly flinched but held myself in check. Zima seemed shocked that I had spoken a word to him, much less his name.

"Listen," I commanded, turning to face forward so the others would not see from the front and try to listen in. "I am still angry with you."

His shoulders slumped in defeat at my words. I now knew he cared for us, at least a little, but it was difficult to shut off the scathing voice in my head that still wanted to hate him.

"I am still angry with you," I repeated, peeking at him

from the corner of my eye. "But I am trying to forgive you because I think I understand your pain."

"You do?" he sounded skeptical. I did not blame him.

"Don't get too excited, Zima."

"Valentin," he insisted. "Please, call me Valentin."

So, I did. "All right, Valentin."

From the corner of my eye, I could see a small smile tug at the corners of his lips, which made me smile a little bit too. Valentin's name would no longer be Zima – cold-hearted – in my mind. Nor in my heart.

"You still need to prove to us that you are loyal and want to try to fix what you continuously refused to repair," I told him, crossing my arms across my chest.

"I'll do anything."

"Anything?"

"Anything."

"Okay," I said, smirking coyly, and gestured to the front of the auto where our teammates sat unaware of our conversation. "Proclaim your undying love for me to our teammates."

Valentin hesitated, looking toward Jax, Himawari, and Félix in the front row of the auto then back to me.

"If I do that, you'll forgive me... For everything?"

"One hundred percent."

Before I could stop him, before I could tell him I was joking, Valentin stood up from his seat in the auto and called for our teammates' attention. When they turned to him, he looked me straight in the eyes and said:

"Everyone, I cannot hide my feelings a second longer. I love Daux Deveraux with every fiber of my being, every cell in my body, and every breath that I breathe. I am unable to cope with the inability to state these passions and feel as if I must proclaim it from the rooftops of Heliorious itself!"

The three of them blinked at him in surprise, not only at his declaration but because we had never known him to be silly or affectionate in any way.

My face *burned*. I had been joking. There was no way in the names of the Gods I would have meant for him to actually *do* it.

"Is he joking?" Félix whispered to Jax who had begun to grin like a clown.

"I think so..." he whispered back but continued to smile. The fool.

Himawari on the other hand said, "That's nice," and turned to face forward with a cool expression on her pretty face.

Valentin, seemingly satisfied with himself, sat back down in his seat and looked at me, grinning hesitantly, but still having that annoyingly confident air about him.

"How was that?" he whispered.

"I still don't forgive you!" I hissed, face still flaming.

Valentin threw back his head and laughed. I realized it was one of the only times I had heard him do so since we had known each other. It made me smile, albeit unwittingly.

When we reached the Overseer's office, we were quickly ushered in by her secretary, without the offer of refreshments. She was in her office this time, waiting behind her heavy wooden desk with her hands folded under her chin.

"Right on time," she commented as I headed the group through the door.

The Overseer's voice was grim, and while she was a normally grave woman, she had an unusually dire tone in her voice.

"Please sit." She gestured to the half-circle of chairs placed in front of her desk. "We have much to discuss."

"Do you have another mission for us?" Jax asked as we all took our seats.

The Overseer shook her head and leaned back in her chair; frustration was written clearly in the lines of her face. It was unusual. Though she was typically serious and hard to read, the Overseer almost appeared guilty when her obsidian eyes fell upon me.

"We've… had some unexpected developments…" she trailed off, looking at each of us closely.

"What unexpected developments?" I asked.

"And why does it concern us?" Himawari concurred.

The Overseer hesitated yet again and pinched the bridge of her nose.

"Deveraux, I don't want to upset you with this news, but I feel like you need to know."

"With all due respect ma'am, just tell us."

The guilt I picked up on earlier shone from her exquisite face in full force.

"We have had reports, specifically from the info you extracted, that several of your father – Governor Deveraux's – close associates are involved in, or at least sympathize with the Coalition's' ideals."

If she was waiting for a gasp or any other exclamation of surprise, she would have been waiting a long time. The silence in the room was palpable. I could feel the stares of the Overseer and my team on me, waiting for a reaction.

"I could have told you that, ma'am," I whispered, crossing my arms over my chest and feeling more than a little uncomfortable.

"You aren't surprised by this?" she asked incredulously.

"No, but I am surprised he and his associates have not been looked into before."

And I was. My father was an obvious narcissist. Conversely, my mother made no secret of her distaste for magic in private. But her status as a Governor's wife should have been reason enough for *someone* to take notice.

"Why would he have been so careless?" The Overseer pressed.

"I, as my younger sister is now, was invisible to him as a child unless I did something he disapproved of. He made no effort to hide his sympathies or ideals at home. As he liked to tell me when I was being punished for pointing out his flawed logic or trying to tell someone about it, 'It's not a crime to show support to the Coalition.'"

"No," The Overseer agreed. "But you cannot deny it is concerning, especially since he has such a high rank in our government."

"It is," I assented gravely.

"As I mentioned, many of his friends and associates share ideals. This leads us to believe they – at the very least – need to be monitored. As well as his family."

Shock flooded through me at the Overseer's words. Me? Under surveillance? And for the crime of being related to my father no less. He was, of course, a hateful bastard but I had no connection to the Coalition, even through him. I said as much.

"That being said, Deveraux, we must know for certain where your loyalty lies."

"With all due respect ma'am," Jax interjected. "That is *insane*."

"I agree!" Félix shouted before the Overseer could open her mouth to object.

"Not to mention tyrannical," Himawari said hotly.

Valentin's reaction surprised me most of all. He stood to his feet and moved in front of the Overseer's desk, towering over her.

"If anyone can vouch for Daux's loyalties, it's me. You're being incredibly hypocritical in the name of safety, accusing Daux of being disloyal when her actions have proven nothing otherwise. She has demonstrated nothing but devotion to our cause, even when she has been terrified beyond reason. I stand by some of my earlier statements, but she is *not* a traitor."

Despite the jab, I could have stood to my feet and kissed Valentin in front of everyone. But I deigned not to embarrass myself or him and stayed seated.

"Regardless, it's protocol. I risk my job even telling

her," The Overseer said, taken aback.

"Bullshit," Valentin hissed, leaning menacingly over the large wooden desk.

They stared each other down, each refusing to show weakness. Dark, fiery eyes met the bright, iciness of Valentin's. When it became apparent neither would back down, I stood, elbowing Valentin out of the way.

"What can I do to prove my loyalty?" I asked, forcing the Overseer to meet my gaze. It was not kind when she did.

I was disappointed. The Overseer was not someone I was close to, but I did trust her. I had hoped she had the same trust in me. She did not.

"I'm sorry Daux," she said, though I now doubted it. "I'll make an exception since your teammates have made some… valid points. You may submit to interrogation, telling us as much information you can, or you can undergo surveillance for an indeterminate amount of time. Your family will remain under surveillance for the time being as well."

"How is that any better?" Félix asked, glowering.

"It isn't," Valentin said, crossing his arms over his chest. "It's unprecedented, cruel, and will tell Spec Ops nothing more than we already know about Daux."

"It's fine," I snapped, refusing to look away from the Overseer. "When do I report for interrogation?"

She smiled, slow and sad. "Immediately."

Chapter Twenty-Two

I had never noticed what color my ceiling was. Off-white, which suited the room, the rose-pink walls, and dark rosewood bookshelves. It looked nice. Stark-white ceilings had always ruined the appearance of some rooms for me. Now I would not be able to look at one without remembering.

I lay on my back, staring upward, trying to force the memories from my mind. Trying to think of anything else. Félix was there, sitting on the floor next to my bed, my hand in his. He squeezed it every so often, just to remind me he was with me.

Jax had popped in a while ago… I had forgotten when – to check on me. He left a glass of water on my bedside table, which was now sitting in a pool of condensation.

Himawari lay next to me, running her fingers through my hair, gently detangling the long strands. Attempting not to hurt me more than I already was. We were all quiet and their presence alone was comforting. I did not want to talk, and they did not want to force me.

"What is your relationship with Chairman Deveraux?" The voice asked.

It was as disjointed and disembodied as the one from my placement exam. I shivered at the memory.

"I don't mean to be impertinent, but I wouldn't be here if I didn't have some sort of relationship with him," I said,

staring up at the ceiling instead of looking around for the source of the voice.

It was white, like the walls. Like the floor. Like the chair I was sitting in and the table which was in front of me. There were no windows, no two-way mirrors, nothing but a white door. The only way to leave this dreadful room. Which I could not do unless I answered their asinine questions.

I sighed. "He is my father."

"Would you consider you and your father close?" The voice asked in immediate response to my compliance.

"No."

A gentle squeeze of my hand brought me back to the present. Himawari was gone now. It was just me and Félix.

"Daux," he whispered. "Are you okay?"

I turned my head and attempted a smile that did not come. "Not really."

"Okay. Do you mind if I go eat something? It's late."

"No, go ahead."

"I'll bring you something?"

"I'm not hungry, thanks."

Félix frowned a little then left, closing the door behind him. I began to fade again, the room closing in around me.

"I already told you," I hissed at the voice. "I. Don't. Know."

"That is not an acceptable answer, Daux."

"Why the hell not?"

"You're hiding something from us."

Rage flooded through me. First, they demand my compliance then they decide it is not good enough once they get it.

"I am hiding nothing!" I yelled, standing from the chair. The screeching sound it produced when it scraped across the floor hurt my ears. "I have told you nothing but the truth. How long are you going to keep me here?"

"Until we get what we need."

It was now Victorisday. I had been gone for three days.

Why Spec Ops' interrogation squad felt the need to keep me so long was beyond me. All of it was beyond me. They had me recount my entire childhood up until my Placement and graduation. And when that was not enough, they sent agents into that room to induce memories.

The agents they sent in quickly grabbed me and injected me with a blocker. I was no match; they had the element of surprise on their side and all I had was a chair and a table. I could have attacked them with the chair, but I was already defeated.

They hooked me up to a machine, which had the same function as the pods from the Placement exam, and I let them. I let them dig into my mind and take my darkest memories and secrets. Anything to get it over with. I had no fight left in me.

"Daux?" A voice called from outside my door.

It was not *that* voice. It was a safe one. A voice that captivated me as much as it irritated me.

"What, Valentin?"

"Can I come in?"

"I suppose."

My eyes were still trained on the ceiling as he entered, I could not bring myself to look anywhere else.

"Félix said you refused to eat." It was not a question.

"I'm not hungry," I mumbled.

"Jax and Himawari are making you something."

"I don't want it."

"Too bad," he said, I could hear the smirk in his voice. "I told them I'd make sure you ate it."

I looked at him then. He was wearing his usual black, but his hair was mussed again, colors riotous like it had been the day I had confronted him. Had that only been four days ago?

My head turned back to face the ceiling.

"Daux…" Valentin hedged.

"What?" I sighed.

"Do you need to talk about it?"

"No."

"Because you can talk to me if you–"

I cut him off. "I said no Z– Valentin."

He stood there, awkwardly silent, for a few moments more before moving to sit by my bed.

"I understand," he chuckled, a sad quality to the sound. "I wouldn't want to talk to me either. Especially about that."

"Don't be self-deprecating," I said, shifting my hand to hang off the bed. "It's annoying."

It should not have surprised me that he took my hand in his – I had wanted him to, as Félix had – but it did. Valentin's hand was so warm compared to mine. I think that was the only reason I noticed. Heat spread through my chest, filling some of the emptiness there.

"I'm sorry," was all he said. I accepted it with a squeeze of his hand. Silence fell over us, comfortable and safe. We sat like that for a while, Valentin holding my hand, offering me the grace I attempted to give him.

Himawari and Jax came in, followed by a hesitant Félix, not much later. They were carrying a variety of sweet things: pastries, ice cream, fruit, anything to tempt me into eating. They were so kind.

Félix – annoyed that Valentin had taken his vacant spot – nudged him out of the way and grabbed my hand. Valentin had the good grace to let him and perched on the edge of my bed by my feet instead. Jax and Himawari also clambered onto my bed, urging me to sit up and eat.

I did so, mostly to humor them because they took the time to prepare something for me and because they were concerned. They pressed a fruity breakfast pastry into my hands, dripping in glaze, and I felt a small pang of hunger. I took a hesitant bite, careful of my traitorous stomach. It was delicious.

Slowly, I ate my way through two small pastries and some sliced fruit, insisting on passing the ice cream around to share. It was nice, all of us in my room, eating sweets. It felt as if things were… Good. It was good. At least, this was.

Eventually, I began to talk. I shared the things the interrogation squad forced from me. Shared the fear and helplessness I felt, being at the mercy of people I trusted to believe in me but did not. Shared the exhaustion, the anxiety, the self-loathing. My resentment towards Valentin, my jealousy of Jax's easy manner, and my initial frustrations with Félix and Himawari.

I told them of my parent's neglect, the forced blockers my mother would administer, about the horrible black bruises my father had left on my skin when my abilities manifested. About him never touching me once after the fact, and never again.

Every ugly little thing I held inside spilled out and I was shocked to find nothing had been tarnished. I wanted them to have everything the Spec Ops interrogators had even if it made them hate me. Instead, my friends, including a hesitant Valentin, wrapped their arms around me and held me tighter than I had ever been before. Félix, who was on the outside of the hug, even reached in to pat my head.

They saw me for what I was and did not shy away. They did not hold me in contempt for my father's abuse – nor his beliefs. They did not judge me for my feelings. And when the topic of our next assignment had to be breached, I was ready.

I would not let my fear, my frustration about the injustice done, control me. Not when I had my teammates. With them surrounding me, we planned, talked, and snacked on the leftover offerings late into the night.

It was not until the next morning I realized that I had fallen asleep. Jax, Himawari, and Félix were no longer there, but Valentin was. He lay on his back on my fainting couch, feet hanging off the end.

I smiled a little at the sight.

"Hey," I whispered to his prone form. "Are you

awake?"

His eyelids began to flutter though he kept them closed. "Yeah, I am now."

"Where did everyone go?" I asked.

"To their rooms, I suppose," he replied, attempting to curl his long legs up onto the small piece of furniture. "I didn't feel like you should be left alone."

"That was kind."

"I'm trying."

And he was. I could tell. He had become so jaded after the deaths of his teammates that it had become difficult to show much emotion or concern. But here he was, curled up on my fainting couch, trying to keep an eye on me. It made it hard to stay angry with him.

"Thank you," I said, and I meant it – more than I could express.

"Don't mention it," he replied. "Seriously, it'll ruin my reputation."

I grinned at him. "I'll be sure to tell everyone I see what a nice guy you are."

"I am *not* a nice guy."

He was glaring at me now, but I could hear the mirth behind it.

"Whatever helps you sleep at night, Valentin," I teased.

"I sleep soundly knowing I'm a coldhearted bastard," he huffed back.

"You're pouting. I cannot believe you're pouting." I started to laugh. It was not like normal – it felt hollow and incomplete – but it was real. It felt good, regardless. He began to laugh too. It was nice, us, together, sort of getting along.

Of course, we shared banter – some of it was thinly veiled jabs at the other, but there was no animosity in them. Not really. Not to the extent that it used to be, at least. But when we quieted down, the mood began to somber.

"I don't understand why they decided I was such a

threat." My throat began to close around a painful lump as I gazed into his eyes.

He shrugged; his eyes were sad. "They see you, magically gifted and strong-willed, related to a powerful man with lots of influence who happens to sympathize with an enemy government. It frightens them and makes them paranoid. They would rather burn the bridges and your trust in them than risk the chance of a leak, or something much worse."

I gritted my teeth against the tears and began to pick at my coverlet. "When you say it like that, it sounds kind of reasonable."

Valentin stood and made his way over to my bed, sitting down beside me.

"You can make almost anything sound reasonable if you use the right words," he said, awkwardly placing his hand over my own. "That doesn't make it right."

"Have you been telling yourself that?" I asked, perhaps cruelly.

A rueful smile. "Yes."

"Sorry," I said.

"Don't be, I deserved it." He squeezed my hand.

"Doesn't make it right."

"Touché."

We were silent for a moment, contemplating many things and nothing all at once.

"What are we going to do?" I asked.

"What do you mean?"

"I want to clear my name."

"Daux," Valentin said sharply and pulled me into a sitting position, forcing me to look him in the eyes. "You did nothing wrong. They have evidence of that long before they interrogated you. You have nothing to prove."

"I- I know. I just wanted... the Overseer wanted... that I was trustworthy." My thoughts were more jumbled than my words, swirling and incoherent.

Valentin's arms enveloped me in a tight embrace. They were warm and strong, just as I had remembered them. Like the few times he had held me before, briefly. It was pleasant and comforting. Like Jax and Félix hugging me. Like a friend. Not an adversary, not a lover. A friend.

"You don't need to prove anything," he said into my hair. "But we can do something."

Chapter Twenty-Three

During my interrogation, the Overseer had tasked Valentin and the others with an info-gathering mission. It would likely entail covert ops, hacking, and observation of known Coalition bases in the area as well as observation of those known and suspected of sympathizing with the Coalition.

It was the push I needed to start working again; the desire to prove my loyalty and innocence. I immediately began throwing myself into our work. Directing small-scale info gatherings, collecting data, and taking observations. Spec Ops had divisions for this sort of thing, but I was willing to do anything to prove I was not a traitor.

Jax and Himawari had mentioned to me – several times – that what I was doing was not healthy. But I had created my entire life around serving the NAF, and if I did not do that, I did not know what I could do. I felt lost, even buried, in work. Confused, even though there were clear goals ahead of me.

Félix, the sweet boy that he was, disabled my holonav which rendered me unable to work on anything while I was in the flat and could have put me as a huge disadvantage in the field. I did not even know holonavs could be disabled, but somehow he did it, leaving a snarky message and smiley face on it as a calling card.

When I went to confront him, I found all my teammates

gathered on the couches in the common area, sitting silently.

"What's going on?" I asked, pausing in the doorframe.

They turned to look at me, but only silence followed.

"Is this some sort of scary holovid thing?"

A weary sigh heaved from Jax before he answered. "Daux, you're running all of us ragged, including yourself."

"I feel fine," I insisted, feeling perplexed.

"Well, you look like shit," Félix grumbled.

"Thanks for that, Fé."

"No problem."

Valentin stood, grumbling under his breath, and guided me to a spot next to him.

"We need to talk," he said, looking weary.

"So, talk," I demanded, crossing my arms over my chest.

"As I said, Daux," Jax began, leaning his elbows on his knees. "You're running yourself into the ground. What the Overseer and everyone else did was completely unfair. You shouldn't be bending over backward to get back in her good graces, or anyone else's for that matter."

"He's right," Himawari interjected before I could argue. "You have nothing to prove, you had nothing to hide, and you have done nothing wrong. Stop killing yourself to try and prove it. This isn't worth it."

"But if I'm not… If I'm not trustworthy in Spec Ops then I'm nothing," I said, voice trembling.

"Don't be stupid Daux," Félix hissed, clenching his fists open and shut.

I looked around me, into each of their faces, all of them lined with fatigue and pity. For a moment, I was angry. Very angry. At them, at the Overseer, at my father, and myself.

I dug my fingers into my arms to prevent myself from shaking.

"You're more than this dumb job, Daux," Valentin sighed, running a hand over his face.

"It's not dumb!" I insisted, close to tears now.

"It is!" he thundered, standing abruptly from the couch, which startled the others. "It is ridiculous, idealized, and romanticized. Each year a handful of new, naive teams are Placed into Spec Ops with dreams of grandeur and praise."

He looked down for a moment before continuing.

"So many of us don't make it past our first year, you all know that."

Our other teammates looked anywhere but at Valentin or me – their toes, the walls, their hands. Why would they Place people in Spec Ops so young if they knew there were such risks? Why would they allow such a thing to happen, to approve and glorify it even?

Because the ends always justify the means to the NAF. I saw that now. It was common knowledge that this job was a dangerous one. The instructors at the Academy didn't sugarcoat anything for those of us hopefuls. We knew the risks.

"We all knew the dangers when we accepted our placements," Jax voiced my thoughts.

"I know," Valentin said, looking each of us in the eye. "But just because something is widely accepted does not mean that it is good. Just because Spec Ops works for the greater good does not mean it is wholly good, and just because there are dangers and oversights does not mean there is nothing good about it. There are gray areas. This happens to be one of them."

"So, you're saying that Spec Ops isn't cruel for what they did to Daux?" Himawari asked in outrage.

"No, what I'm saying is that Spec Ops – and our whole system of government has gray areas – like everything else," Valentin said placatingly, reclaiming his seat next to me. "You all need to be able to see the distinctions and make up your mind whether to support them or not."

Silence fell upon us again, weighing heavily on our shoulders. I truly believed I was doing good in Spec Ops, and that the organization as a whole strived to be morally superior. Perhaps, even though they did cruel things, they believed they were. Then the Coalition… the people who supported them also believed in the principles they upheld. Did they also agree with these "gray areas" as Valentin put it, or did they accept those parts of their ideologies to achieve the shared goal?

I suppose I should not have been so shocked. It was obvious to me from a very young age that the NAF and its territories was not a combined utopia as most thought it to be. My father was a bigoted Coalition sympathizer after all. Not to mention that I – a loyal citizen with very little ties to my sympathizer father – was subjected to an invasive interrogation reserved only for the worst of criminals and traitors. These facts did not erase the sting of betrayal.

"I could have undergone surveillance…" I began, clenching my hands into the fabric of my sleeves. "But any slip up – any ambiguous comment – could have been used against me. They could have used anything to prove I was brainwashed by my father. I agreed to the interrogation only because I feared that outcome."

"They could have just believed you," Himawari argued, her dark eyes flashing.

I frowned at her. "But what sort of precedent would that set? That since I'm good at my job, I'm infallible and completely trustworthy?"

"Do you even hear yourself, Daux?" Jax ground out. "You're defending them, even though they were wrong and made you undergo an incredible amount of pain!"

"I'm not defending them!" I cried, standing to my feet. "I am agreeing with Valentin. Yes, Spec Ops did a bad thing and treated me unfairly. It is unforgivable, but I understand why they did it."

"Well, we don't!" Félix yelled. "You were a mess after the interrogation Daux, and now you're destroying yourself just to appeal to the same people who hurt you!"

"You're right," I agreed, softly. "I was a mess. It was

bad. You were the only thing that brought me back, and I am thankful for it. And I have been running myself into the ground to win some favor back, which is unfair to all of you. I'm sorry. But I still understand, to an extent, why they insisted on being sure. Was it fair? Absolutely not. But we can still do good with our positions, and I intend to keep doing good as long as I can."

"So, you're going to stop this manic overworking?" Jax asked, skepticism apparent in his voice and expression.

I nodded. "Yes."

"And you're sorry for worrying us?" Félix demanded petulantly.

"Yes."

Himawari looked between Valentin and me for a moment, appearing to contemplate her words carefully. "I'm not sure I agree with you brushing this off so lightly, Daux. But what Zima, sorry," she glanced sheepishly in his direction. "*Valentin* says makes some sense. Nothing is completely black and white, and while we need to hold people accountable for injustices, we can't disparage a whole for the faults of a few. In the sense of Spec Ops, I mean. The Coalition can go to hell."

That brought out a few laughs, though they were not all mirthful. I had been wrong in my desire to be accepted by Spec Ops again after the interrogation. They had proven to be on the side of protocol rather than those who work for them, or the average citizen. And while that was not entirely bad, it was not something I wanted to strive for.

I wanted to help people. And while I believed protocol is important, someone's actions should speak for them. I had not once strayed in my quest to aid our union, and I was repaid with distrust and treated like a criminal, which affected my teammates in turn.

There was more to be done, but I now saw I did not need the approval of those I once, and perhaps still, idealized to do good.

"What do we do now?" Jax sighed, leaning back into the couch.

I smiled. "I think I have an idea."

Nostalgic– a restaurant near the Spec Ops housing complex – was dimly lit and busy this warm Gravesday evening. Spec Ops teams, military personnel, and local civilians filled the many booths and tables lining the dark vinyl floors. It was an antiquely decorated place, with dark paneled walls lined with old movie and entertainment memorabilia. It was a popular gathering place for homey cooking and relaxing with friends and colleagues.

No one would suspect our intentions. No one would even think we were here to discuss the growing tension my father and his associates were causing in the government. Nor the suspicion I had been put under.

The pretty hostess led us toward the back of Nostalgic, to a private room where several other teams were sequestered. We had booked it under the guise of a party for a team member's birthday. Thankfully, it *was* one of our group member's birthdays.

Talia grinned up at me as we walked into the room, brown eyes sparkling. I was glad to see her again. It had been too long since we had gotten to hang out. I hated that it was under such circumstances.

"And the guest of honor arrives!" she crowed, lifting her frothing drink in salute.

"Why is *she* the guest of honor, Tali?" One of the twins grumbled with puppy-dog eyes turned on her in full force.

"Because," she said with a haughty air, turning her button nose up at her teammate. "Daux is my best friend, and it's *my* birthday."

I grinned at Talia and took a seat across from her at the long table. She grinned back and shoved a full mug of whatever frothing liquid she was drinking at me.

My teammates seated themselves next to and around me as I took a sip of the drink Talia had pushed at me and nearly choked. It burned and crackled as it made its way down my throat, settling in an unpleasant pool in my stomach.

Valentin, to my right, shot me a concerned look and took the mug from me. He swirled the liquid around and took a sip.

"Daux," he said, I could hear the amusement in his voice. "It's sparkbeer."

"Sparkbeer?" I sputtered, shooting a glare at my very best friend in the whole world.

The beverage was often an acquired taste, but many found the sparking and crackling sensation the magical imbuement provided invigorating. I was not one of those people.

"I think I'll keep this," Valentin laughed and took another large gulp.

I ordered myself a juice.

Talia chattered endlessly, introducing her teammates – Alexis and Dimos Spyros, the twins, and team leader Gwyn Hier – to us, and generally being exuberant.

When Riannan and her teammates showed up, Talia's liveliness amped up even more. She, already tipsy from the sparkbeer, launched herself up from the table and nearly suffocated Meera in a bear hug. A pang of jealousy shot through my chest; she had not greeted me that way. I had not even realized they knew each other.

"This girl saved my ass the other day!" Talia sang, one arm still slung around Meera's shoulders. "Without her earth-rending magic, I would've been toast!"

Meera had the decency to look embarrassed. "It was an accident. We had no idea another team was dispatched to the area anyway."

Instantly, I began to feel sorry for her. Talia's, albeit

friendly, praising would have made me uncomfortable as well. And I had no right to be jealous, as I had also made new friends.

As Talia continued to brag about Meera and her team, Riannan approached and hugged me from behind, her riotous curls nearly enveloping me. She smelled of sunshine and wildflowers.

"Hi!" she greeted cheerfully and took the empty seat to my left. "I didn't know you all knew Gwyn's team."

"We don't," I answered, still tense from my bout of jealousy. "At least not well, we just met most of them this evening. Talia is a friend from the Academy."

"Ah," she said with a knowing smile and patted my arm. "Talia is quite a friendly person. Gwyn says she could make friends with a psychopath."

I nodded, finding that the smile that crossed my face was no longer forced. "And you know Gwyn from the Academy too?"

"Yeah, we had several classes together. We bonded over our unrequited crushes on certain classmates." She winked knowingly at me as we observed the tall, brooding man across the table from us.

He was handsome, I supposed, in a grouchy sort of way with long, dark hair and eyes and a face that would make a novelist swoon.

"He's nice," Riannan whispered to me conspiratorially. "You just have to get past the permanent grimace."

I laughed softly and peeked up at him again. He was now looking in our direction. I couldn't imagine him having a crush on someone, much less bonding with Riannan over it.

"Hey Gwyn," Riannan trilled, wiggling her fingers.

"Hello," he replied with a shy smile before turning back to continue speaking with one of the Spyros twins. It was difficult to tell them apart.

"We ran into them on a mission, like Talia said. We were sent to extract some info and bring it back to decode," she explained, taking a swig of a syrupy, dark liquid. "And they were there, apparently doing some sort of extraction or hit? I wasn't sure and they never said. Anyway, during their mission, Talia got separated from them somehow and Meera ended up saving her butt with a quickly improvised earthquake."

"Wow."

"I know right? The Berry's specialize in reality-bending magic and Meera's ability is for earthrending. We're pretty hard hitters for an intelligence team, huh?"

From Riannan's expression as she looked down the table at Meera, it was obvious she admired her.

"Do you…" I began, but Valentin stood to his feet, asking for everyone's attention.

"Now that we've all gathered here, I think it may be time to get the important things out of the way," he announced.

Often, I wondered why he was not our team leader. He seemed better suited for it. His presence alone commanded respect. He was imposing, smart, strong, and had more experience than me. And now, watching Valentin capture the attention of everyone in the room so easily, I began to doubt myself again.

"I'm sure you all know who I am," he continued. "So, I won't waste your time introducing myself. I'll let my team leader do the talking, but I want the teams to introduce themselves to each other, so we can all know who's talking, and which tasks each team will be delegated."

Despite my admiration for Valentin's strong presence and voice, the somber nods that followed his speech made me realize what a buzzkill he was. I suppressed a smile.

Talia's team went first, Gwyn taking charge as team leader and introducing himself, and gesturing for his teammates to do the same.

"Alexis and Demos!" The twins shouted in unison, refusing to indicate who was who.

Talia rolled her eyes and said, "The one on the right is Alexis and the one on the left is Demos. I'm Talia."

I winked at her, and she grinned back. Riannan's team went next, first with the Berrys.

"Willow," The elder sister stated simply, while her sister Hawthorn introduced herself sweetly and serenely with a greeting and a small wave.

Meera went next flashing a dazzling smile. "I'm Meera, but Talia has already introduced me." Talia had the decency to look sheepish.

Then it was our turn.

"I'm Daux," I introduced myself and gestured for Félix to go next. Himawari followed, and finally Jax.

"So now that we've all been introduced," I began, looking around the room at my old and new friends' faces. "We should get to why we're here. There have been reports of treason among high-ranking members of the government. We – my team and I – did not know who to turn to, as our suspicions could get back to these people if we went to others working in Spec Ops, or the NAF, who may have pertinent info."

"And we were what you came up with?" Riannan asked, her deep brown eyes clouded with confusion.

"As you are aware, I asked each team for condensed dossiers before we set up this meeting. Talia's team is experienced in covert operations, and other more dubious endeavors," I explained, sending a knowing look in my old friend's direction, which she returned.

"And from what your dossiers tell me, your team is a mix of intelligence decoding as well as expert spies," Valentin told Riannan, who blushed at his attention.

Riannan's memory magic allowed her to remember nearly everything, making her invaluable to Spec Ops' spy network and decoding core. She was a natural team leader for the three other girls who had similar skill sets. They made a terrifying team together.

Talia's team, on the other hand, was focused more on assassinations, and retrieving information which would be passed on to different teams. Our team was more multipurpose, the ones who would blast open the door but also run in behind the scenes.

"We will need all of you if this plan is going to work," I said gravely, looking around the room again.

I was nervous. Any of them could walk out at any moment, deciding that this was not worth their time, or lives. Talia would stay, without a doubt, and the rest of my team. But I was concerned about everyone else. Especially when they found out just *who* was under suspicion.

A sudden squeeze of my hand under the table made me jump. I looked to my right and Valentin was looking at me from the corner of his eye.

"You've got this," he whispered and squeezed my hand again.

His confidence in me made my chest swell with indiscernible emotions, and I took a deep breath, wrapping my fingers boldly around his.

"One of the people under suspicion is Governor Deveraux," I said, bracing myself for the reaction of the table.

Gwyn's chair screeched across the floor as he abruptly stood. Gasps and sounds of disbelief were heard from around the table. Talia just looked at me with a sad expression on her typically impish face.

"You," Gwyn pointed directly at me, ire in his handsome face. I forced myself not to flinch. "I know who you are now. You're Governor Deveraux's daughter. Why should Spec Ops trust any info you give on him or anyone else involved?"

Félix and Jax stood to their feet, eyeing Gwyn down. "Down boys," I commanded softly, not taking my gaze off

Gwyn. "I can handle this."

But Willow and Meera had been nodding along with what Gwyn had said and my heart began to sink in my chest. Nevertheless, I persisted.

"You are right to mistrust my intentions. You don't know me. I could very well turn any info we find into my father and alert him to Spec Ops suspicions. But you do know Tali, and she knows and trusts me."

"That's right," she snapped, standing to her feet to face Gwyn. "Daux wouldn't do something like that. Besides, she hates her dad."

"If my father is truly guilty of treason, I want him brought down as much as any of you would. Perhaps more so," I defended myself, letting my eyes roam to the others who doubted me.

"And why should we believe that?" Willow asked in her soft, childlike voice.

"You're all free to access Spec Ops databases and read my interrogation reports. The Overseer herself has decided I was not a threat, so I don't see why we have a problem here."

Crossing my arms over my chest, I sat down, refusing to curl in on myself. I would not be afraid of these people's judgment, I would not be afraid of the memories of my interrogation, and I would not be afraid of this mission.

"Tell me you're not serious," Talia said, her sun-kissed skin paling at my words.

"Completely," I replied, meeting her honey-brown eyes. They started to redden and brim with tears.

"They interrogated you? *You?* And your teammates just let this happen?" she shouted incredulously. The other teams began to look a little green – Willow, Meera, and Gwyn refused to look my way.

"Hey!" Jax protested, dark eyes flashing dangerously. "We did all we could. Where were you when she was in recovery?"

"I- I was…" she could not answer.

Jax's smile was not pretty. "Exactly."

"That is enough." Valentin gestured for Jax and everyone else to return to their seats. "Yes, because Governor Deveraux is being investigated for treason, Daux chose to be interrogated to clear her name, instead of undergoing an indefinite period of surveillance and suspicion. She spent days in recovery with her teammates by her side every second. But go ahead, check the records and footage if you don't believe us."

The room was silent. No one would meet our eyes. Then Riannan placed her hand on my arm. "I believe you Daux, and I will help you, even if the rest of my team won't."

Her soft, but firm declaration sent a jolt of confidence through my chest. And like her, Talia followed, shaking the shock and hurt from her face. "You know I'd follow you anywhere, Daux."

Hawthorn, to the dismay of her sister, also pledged her support. After which Willow did as well, though less ardently. I did not blame her, but I could not say I was not a little put off by her reaction.

Meera and the Spyros twins also agreed to help, and once everyone at the table had determined to help with our plan, Gwyn did as well with a sigh. "What is this plan then?"

"I'm so glad you asked..." The corners of my mouth twitched, but I refused to smile lest it make him angry, and he recant his decision to help.

As carefully as I could, I explained that I wanted those who specialized in surveillance and intel gathering to focus on suspected sleeper agents and potential sympathizer meeting places, which I would be sending to their holonavs. Hacking personal files was not currently permitted by Spec Ops since this mission was completely our initiative. I explained that it would be best to wait until we have enough evidence on these individuals before requesting permission to gain that intel.

For these surveillance missions, I stressed the

importance of having backup since it was likely the sleeper agents or other individuals we were shadowing likely had backup or bodyguards. We were all highly trained and capable, but we could never be too careful. Especially when it came to the Coalition.

"Once enough evidence against these individuals is gathered, we will submit it for review and take it from there," I concluded.

"Why ask us though?" Meera questioned; arms crossed.

"I and my team want this done quickly and quietly. We cannot handle it alone with those restrictions. We had no one else to turn to that we could trust." I chose vulnerability over waspishness. A good leader earns trust, she does not demand it.

I repeated that like a mantra at each mistrustful glance.

"I think it sounds simple enough," Talia said excitedly. "I mean, it isn't *simple,* but it sounds like we should be able to do it and do it well."

A murmur of agreement ran around the table, and I stood, the others followed suit quickly after. Goodbyes were said, hugs were given, and by the time we had exited the restaurant out into the cool night air I realized how relieved I was. We could do this.

Chapter Twenty-Four

To say I felt exhausted was an understatement. I felt the weariness in my bones, in my very soul. And yet I could not stop myself from moving on to the next objective. The next round of training. The next action to take against my enemies and those who wished to see me fail. I was moving on spite and the overwhelming fear of failure alone.

After our meeting in Nostalgic, we had taken every waking moment into investigating our targets, looking into lead after lead. Each time, we would come to a dead end, or the person would end up not even being associated with my father or the Coalition. Most times they weren't even Coalition sympathizers, just happened to say something innocuously to the wrong person or posted something on social media that was a little off-color.

With each dead end, I deflated, my momentum running on its last dregs.

"Daux?" Himawari asked, concern lacing her tone.

I barely heard her, sending another blast of flame toward my simulated target. One that I barely had the energy for. It was weak, hardly more than an ember. I had been using my magic far too much recently, keeping my foresight on almost every waking hour to make sure I didn't miss a single thing on reconnaissance.

"Daux," she repeated, her worry increasing. "Are you

listening to me?"

Doubling over with a hand on my knee, I wiped the sweat from my brow – my breaths coming in quick, heavy gasps. "Yeah," I said once I had enough air in my lungs. "What's up?"

Himawari's face flicked through a range of emotions before settling on compassion. Or pity. I could hardly tell which was which anymore.

Tamping down my annoyance, I straightened to look her in the eye.

"What's up?" I repeated.

"Oh, nothing," she waved me off. "I was going to suggest taking a break. The rest of us are pretty beat."

Tired? We had a potential government coup to uncover and they were tired? Aggravation flared up within me, but I refused to let it show. They wouldn't understand. Their loyalties were not being called into question because of their parents' connections to the Coalition. Training and recon were indispensable.

But as I looked over them, each one of my team members was covered in sweat and grime – their appearance tired and haggard as I knew my own to be.

"Right," I said slowly, nodding my head. "Okay. We can take a break for today. We should get back at it before recon on Sorrowsday though."

Jax and Félix's elation at the prospect of a break ended in groans of defeat when I finished speaking. I couldn't bring myself to be mad at them. They had been working very hard lately – and they did it all for me. I had no right to push them further.

The sounds of the vid Jax, Félix, and Himawari were watching in the common area carried down the hall and filtered through the door of my bedroom. I contemplated telling them to turn it down, but couldn't bring myself to walk all that way much less message them with my holonav. They deserved a movie night after today anyway.

Besides, I needed to finish our latest recon report before my eyes decided to close permanently for the evening. My bed was soft and comfortable, and I could feel myself fighting to keep them open.

"Knock, knock," a familiar tenor said from my doorway.

I jumped and looked toward the sound.

Valentin stood there, hair wet and glistening on his brow, smirking. He was clothed, thankfully, but it was plain that he had just finished showering. I hadn't even heard him…

"What?" I snapped, turning back to my holonav only to see that the holoscreen had shut off and the device ha powered down.

"You were snoring," Valentin teased.

"I was not!" I exclaimed in indignation.

"You were."

My brows furrowed at him, and my lips pursed. I was just filling out a report, I couldn't have been snoring. Maybe he had heard the movie? I asked him as much, ignoring the fact that I could no longer hear it myself.

Valentin shook his head. "I came to confirm the plan for tomorrow, but you didn't answer. The light was on, so I opened the door to see if you had headphones on."

I commonly filled out reports with my music on when I did them at the flat, so it wasn't an unfair assumption. But that didn't explain the snoring comment.

"You were asleep," Valentin continued wryly at my confusion.

Heat flooded my face and I stood unsteadily on my feet, marching toward him. His amused expression never left his face, even when I pushed him outside of my room.

"We're still on for tomorrow," I snapped and slammed

the door in his smug face.

Then I finished my report and went to bed.

I had slept deeply and dreamlessly, but when I awoke to my alarm I felt the same bone-crushing exhaustion as the night previous. Aches and pains jolted through my body as I dragged myself from my bed. It was almost agonizing to move through the stretches I knew would loosen up my muscles and joints.

Valentin and Himawari were already dressed and waiting when I exited my room to make tea and breakfast. My stomach was in knots, but I forced a protein bar and an apple down my throat while he sipped on a cup of cold coffee and she a smoothie. Once we were finished, and I was ready, we left.

Jax and Félix were still sound asleep when we exited the building, but we had planned it that way. They had been doing too much on my behalf, and they deserved to sleep in. Valentin had insisted on going with me to make sure I didn't pass out, and Himawari was going to be a much-needed third set of eyes.

I scoffed at them but agreed to let them come along anyway. I needed someone to watch my six, and Valentin was the only one on our team that didn't look like he was going to pass out at any moment. Himawari thought we needed a chaperone, which was a preposterous notion in my opinion. I was more likely to punch Valentin than I was to kiss him – or any sort of action like kissing.

But as I looked at him from across the shuttle's aisle, I once again noticed how pretty he looked. I didn't know how he did it, running on fumes like we all were. He still managed to look like he was airbrushed onto a holozine. Maybe he used a glamour.

He probably used a glamour.

Though try as I might, to dispel it with foresight on our way to our coordinates, I couldn't. This frustrated me to no end.

A small smile curled at the corners of his lips when he caught me staring and the dreaded blush crept back into my face. I turned sharply away from him and refused to look at him for the rest of the shuttle ride.

Our mission was simple. We were to sync our holonavs to the files of the Governor's office after a brief meeting with the secretary and do a sweep of my father's offices. The three of us decided on glamours since my presence in the Governor's office would attract suspicion even if my father was not in today. Since the Governor's offices had anti-glamour magic tech in place to protect against similar scenarios as this, we would be using tech glamours invented by the R&D department of Spec Ops. The tech was so new that my father's offices would not have precautions against it yet.

The Governor's offices were in Heliorious, but the capital of New Palogenia was a large one. We had to shuttle for over two hours, barely making it to our appointment with my father's secretary. And that was with good traffic.

"Welcome," Hayley the secretary said brightly as she received Valentin and me into my father's inner offices.

They hadn't changed much from when I was a child. Expensive hardwoods lined the walls and bookshelves, giving the rooms an oppressive feeling. Plush rugs and furs from non-mutated animals lined the floors. The heads stared down at me with hatred, as though they too judged me for my father's sins. The fact that he had hunted these creatures was abhorrent to me, and the fact that it had been legalized even more so.

The secretary was tall, blonde, and bright-eyed. If I didn't know better, I would have thought she looked like my mother. But I did know better, and I knew my father chose this young woman for a reason.

He had a type after all.

What upset me though was that he wasn't hiding his preferences anymore. Not that I felt bad for my mother, but she didn't deserve this type of torment. The kind where one's husband surrounds himself with attractive young women who looked like you did once upon a time – just because he could. No one deserved that.

Our questions for Hayley were routine enough. Frequency of audits, efficiency, and if the employees were treated fairly. I knew by the opulent furnishings in my father's inner offices that two of those things were lax. I could see it as though it had been painted in bright neon on the dark walls.

"Governor Deveraux is a fair lawmaker," Hayley said diplomatically, but her smile had faltered.

I just hoped Valentin and Himawari could not see the embarrassment on my face. It was bad enough that I was here again, in the place my father committed treason against the NAF. The office he was supposed to uphold for the good of our allied nations. I could hardly stand being here again, but I had to do this. I had to uncover his crimes not only for myself but for Amalie and for everyone else my father had wronged.

"And there is nothing about Governor Deveraux you would like to report? Personal grievances and the like?" I asked gently, trying not to cringe at the sound of the new voice coming out of my mouth. Glamours were always uncomfortable for me.

Hayley looked between the three of us, apprehension shining in her bright eyes. Then she covertly activated her holonav and tapped on it for a moment. Seconds later, the cameras in the office blinked off and retracted into the walls. Her nervousness was palpable, mingling with my own in the tension-filled space.

"This doesn't feel like just a routine inspection," Hayley whispered, clutching a hand to her chest. "What has

Governor Deveraux done?"

"We can't disclose any information pertaining to our inspection. You are familiar with the process," Himawari replied with genuine regret, as Hayley looked downright terrified.

Swallowing a few times, Hayley answered my question. "He… He, uh, sometimes speaks to me in ways that are not appropriate for the workplace. And he makes me uncomfortable. He has a bad temper and will behave abominably if one of his proposed bills or laws does not pass."

Hayley went on for a few more minutes, detailing my father's mistreatment of his aids, secretaries, and employees and his abuse of power. Himawari looked greener the more of my father's actions spewed from Hayley's mouth. Valentin only looked angry.

I knew my expression was schooled into a cool mask, though I could feel my jaw twitching with rage. My father was sinking lower and lower with each word that fell from Hayley's lips, and I could feel the guilt washing over me in waves. Staining me with its scummy waters, filling up every crevice with its mold.

What if I had said something about my father sooner? Why hadn't I said something sooner?

Because I was a coward who didn't want my chances of being Placed in Spec Ops to be ruined by just being associated with my father. I had not said anything because I assumed my father's poison was only directed at me – only affected me. I had not thought he would be directly harming anyone else, even if he had not laid his hands on them.

"Hayley," I said, my voice rasping out much harsher than I had intended and causing her to jump. "Would you be willing to let us have access to my—Governor Deveraux's files and the office's data? We want to stop him from harming anyone else, from bullying and exploiting more people."

Her lips pressed together in a thin line, but she nodded her answer, pulling up her holonav's screen once again and leading us to the ornate wooden desk that sat in front of the picture windows at the back of the room. Soon, she had the holonav connected to the data system there and began transferring everything straight to our holonavs.

"I won't be held responsible if I'm found out? I will be protected?" she asked nervously.

"To the best of our ability," Valentin promised as the data finished uploading.

Nodding again, Hayley shut down the system after wiping the activation from the device's history and slowly walked toward the door, indicating we were free to search the interior offices on our own. We did so quickly, but thoroughly and soon we had everything we needed. The rooms themselves yielded nothing but my father's opulent spending habits with taxpayer's dollars, which in itself was not something illegal. Though it was very telling about the kind of lawmaker he was.

Once again, I wondered how he came to be Placed in such a station.

Now was not the time to worry about that though. We had to leave and leave quickly. There was a lot of data to go over, and I wanted anything incriminating in the Overseer's hands as soon as I could put it there.

Chapter Twenty-Five

Valentin, Himawari, and I had just set down our gear in the living room after the shuttle ride home when my holonav buzzed with a notification for a holochat. It had been a little over a week since our meeting with Talia and Riannan's teams requesting their help with the mission we had been tasked with.

"You're not going to believe this," Talia said when I answered, her face flushed with excitement. "Well, actually, you probably will, but you get what I mean."

While my team and I had been performing missions as we normally would alongside our data gathering, Talia and Riannan's teams had been out carrying out covert operations. They were trying to connect evidence with the many suspects we had to any terrorist involvement.

"After tailing and failing multiple times, oh hey–" she sniggered. "I rhymed, anyway – one of the targets you asked us to observe led us right to an underground Neo-Traditionalist rally!"

"And this is good, how?" I asked, affectionately exasperated with my friend.

"*Because,*" she said, rolling her eyes. "It means he is, at least in part, a sympathizer to the Coalition's cause."

"Obviously," I sighed, making notes in my holonav on some of the data we had collected earlier in the day. "But we knew they were all at the very least sympathizers."

"But we have never had concrete evidence of any of them associating with the group before now."

"True…"

"Which leads me to my next big reveal!"

I was about to reply, to play along with Talia's theatrics, when Alexis, or Demos, I still could not tell, burst into her room.

"Have you told her about her dad yet?" he asked enthusiastically.

My stomach sank. Had they been investigating my father today? Was he not in his office because of this rally? It had to be the worst news, but that was something I had been preparing myself for. I schooled my face into one of neutrality as Talia glared at him.

"What about my father?" I asked.

Talia turned back to me, and all the excitement drained from her when she saw my face.

"Sorry Daux," she apologized. "I didn't think, and it was insensitive of me to bring it up like that."

"What *about* my father?" I repeated, anger seeping into my voice.

Talia took a few deep breaths before answering – mirroring me.

"While he wasn't leading the rally – like we hoped he would, you know, so we could stack up more substantial evidence against him – he was there, in secret. He was in a secluded box applauding along with several of the other officials we were investigating while the speaker incited violence against multiple branches of government and those who disagreed with their cause."

I closed my eyes and breathed in slowly through my nose. Then out. Talia was quiet on the other end of our call, giving me time to process. Valentin and Himawari were also silent. I could tell, even without opening my eyes, that he was standing as still and ridged as I was. That Himawari was holding herself back from embracing me.

"And you're sure it was him?" I asked, willing the tremble from my voice.

"He was in disguise," Talia hedged, but she knew him; she knew *me*. She wouldn't have mistaken him, not with her eagle eyes. "But it was him. We used our glamour detectors to covertly check. I'm sorry, Daux."

Shaking my head as if to clear it, I allowed myself a few heartbeats to grieve. To process this information and what it meant for me, my sister.

"Okay," I said, finally allowing myself to look Talia in the face again.

"Okay?" I could not tell if she was asking if I was all right or questioning my response.

"Yeah."

"Okay."

Another round of breathing. "Send me everything you've got, and I'll give it to the Overseer for review."

"I'm sending it over now," Talia sighed. I could hear the clicking of a monitor through the audio. "Daux, I'm sorry. Are you going to be all right?"

I nodded my reply and ended the call without saying goodbye. Without a word to Valentin, or any of my teammates who had gathered in the room while I was speaking, I turned on my heel and left.

"Here," I snapped, barging into the Overseer's office unceremoniously, and tossed the holofiles onto her desk. Her secretary trailed after me, halting in the doorway.

"What are these?" she asked in a cool tone, though her eyes were brimming with black fire at my intrusion.

"Evidence on my father, as well as a few other high-ranking members of the government. This should be enough to further investigations."

The Overseer quickly downloaded the files onto her

holonav and swiped through them, her rich brown skin becoming paler with each passing second.

"Daux," she said hoarsely. "I'm so sorry."

"I'm not," I replied coldly. "Let me and my team find out if he's actually breaking the law. That's all I care about."

"I meant…" she began, then seemed to think better of it. "You're right. This is evidence enough to investigate further into your father and his accomplices."

"Good." It was all I said before I stormed from the office.

When I returned to our flat that night, my teammates were unusually quiet.

"What's going on?" I asked as I entered the dining room.

Félix, Jax, Himawari, and Valentin were sitting around the dining room table, barely picking at the chicken stew Jax had prepared.

"We were waiting on you," Himawari said.

"You all can eat without me you know."

"Yes," Jax sighed. "But we needed to talk to you."

I sat in my chair, gesturing for them to begin. "Go ahead."

"Daux," Himawari began. "We don't want you overworking yourself again now that there's been a break in the investigation."

I looked at them, their worried faces and tired eyes, and felt guilt. I had caused them pain again and caused them distress. I sighed.

"I will do what is necessary, nothing less, and nothing more," I promised, watching their expressions which ranged from angry to solemn. I held up a hand to silence any bursting opinions. "I promise I will *only* do what is necessary."

Valentin, whose face was still vaguely stormy, relented. "I suppose that's all we can ask for. Just don't run yourself into the ground."

"We will continue working with Gwyn and Riannan's teams to lessen the load. Don't worry," I reassured them all gently. "Was that all?"

"No," Félix said. "How did it go with the Overseer?"

The weariness I had attempted to keep at bay until that moment hit me all at once. I slumped down in my chair, drained. "As well as to be expected. She still doesn't trust me, and it's really starting to get on my nerves."

"Well Governor Deveraux is the number one person of interest in this case," Jax hedged. "You said yourself you understood their mistrust."

"Yes," I agreed. "But I've been proven innocent, so it's stupid to keep treating me with suspicion."

"It sucks." Himawari slapped the table with her hand.

"Yes, yes," Valentin interjected. "It sucks and Daux's father is a terrible person, but let's get to the point. What is our next move? The investigation is still ongoing, and every moment we waste we lose an opportunity to stop the Coalition's plans."

"All right, all right, calm down, Valentin," I laughed.

Now that we had the clearance to continue the investigation, The Overseer had assigned us a mission on the Cassacania coastline near the small port town of Portnith. Through the info we and the other teams had gathered, we discovered a Coalition base set up inside a shipping warehouse.

"How do these bases keep popping up unnoticed?" Félix asked irritably.

"Well," I said, pausing a moment. "It's likely because we have Coalition sympathizers in the government. If they're as high up as the governors – like my father – then it stands to reason that there are moles in our military and boarder security as well. It's also difficult to regulate, especially when the NAF has so few territories compared to the Coalition."

"Well, that sucks," he grumbled again, pushing

legumes and meat around in his bowl.

"Okay, walking encyclopedia," Himawari joked, "what's our next move?"

I stuck my tongue out at her. "We're going to finish this nice meal Jax prepared, then we're going to rest and prepare to leave tomorrow morning."

And we did, discussing the details while we ate. We would leave early in the morning and arrive at our destination in a day. Heliorious, the capital city of New Palogenia, was located within a day's travel from the coastal cities so delegations and other political guests could easily travel to the city. Air travel was strictly monitored and usually reserved only for Spec Ops and military activity within the NAF territories.

Once we arrived, along with the other two teams, we would infiltrate the base and take out as many of their systems as possible, extracting as much info as we could, as well as incapacitating soldiers.

It was to be an all-out assault on their system and organization. And hopefully, bring in some damning evidence to convict my father, and the other Neo-Traditionalists who supported him.

Sleep did not come easily that night. I contemplated waking Jax, Himawari, or Félix to sit with me and calm my nerves. But I did not. I knew Valentin would still be awake. He ran on caffeine and rage apparently and was always up late, so I gathered up my courage and knocked on his door.

He opened it surprisingly quickly, looking down at me with his bright eyes which seemed to shine in the darkness. "Can't sleep?"

I shook my head.

"C'mon," he sighed, gesturing for me to step inside his room. Somehow it was even darker in his room than it was in the rest of the flat. Likely due to all the black used in the décor.

I stood awkwardly in the middle of the room while

Valentin flicked on a small bedside lamp as he climbed into the large four-poster, which barely illuminated the space.

"Come here, Daux," he grumbled from his spot on the bed. "I'm too tired to bite."

I gave a nervous chuckle and joined him on the bed, hesitantly.

"You want to talk about something?"

"No," I said.

"Read?"

"No."

"You going to just sit there and stare at me?"

I shrugged, feeling quite miserable.

"You really are weird, Daux," Valentin snapped. "You know that?"

"Yeah," I said, smiling wanly.

He shook his head. But we were quiet for a while, neither of us looking at the other. I stared at my hands, which worried Valentin's soot-colored coverlet into tiny wrinkles, and he stared past me to a dark corner of the room. We sat like that, until my eyes began to droop, and my hands began to still.

"I'm scared," I declared softly.

"About?" He turned the full force of his eyes onto me.

"Everything. I'm always scared. That I'm going to fail and disappoint everyone, including myself. Or that someone will be hurt because of me. I'm just so scared all the time, and I'm sick of it."

My eyes began to burn. I hated the sensation. I hated myself for being quick to cry. My weaknesses and fears. I was ashamed of them, and I hated that I was baring them to Valentin. Vulnerability was something I had been taught to cut out and thought I had, for the most part.

There were times when I shared my tears with my friends, but I had never told them how scared I was. Of everything. It was too difficult to talk about. Too hard to put into words, even if it seemed simple.

The thickness at the back of my throat and the burning in my eyes would always stop me before I could even utter the first word.

"Come here," Valentin commanded, repeating his words from earlier. He had his arms held out to me, inviting me into an embrace.

I hesitantly shifted and moved next to him, letting him put his arms around me awkwardly. Despite the unease, it was nice to be held by him. Valentin was all lean muscle and had the ozone smell of ice magic and mint. He felt safe.

"The only way you can fail, Daux," he said softly. "Is if you never try."

He was right, of course, and what he said helped. A little. That nagging, fearful voice in the back of my head filled with doubt and anxiety. I would take what Valentin said to heart though. I would remember it and refuse to forget it when I felt the fear overtake me.

"I know it's kind of a platitude—" he started.

"No," I interrupted. "You're right. If I don't try, I don't give myself the chance of success. I mean, words are not going to make the fear go away. But you are right."

Valentin gave a soft chuckle, and I realized just how much I liked it when he laughed. It was nice, being able to be friends with him. Things were not completely smooth between us, even now, but we had become friends since that day in the rain, and I was glad for it.

"Are you… happier now?" I asked, looking up at him.

He was quiet for a moment, then spoke. "Yeah, I think I am. Some days are still harder than others, but this team has given me a purpose. It's easier when I focus my energy into it, into you guys, rather than being angry."

"I understand that completely." I smiled, finally beginning to feel sleepy.

I knew at that moment I was ready for anything. With Valentin at my back and my friends at my side, I knew I could handle the upcoming mission, despite the dread that still ate at me. Fear could not overtake me; I could not let it. My team, my friends, and so many others were relying on the success of this mission, and I had to see it through.

Chapter Twenty-Six

A loud pounding on the door woke me from a deep, heavy slumber. The warmth my body was nestled into suddenly disappeared. Perturbed, my arms pushed across the empty space, searching for it.

"Hey, Valentin— Oh, crap, sorry!" Félix shouted from the doorway.

"Damn it, Félix, do you ever knock?" Valentin hissed, pushing him from the room.

Valentin? What was he doing in my room, in my bed?

"Well, if I had known you were having a *sleepover*, I wouldn't have interrupted. I was looking for Daux anyway, she's always up first."

I sat up straight then, realizing I was not in my bed. My eyes darted to Valentin, then Félix, in shock and mortification. They were still bickering as I slid out of Valentin's bed and ran past them into my room. My heart was pounding. There was no way I had spent the entire night in Valentin's room, his bed. No way. But I had. Oh Gods, I would never hear the end of it.

And I did not. The entire time we prepared to leave and the entire trip to the coast, I heard nothing but ribbing from Jax, Himawari, and Félix. Valentin was decidedly silent the whole time, looking incredibly like himself, moody and annoyed. I prayed they would not continue when we met up with the other teams. I could handle teasing from them, but

I would likely die of embarrassment if anyone else knew.

The air this morning was jovial, mostly because Félix couldn't keep his mouth shut. But a ball of lead was forming in my stomach. We were about to infiltrate a Coalition base within our borders. They had weapons of mass destruction. They had important intel to extract. People were more than likely going to be injured, or even die, and we were sitting in the auto joking around.

The ribbing didn't last too much longer, and my distress only grew. Once we met up with Riannan, Hawthorn, Talia, and Gwyn at our navpoint, my teammates had let up with their torment. Valentin was finally able to relax the grimace on his face.

"So," Talia said cheerfully. "What's the plan?"

"First things first, we need to gain entry to the base. Once we do that, we will split off into two teams. Jax, Valentin, Tali, and I will head the assault group. Gwyn, Riannan, Himawari, Félix, and Hawthorn, I want you all to hack into the system and after downloading as much info as you can, wipe the system and put them in the dark. I don't want any outgoing communication from this base."

Riannan timidly raised her hand. "Are we killing anyone on this mission?"

At her question, my heart shuddered to a sudden halt. Then it started back up in earnest when I took a deep inhale to steady myself.

"I-I… Um…" I began, licking my lips nervously.

How does one answer a question they don't even really know the answer to? We would need to destroy the base, so of course there would be casualties. But 'casualties' was an easy word to say when you didn't have a body count to back it up.

Steeling my spine, I started again with guilt and regret flooding through me. "It's a high possibility and not one that I look forward to. We will be destroying this base completely because of the weapons they have stored there, and to do that, lives will more than likely be taken," I paused, refusing to let my hands tremble. "I don't like this – I don't want to kill anyone – but the Coalition has given us no choice."

"I've never killed anyone before," Riannan murmured, eye downcast.

At that moment I nearly regretted bringing her on this mission. Other than Valentin or Gwyn, I doubted any of us had directly killed anyone on our missions. Death, faceless and anonymous, loomed before us, and I was sure it would find somewhere to take hold. If not today, then any other. I did not look forward to the moment I met with it.

"Neither have I," I replied. "And I don't relish the thought, but now is not the time for that discussion. We have a mission to complete." I signaled to the group it was time to head out.

The pseudo-warehouse rose before us like a behemoth. I swallowed back the fear I felt and lead the group onward. Try. All I had to do was try and do everything in my power to make sure this mission was a success. Easy right? I gritted my teeth and headed forward, to the mouth of the beast.

Once we had made it close enough Talia, Hawthorn, and Félix had disrupter software going which would ruin any surveillance footage. This would ensure we could make it through the building before the cameras detected us. The rusty side entrance was left unguarded, something that surprised me. How were these soldiers so comfortable in enemy territory?

Splitting off into separate groups would be the difficult part. Gwyn and Riannan were capable leaders and I trusted them to protect their group, but this was such a high-stakes mission. We had to keep in constant communication.

Before we went our separate ways, Himawari grabbed me by the wrist. I turned to look at her in surprise. A fierce light shone brightly in her dark brown eyes, it was encouraging and filled me with hope. She clasped my forearm in her hand, gripped it tightly, then turned and headed off with her team.

"What was that about?" Talia asked, coming to stand beside me.

"A wish for good luck," I said smiling, and headed off in the direction of the generators.

While the other team was to download intel and shut down the building's communication systems, we were to lead the assault on the building. First order of business, we were to set up explosives at the buildings' generators, incapacitating as many Coalition soldiers as possible along the way.

Stealth was the main priority, and we swept down the halls cloaked with Jax's light manipulation magic. We made quick work of the soldiers we saw, stealing the air from their lungs with Talia's wind magic, freezing them with Valentin's ice magic, and knocking them unconscious. We stashed them in darkened corners and supply closets, praying they would not wake before the others could shut down the comm systems.

This had to be timed precisely. There were too many variables again. Too many variables meant too many ways for our friends to be captured or killed.

I shook my head. Yes, many things could go wrong, but I could not allow such thoughts to make me falter. I had to be strong. My teammates needed me to be strong.

Carefully and quietly, I slid through the generator room doors. The hum of the machines was loud in my ears. The vibrations resounded deep in my chest, making me feel slightly ill. A quick scan of the room with my foresight told me there were no other people in the room with us. Yet. I signaled to the others that it was clear, and they quickly set to work on the explosives.

It was a large, rectangular room with tech lining the walls and generators lining the floor. I did not have to use my imagination to figure out what they were powering. Intelligence told us that the base held at least one weapon of mass destruction including other, less powerful, magical devices. Our neutralizing virus would render them useless.

The intel team would be working to extract the data while simultaneously uploading a virus that would trigger a "self-destruct" mechanism within the WMDs to neutralize the explosive compounds, rendering them useless and completely safe when we demolished the building with our smaller-scale explosion.

Talia and Jax bickered softly as they worked on their generator, rigging the delicate bomb to the machinery in such a way that it would be hard to detect. At least before it exploded. A sad smile graced my lips. I hated that we had to reduce this place to rubble. Hated that we would likely be taking lives in the process. The Coalition was dangerous, that much was for certain. But to fight under the same tactics as they did felt dirty. As if we could not outsmart them, or that we could not be better somehow.

From what I had recently experienced was that the NAF was not exactly the ideal society I had thought it to be. It was my dream to be in Spec Ops, to help people by serving the NAF. To use the magic the Gods had gifted us with for good. Despite these doubts, these fears, I had to believe that what we had was better than the totalitarian control the Coalition excised over its territories. Otherwise, my team and I were doing something reprehensible.

As if he sensed the anxious turn my thoughts had taken, Valentin patted my shoulder gently before he moved to the next generator. We had completed three of the four largest generators during my reverie and a quick check of the time on my holonav told me it was time for the other team to report in.

Touching the device at my ear, I listened for Himawari's soft voice. I waited a minute, then two. No response. No big deal, maybe they were trying to get past some guards.

They should be at the main hub by now, though. Not

sneaking past guards. A memory from the Gladwin base infiltration flashed through my mind. Jax had nearly been discovered and would have been killed – or worse. What if something similar had happened to the other group?

I touched my finger to the device again as I attempted to help Valentin wire the explosive to the last large generator. Still no response. He caught my eye and nodded. He knew and understood.

I waited for a second more before I spoke. "Deer to Shade. Deer to Shade, please respond."

Noise crackled over the line before Himawari's voice sounded, sending a blossom of relief and warmth through me. But that was before I registered what she was saying. "You're not going to believe what we're finding."

She did not sound enthused. There was a terrified note in her tone that made my blood run cold.

"Shade, is all well on your end?" I asked, trying to keep *my* terror from leaking into my voice.

A shuddering breath. "Yes, we are all safe. Nearly done extracting the info. Fé and Thorn are uploading the virus, weapons neutralizer, and the shutdown software as we speak."

"Why have none of you checked in? It's way past the agreed-upon time."

"We are all a little in shock, sorry."

I gritted my teeth as Valentin finished hooking up the bomb. How many times had she done this before? "Please, just report at the appointed times. We're all under duress right now, but if we don't communicate then this whole thing goes belly up."

"Noted," Himawari said, sounding apologetic.

"Deer out."

"Roger."

With a flick of my hand, I ended the conversation. Valentin, Jax, and Talia had finished rigging the largest generators while I spoke with Himawari. It was time to get out of there. Once the bombs went off, the explosions would spread to the smaller generators and other machinery in the room, creating a massive inferno. We would need to hurry.

I signaled to the others and Valentin started the countdown with the detonator. Once we were clear of the room, we headed in the direction of the others. Hopefully, they had managed the blackout.

Through the winding, monotonous halls we ran. The red light of the security cameras was not shining. I prayed that meant they were shut off. Jax kept up his cloaking magic regardless. It would not do to be discovered prematurely, and I was not taking the risk of alerting the enemy before we knew the comm system was shut down.

"We have to be heading in circles," Talia groaned as we made our way down another stark gray hallway.

A commotion coming from up ahead punctuated her grumbling.

I cursed and sped up, ramming my way through the double doors at the end of the hallway. This mission could *not* be compromised.

The sight before me was nothing other than absolute chaos. Our friends were going head-to-head with a group of Coalition soldiers, taking them down left and right. Felix had smashed one soldier to a bloody pulp, leaving an unrecognizable mess behind.

Shadows swarmed the room, attacking the soldiers as grotesque shapes made from nightmares. From the sound of their screams, they believed so too. Himawari stood in the center of the swarm manipulating every movement, every attack.

Hawthorn and Riannan fought back-to-back, shooting and slashing with guns and blades at any who came too close, creating a deadly circle of carnage. Gwyn seemed to appear out of thin air, materializing for a second to attack before blending back in with the swarm of shadows.

Talia, always quick to act, sent a gale of wind onto the

battleground, disorienting the soldiers. But she also distracted *our* people in the process.

"Nice, Talia," Valentin chided and leaped into the fray. She shouted her protest and followed suit, notching an arrow into her bow.

Jax caught my eye, and I nodded at him. Together, we joined the fight. He charging his knives, and me allowing the world to melt away as I sharpened my foresight.

My sword felt light in hand, an extension of my arm, and nothing more. The sounds of the fight, though still loud in my ears, were no longer a distraction. I could hear each jibe of my friends and each command of the soldiers' superiors. It became exhilarating.

A jab to my left, a quick swipe to my right, under, over. Breathing even. I wove through the carnage, cutting down each soldier who was unfortunate enough to make their way into my path. We would have to fight our way out if we wanted to escape before the bombs detonated. I would have time to reflect on the death I was causing later.

For the first time, I was grateful for the emotion-numbing effect my foresight had. Especially as my rapier made its way through the chest of a soldier who had charged me, splattering my armor, my face, and my helmet with deep red blood. As I cut the limbs of another who reached to grab me.

I spun and whirled, taking in the desolation around me all at once. Had I not activated my magic, I would be a mess. Later was another story, but now I had to make a path to escape.

A loud, ear-splitting sound shook the building, knocking several people off their feet. Riannan, who was closest to me, had fallen. She looked up at my blood-splattered helmet in horror but accepted the hand I offered her.

"We need to get out of here," I commanded at her paling face.

"Was that what I think it was?" she asked as we fought our way through the throng of soldiers.

Screams of terror sounded all around us as another explosion shook the building.

"We need to get out *now!*" I screamed, hoping my teammates and friends could hear me.

My movements became less precise in panic. I had to get everyone out. I shoved Riannan ahead of me. "Run for the nearest exit! Grab any of our teammates you can, I'll get the rest."

She nodded, a determined look I had yet to see crossing her lovely features. She had a split lip and swelling above her left eyebrow, but I had never seen her animated features so alive. Without a moment's hesitation, Riannan grabbed Hawthorn by the elbow and ran, shouting for the others to follow her.

Thankfully, I saw Gwyn and Talia follow close behind, fighting off frantic soldiers every step of the way.

Himawari was easy to spot in her hoard of shadows, a look of pure terror on her face as a third explosion blasted through the building. The way we had come from had begun to crumble. Jax, quick as lightning, appeared beside her and lifted her into his arms. As quickly as he had appeared, he vanished, taking Himawari and her shadows with him.

A loud, metallic screech filled my ears, and I twisted away from my opponent, yanking my sword from his chest, to see where it had come from. Yards behind me was a soldier holding an automatic firearm, still smoking. I reached my hand up to feel my helmet. A small groove where a bullet had passed now marred the durable metal. He grinned wickedly at me and opened fire again.

I let him, feeling the bullets ricochet off my armor as I strode purposefully toward him holding up my left hand. The feeling of flame grazing my skin was a welcome sensation as the magic left my palm, engulfing the soldier. Barely registering his agonized screams, I turned away. But another explosion knocked me from my feet, sending me flying.

"Daux!" came a far-away shout.

My mind was reeling. The next explosion should not have been for another minute, even if the fires had reached the last generator. It wouldn't be long after that the whole building would go up in a raging inferno, but we should have had at least a minute.

I was not going to accept death. Not yet. Struggling to my feet, I felt a strong arm wrap around my waist, pulling me along. I fought it for a moment, before realizing it was Valentin, face pale with strain and worry.

"Hey," I rasped.

"Hey yourself." There was that cocky smirk I hated. I was never happier to see it.

"We gonna make it?" I asked, limping alongside him.

"Yeah, that explosion was Félix blowing a hole in the exterior wall."

"Nice!"

The smirk again. "It was good improvising."

"Would it kill you to give someone a regular compliment?"

"Absolutely."

The building was shaking and groaning. No time for laughter. Through the smoke and rubble, we ran, pulling each other along until we cleared the giant hole Félix blasted in the wall. Fading sunlight washed over us, bathing us in its reddened glow. We ran as far as we could, hoping to be far enough away from the blast radius when the building blew.

With a deafening roar, the Coalition base behind us began to collapse in on itself, flame erupting from it in angry bursts as if it were a dying, angry god. Shouts from behind us caused me to whirl around, raising my palm and sword defensively.

"Whoa, Daux," Jax said, holding his hands up placatingly.

"Oh, sorry."

"It's okay," he sighed in relief. "We're all on edge right now."

"That is the understatement of the century."

A soft, pained groan interrupted our banter. Valentin was holding his side, kneeling on the ground as if he were in pain. "Now is not the time for humor, guys. We still have to get away from here."

Blood was seeping from between his fingers where his hand was pressed, dripping like liquified rubies over his quickly paling fingers. My pulse, which had just started to calm, began pounding furiously in my ears. Louder than the explosions that were still going off behind us.

"Valentin!" Jax exclaimed and rushed to Valentin's side. "What happened to you?"

Valentin winced as Jax helped him to his feet, strain whitening his face. I had not realized he was injured. He had gotten me out of the base, and he was *injured.* He had not told me – had given no indication. We had been incredibly lucky to have gotten this far in our Spec Ops careers with only minor scrapes and bruises. I did not know how to handle this.

Hawthorn, a blur of tanned skin and sandy hair, rushed past me.

"I can help!" she said, pulling off her filthy combat gloves. "I know some basic healing magic. Our mom is a healer."

I wanted to snap at her, to push her away from him. She was not trained to deal with trauma situations. But the pain in Valentin's face was unbearable. He needed a healer, and Hawthorn was the closest thing we had. I could not let my panic get the better of me. So, I held my tongue.

When Valentin removed his hand from the wound – when I saw the extent of the damage – bile rose in the back of my throat. Shrapnel from the explosion, or the building's collapse, had embedded itself into his side, ripping through the typically durable fabric of his tactical armor. The flesh around the wound was torn and puckered around the piece of metal.

"You shouldn't have messed with this," Hawthorn chided him from what sounded like far away. "If you had left it alone it wouldn't be bleeding so much."

A pained bark of laughter escaped him as she removed the debris, cleansing the wound with water and a small vile of disinfectant. Black danced across my vision, and everything seemed to tunnel.

"Somebody help her," Valentin ground out through clenched teeth. "She's going into shock."

"What can I do?" I asked, holding my hand out as if to help. A tan, long-fingered hand clasped my extended one and held it to my side.

"It'll be okay, Daux," Félix whispered, squeezing my hand. "Just breathe with me."

"Will that help?" I asked, my voice sounding thick like I was underwater.

"It will help me, and you."

"Okay."

I swallowed around the lump in my throat, breathing deeply. In, as Hawthorn pulled the last piece of foreign matter from Valentin's side, dousing the bleeding wound with more disinfectant. Out, as she placed her hands over the torn flesh.

"This may scar pretty bad," she informed him. "I'm not the most talented healer."

"Just do it," he demanded, gritting his teeth.

I almost lost the contents of my stomach as the skin and muscle began to knit back together under Hawthorn's small hands. Félix gave me another squeeze, and I took another deep, shaking breath through my nose.

Soon, the gruesome wound was nothing but a crude sunburst-shaped scar, pink and shiny against the rest of Valentin's skin.

"Now," he said wearily, grinning in my direction.

"Was that so bad?"

Despite my stomach roiling and unsteady legs, I rolled my eyes. "We should have let you bleed out."

Turning on my heel, I ignored Valentin's pained laughter that rang out behind me. The others followed close behind. We had a mission to report.

Chapter Twenty-Seven

Though Hawthorn insisted Valentin rest as much as possible, he refused, discussing the details of the mission with Gwyn and Riannan. Something I should have been doing. Instead, I was gazing out of the open window of the auto, ignoring everyone, and trying not to vomit.

Everywhere I looked, I saw the gaping hole in Valentin's black combat gear. The flashes of blood and torn flesh. I resisted the urge to vomit all over again. There had never been a serious injury on a mission I had led. Statistically, it had to happen sometime; I was not prepared for it to be today.

After my initial and irrational anger at Hawthorn, I was grateful she was there. I resolved to have us each learn a bit more basic trauma care in case this were to happen again. At least if we were capable of doing so. I hated the thought of one of my friends getting hurt like this again.

So lost in thoughts of self-pity was I, that I barely registered what the others were saying.

"Among the countless data files we recovered, we were able to establish Governor Deveraux's," Himawari said, glancing warily in my direction. "The file contained information on Daux, her sister, and her mother. He doesn't see Daux as much of a threat to him, vastly underestimating her abilities. But that is beside the point.

"He is without a doubt a high-ranking official in the Coalition. A double agent who has been funneling important NAF secrets and information into the ears of the Coalition. He abused his position as governor to gain access to this information and use it against the NAF. Against his *daughter*."

The others were stunned, staring dumbfounded at each other, the walls – anywhere but me. I, on the other hand, was enraged. My father was already the worst kind of man in my eyes, but somehow, he was able to sink even lower. Clearing my throat, everyone's eyes reluctantly turned to me.

"What else?" I asked.

"Daux…" Himawari hesitated.

"I said, What. Else."

A heavy sigh. "We already know the countries aligned within the NAF defected from the Coalition because they disagreed with their totalitarianism, along with their more… cruel ideals."

"Go on."

"The Coalition's countries still employ the use of the slaving market and labor camps," Himawari shook her head in disbelief. "Spec Ops and the NAF knew this, of course, but we were able to recover top secret info on slaving routes, market locations, and locations of the labor camps."

"And," Hawthorn spoke up hesitantly. "There is evidence of high-ranking Coalition officials using magic for personal gain."

"This was worth it…?" I hedged. Of course, it was. This information was invaluable.

"Yes!" Himawari exclaimed. "Yes, it *is* good that we got it. But the images… They were awful. And they will likely be changing tactics once they learn of our attack."

"They may," I acquiesced. "But the Coalition government won't view us *personally* as a threat. The NAF maybe, but to change months – or even years – of planning because a small group of Spec Ops agents destroyed *one* covert base?"

"Many in the government won't, but they won't take this attack lightly. Especially when it is connected to the other places we've raided over the course of the year," Valentin explained, drawing my eyes to him for the first time since I entered the auto.

He was haggard. Sweat slicked pieces of his hair against his forehead, smearing the streaks in a blur of color. His skin was paler than usual, waxy, and pain burned in his eyes. Hawthorn was right, she was an inexperienced healer. I felt anger flare up in me again, settling in the gnawing hole in my chest.

"So," I said slowly. "My father is a double agent and a piece of shit, the Coalition is still doing things we already knew about, and they may retaliate. Did I get all that?"

"There's no reason to be so waspish, Daux," Valentin chided gently. "We've gleaned important information on this mission and destroyed the source of a major threat to New Palogenia."

Heat flooded my face, and I looked away in shame. It was uncalled for, I would admit. But I was so angry. Angry with my father for being exactly whom I thought he was, and worse; angry at the senseless loss of life back at the now ruined base; angry with Valentin for daring to get injured. At his stupid face and the pitying glances I was getting from others in the group.

I wanted to scream, to yell. I wanted to hit something. There was nothing I wanted to do more than curl up into a ball and cry. Emotionally, I knew I was a wreck. That was evident before I was even Placed, but I thought I had been healing.

Now, it felt like any progress I had made was undone. I felt seven years old again when my father had forbidden my grandparents from seeing me. Empty. Angry and empty. Like the void inside my chest had grown tenfold and would swallow me whole, destroying everything I had ever let myself love along with me.

Before I could even attempt to issue a half-hearted apology, the auto lurched like it had been struck. From the windows, I could see nothing but the world flying by us, underneath us, as we flew through the air. My head slammed against the inner wall of the auto, black dancing across my vision for the second time that day. A loud crunch.

Everyone was screaming. Someone was crying. I could not move. Why could I not move? The darkness, the void inside my chest reared its ugly head, snapping its jaws. It devoured me, and I knew no more.

When I awoke, I was still unable to move. I lay on my back, my arms beneath me, and legs straight out along the cold hard ground. Ground? Where was the auto? Had someone carried me here? Where was here exactly?

My eyelids creaked open, feeling gritty and heavy. The room was completely dark, but I could make out vague outlines of other people laying on the ground in the dark. Attempting to sit up to get a better look was difficult, and I realized my arms and legs were bound.

We could not have been here long, a few hours at the most. There were the beginnings of hunger pangs but no urge to use the bathroom. What puzzled me was *how?* My team had told no one of this mission and hardly anyone from Spec Ops knew of it at all. So how had anyone learned of our whereabouts and taken us to this unknown location?

A soft creak captured my attention, and I went still. There was no light spilling into the room. No light at all. Heavy footsteps thudded across the floor, thundering in my chest. I did not move, keeping as still as possible. That was until a sudden kick landed in my stomach.

A low grunt escaped me, and I descended into a coughing fit.

"Shut up girl," a gruff, hateful voice said, and I was pulled roughly to my feet.

"Screw you," I rasped, receiving another harsh jerk.

"Walk," he demanded. When I found my legs, I realized that though my ankles were bound, they were only tied enough so I would have trouble running.

Shouts of protest followed as I was dragged from the room. I was not alone. Valentin, Jax, Himawari, and Félix were hauled out soon after.

"What do you want with us?" I demanded as we were led down a long, dark hallway.

"I said shut up," the man growled.

"Hey Daux," Jax called from behind. "Tell that asshole to suck my–"

A scuffle arose as Jax's handler attempted to quiet him. He hit Jax with something that created a loud whack. The butt of a gun? Jax laughed mirthlessly and – encouraged by his tenacity – I held my head a bit higher.

Soon I could see a light at the end of the dark hall. I was quickly shoved through it, unable to see clearly. The transition from dark to light burned my eyes to the point of tears, and I realized I was still using foresight. That was why I had been able to see the others in that pitch-black room.

Once the tears were blinked away and my eyes could focus on the light, I was able to discern a tall figure, standing with alert and elegant posture at the back wall of the small room. The light hair, handsome face, and ocean-green eyes came into focus. My stomach lurched.

"Daux, Daux, Daux," my father crooned as he strode towards us. "I can't believe you would stand against *me*, your father!"

My lips curled back in a sneer, blatantly allowing my disgust for him to show.

"Father?" I spat. "You've never been a father to me."

Pain shot through me, and I fell forward, knees barking against the concrete floor. I heard Valentin shout. The only thing keeping me upright was one of my father's followers holding me by my shackled wrists. He must have kneed me in the back. I reached inside me for that burning ember of fire magic to retaliate, to free myself, but found it nearly extinguished. They must have used my magic-blocking cuffs on me. Perhaps even the rest of us. I shot a warning look at Valentin to keep quiet.

"Now," my father said, smiling down at me. "Why don't we talk business?"

"What business would we want with you?" Valentin growled, seemingly ignoring my silent command.

"Oh, I think you will want to hear what I have to say, Valentin Angelov."

"Unlikely."

My father's smile never faltered. It stayed plastered on his face even as Valentin goaded him.

"My *'friends'* and I want something," he said, turning away from me to pace in front of my team and me. "And that something is freedom. Freedom of expression, freedom of ideas, freedom to live how we see fit."

"Except your idea of 'freedom' oppresses others!" Félix shouted. "How do you expect people to want to listen to you, much less give you what you want, when it will persecute them in the end?"

Then the smile dropped from my father's face. It was like the removal of a mask, showing his true self underneath. Rage was evident in every corner, a rage I had never, in all my years had the misfortune of observing.

Fear filled me, and I watched as my father's slender, manicured hand roughly grabbed Félix by the jaw and jerked him upward, forcing him to meet his eyes.

"Boy," my father growled. "*We* are the ones who are persecuted just for our ideals alone. The Gods cursed us with people like you. Those outside of this oppressive country realize this and wish to help."

My fear slowly turned to horror as I took in my father's

words. We knew he had been in contact with some from the Coalition. Hearing him confirm that they had responded and offered assistance was beyond terrifying. He had opened a crack in our defenses, and the Coalition would soon be pouring through.

"The information we stole from your base is already in the hands of Spec Ops," I bluffed desperately. "Whatever you do to us here will be in vain."

"Daux," my father taunted, turning to me with his hand still on Félix's jaw. "If I didn't know any better, I'd think you were lying to me. You know what happens when you lie to me, right?"

I swallowed thickly. Flashes of past punishments danced across my mind's eye. The denial of food and leisure activities were easy punishments to bear, but he knew where to hurt me. The memory of that day drew itself up, unbidden. He had not taken me from my grandparents to punish them, though that was an added benefit. My father did it to hurt me because he knew that hurting people I loved was the best way to control me. He didn't need to lay a finger on me.

"Where is Amalie?" I demanded breathlessly. He had to have her here, planning to use her in some way to get to me.

"Oh, my little deer." He grinned dazzlingly, the 'pet name' he used for me making me shiver in disgust. "What an excellent idea! Too bad I didn't think of it myself. No, I don't need your sister to get what I want. I just need these new friends of yours."

As he spoke, his hand tightened on Félix's jaw, veins protruding with the tension. "I could break this child's jaw right now, and all of you would be powerless to stop me with your weapons gone and no way to conduct your magic."

Despite the pressure on his jaw, Félix's expression betrayed nothing but hatred. No pain, no fear – only rage and hate.

"Hurting us to upset Daux will accomplish nothing!"

Himawari shouted, standing tall and proud despite the large man behind her holding her captive.

My father turned to her, his grin widening in a frightening display of even white teeth. "It will accomplish plenty."

"That is enough!" I yelled, but my father did not relent.

"You, *daughter*, do not get to command me." He squeezed harder and Félix's deep brown eyes began to well with tears of agony.

A soft breeze floated through the room before darkness descended upon us. Cries of surprise and pain rang through the room, and I found myself knocked to the ground. A yelp of fear escaped me as hands grasped my ankles and wrists. But they were not there to harm me, and my bonds fell away before I was pulled to my feet and into a crushing embrace.

"Heya, Daux," said Talia's mirthful voice, and then I was released.

The darkness began to recede, and I squeezed my eyelids shut. A strong, small hand clasped mine. "You can open your eyes now, Daux. We have to escape."

When I opened them, Talia was at my side grinning triumphantly – Gwyn and the others off to the side releasing my teammates from their bonds. *He* had caused the darkness. Our captors had not considered that we had another shadowmancer in our group. I smiled back at Talia, relief coursing through me.

She pressed my rapier into my hands. "When they escaped, they found our weapons."

"Let's grab my father and get out of here," I turned in his direction but he was nowhere to be seen. Neither was Félix or Valentin. The guards in the room were all incapacitated with Gwyn, Riannan, Talia, Jax, and Hawthorn standing over them. Where had my father gone? Had Valentin and Félix pursued him?

A loud boom shook the building we were in and the panic from earlier began to resurface. It has only been mere hours since the explosion at the base in Cassacania, and it was still fresh in my mind.

Without waiting for the others, I ran, allowing my foresight to take over, to predict the easiest route out of the building. I had to find Félix and Valentin. My father needed to be apprehended. I could not let him escape – they could not have gotten far.

When I burst through the exit door, hot sea air rushed into my face, searing my eyes. Before I could blink away the tears, another earth-shattering boom shook the ground knocking me to my knees.

I attempted to right myself, swiping at my burning eyes. A few blinks later, I saw that we had been taken to Portnith, the port town near the Cassacania coast. Portnith was named for the Nith family, who had founded it centuries ago before the war. But what I noticed a mere second later was that the whole town was engulfed in flame.

Chapter Twenty-Eight

*F*ire.

Where was Valentin? Félix, Jax, Himawari? Or Talia and the others? That's right, I had left the others behind in my haste. This was bad, very bad. And I did not know how to fix it.

An explosion erupted to my left, sending another gust of hot, salty air rushing into me. It seared my face and burned my lungs as I huddled close to the ground, trying to keep from being blown away.

Then it hit me. *An explosion!* Where there was fire, there must be Félix. Once the burning gusts had subsided slightly, I dragged myself to my feet and began running in the direction of the blast.

All around me was destruction, flame, and rubble. Surely, he had not caused this all himself. Félix could have meltdowns if overstimulated or upset, but never to this magnitude. Panic began to slither up my spine and settle in my chest like an oily, disparaging snake.

Through the smoke and flame it was difficult to make out the ever-shrinking threads that were Félix and Valentin's magical signatures. It felt like hours and hours I searched for my teammates, though it was only a few minutes. My fear and anxiety were nearly crippling me as I called Félix and Valentin's names over and over.

Eventually, through the sound of my frantic cries, I

heard screaming and shouting. Without a second thought I dashed toward the noises, arms pumping at my sides, willing myself to go faster as the scorching air burned my lungs. The threads began to widen into ribbons of bright orange and icy white. They were close.

I found Valentin first. He was kneeling in the dirt in front of the burned skeleton of a building. His hands were at his side, clutching at his wound which had been healed only hours earlier.

Rushing to him, I fell to my knees at his side. Dirt and ash rose around us in a cloud. That was when I noticed the blood. His wound had reopened.

"She warned me about this," he said weakly, attempting a wry smile.

"*Shit!*" I cried. My arms would not stay still and my body buzzed with panic. What do I do? What should I do? Valentin was hurt, he was bleeding, again. And – just like last time – I did not know how to help him.

"Daux," he said in a stern tone, drawing my eyes to his. "Where are the others?"

"I ran after you and Félix, I don't know," I told him honestly, uncaring whether I received a tongue lashing later or not.

Gritting his teeth, Valentin shook his head. "You need to go after Félix. We were chasing after your father, and my wound reopened."

"What about the citizens?" I asked. Many had passed me during my search, fleeing the burning town.

"I'll radio the others and give them instructions."

"What about you? Will you be okay?"

Valentin's smile was small and still weak, but his eyes held a strong, pale fire. "I'll be fine, go find our teammate."

I nodded – tension building in my chest – and before I could lose the courage to do so, I pecked him quickly on the cheek and ran for it. If I had stuck around for a second longer, maybe I could have relished in the shock on his face, but I had to find my friend. Who knows what my father was up to? An escape? Suicide? He may suffer from hubris, but I doubted he would allow himself to be captured and brought to shame.

The further into the burning town I ran, the hotter the air grew. My lips began to crack, and the smoke-tinged air burned my eyes. I needed to invest in some eye gear when we got back to Heliorious.

Just as I was about to call for Félix again, an explosion erupted to my left. Without a moment's hesitation, I ran in that direction. Where there was fire, there was Félix. As I followed the most recent trail of smoke and debris falling from the sky, I observed the destruction around me.

Buildings were decimated. People's homes and businesses were all destroyed. A statue of one of the Gods lay in ruin across the square. Abandoned toys, books, and other personal items were strewn about the streets, left in the citizen's haste to escape and blown from the buildings. I tried not to focus too hard on them. This could not have been our doing. It was not physically possible for Félix to cause this much destruction in such a short amount of time even without his conduits. None of the others possessed the power to cause such devastation.

It had to be the Coalition, part of my father's plan. Something. They had to be manipulating the situation to prove we were the dangerous ones, that magic was destructive and unnatural. That we were a curse from the Gods. They hated us, and they wanted the rest of the NAF to see how dangerous we were. How deep we were in our sin.

Whatever this was, I needed to find Félix. Valentin, though injured, would be fine. He had been in these situations before. Félix, on the other hand, had not. He was only fifteen, and any danger he had been in previously, we had been in together. I *needed* to find him.

The sounds of decimation roared in my ears. The panic I felt was overwhelming. Not only was my friend in danger, but so were thousands of people, and I had no idea how to help them. Fire brigades, water magic users, and healers were out in clusters attempting to right the damage as civilians ran for their lives, clutching personal belongings and children to them in their flight.

I remembered Valentin's insistence that I find Félix, but it was so difficult to see all these people in fear. The desire to help was nearly overwhelming, but what could I do besides stop the man who destroyed the town in the first place?

Instead of guilt, the terrified people I passed began to give me renewed strength. I needed to not only find Félix, but my father. He must be stopped, and captured, at all costs.

Sounds of gunfire rang out in the distance. Rapid and growing louder with each step. Explosions erupted intermittently through the loud, popping of the firearms. That was where Félix had to be.

Though my body was weary, I pushed myself just a little bit further. And further.

And further.

Through the rubble and crumbling structures, I ran. There were no more civilians around attempting to escape; their cries were farther away now. I tried not to think about any who had been caught in the blasts or fire. I couldn't do anything for them. And Valentin would have sent help after me, so long as he was able to.

Oh, I hoped he was all right.

There was no time to worry about him, no time to think about him. About how less than a few hours ago I was in his bed, curled into his warmth. How confused he made me. Angry and confused.

I shook my head. No distractions. My lungs burned and felt as though they would give out at any moment.

Then, finally, I made it to the source of the gunfire: the town's center. Nearly every building had been decimated and riddled with bullet holes. A thrumming I had not noticed before now had begun reverberating in my bones.

Looking to the sky, I saw my father, holding a large semi-automatic firearm in the safety of a helicopter. My heart sunk to my toes.

"No…" I whispered, hands clenching into fists. "NO!"

He was getting away. He *would* get away! No, no, no, no, *no!*

Even from this distance, I could see the whiteness of his teeth as he flashed a triumphant grin at me. The wild brightness in those ocean green eyes which were so like mine.

I felt him pull the trigger before I heard the shot. Somehow, I just knew he would. I fell to the right, rolling quickly before shoving myself back to my feet running to find cover. But I need not have worried. My father had not shot at me.

A gangly figure lay, prostrate on the ground. Orange glowed all around him and before I could get to cover, he exploded. Blown back by the blast, my head cracked sharply against a destroyed shop window. I knew before I could even reach back to feel, that my scalp and the back of my neck had been sliced in multiple areas. Hot blood ran in rivulets down my neck and I could feel that glass and debris had become embedded in my skin.

When I stumbled to my feet, lungs heaving and head throbbing, my father's helicopter had started its ascent.

"Goodbye my little deer," he said, voice amplified by a radio system in the helicopter. "I did so enjoy our time together. Too bad you failed and allowed your friends to get hurt."

"Shut up," I cried, willing back the tears of anger and defeat in my eyes.

"Au revoir!" he called with an arrogant wave. "Next time we meet, you and your wretched idealists will be in chains."

In a rage, I flung my hands toward the helicopter,

willing the flame to my fingertips. Air, ice, anything to ground him. But nothing would come. There was not enough oxygen in the air to breathe – let alone start another flame – ice melted as soon as I could cast it, and my magic was too depleted to use such a wild magic as the air. It was not my affinity. Any arrows I could attempt to shoot would not reach. Not now.

I sank to my knees, ignoring the voices in my head urging me to rise and fight. I could do nothing else to stop my father. Nothing I could do but watch as Félix smoldered and bled out on the ground. Watch as the city crumbled and fell to flame.

The world was burning, the image seared into my memory, and I could not shake it. I could feel the fire, everything, and hear the screams of the people I could not save. But what horrified me the most was the boy in front of me. Félix was prone on his back, broken and bloodied, screaming. Just screaming. Blood was pouring from his mouth, his wounds, and pooling beneath him in the dirt. I should have comforted him. I needed to comfort him, to help him. But I just knelt there in the rubble, listening to his screams, as fire razed the world around us.

I remember vomiting. My stomach was mostly empty – not much in me to rid itself of – but it kept heaving. And heaving. Until I was gagging on the ground, covered in dirt, blood, and bile. I had killed people today. Let others die. For what? Everything was ultimately a failure.

Valentin and the others found us eventually. Other Spec Ops agents were with them. They loaded Félix onto a stretcher, forcing pacs into his mouth as healers swarmed his burnt body.

I refused to let anyone touch me. Not Talia, Himawari, Jax, or even Valentin. Eventually, I was forced onto a stretcher and a pac was placed into my mouth. My teeth pierced the soft exterior involuntarily and the medicine poured into my mouth. It was bitter and tangy, like the bile I had just expelled. I gagged again, but the healers jabbed a needle into my arm, injecting me with anti-nausea medication.

The last thing I remember before I blacked out was the Overseer leaning over my stretcher, a pained expression on her face.

"I'm sorry…" she whispered and that was all I knew.

Chapter Twenty-Nine

In stories when the heroine is captured by the villain, she is left in a dark, damp dungeon awaiting torture and other romanticized notions. A handsome savior would come and rescue the poor girl from the nefarious people who had captured her, and they would ride off into the sunset, living happily ever after.

The cell I was in – if you could call it that – was bright with simple furnishings. I was told I would only be here for a few days, "Until we figure out what happened". That had been two weeks ago, and no prince was charming in sight. Two weeks on Godsday, when I had been pulled from my hospital bed, still groggy from the anesthetic they used so they could stitch up the back of my head and neck. Then I realized they had sheared my long hair to be able to care for my injuries.

No torture had taken place, I was being fed well and was allowed many freedoms, except I could not leave the confinement of my room. No one came to visit me, save the interrogators who made me relive those horrific memories over and over again until I was dry heaving and weeping on the white tiled floor. The smell of Félix's charred flesh still burned in my nostrils and came back stronger each time.

No one had deigned to inform me of his condition, and I tried not to think the worst, though it came to me in dreams. His burned skin and bullet-riddled body, crying out for my help, but I could not move. My father held my wrists behind my back, forcing me to watch as Félix succumbed to his injuries.

I would awake in a cold sweat, begging anyone listening to tell me if he was all right. No one would answer. After a while I stopped asking.

That was until a familiar face appeared in the small window of my cell door. It was unlocked quickly and urgently, and he came sweeping into the room with his comforting icy chill.

"Hello, Valentin," I said as I sat on the small cot in the corner of the room. I attempted to breathe carefully in and out.

"Daux," he responded hoarsely.

The dark circles under his eyes were like bruises and his normally handsome face was haggard. It appeared as if the past few weeks had taken a toll on him too.

"How is he?" I did not need to specify who.

"Recovering."

"Did they send you here to interrogate me?" I asked, trying to keep my tone neutral. I prayed that was not the case.

"No." He sounded hurt.

Despite myself, I felt relieved. "Then why have they let you in?"

He lowered himself onto the pristine floor, his black clothes like an inky stain against the white tile. The colors in his black hair seemed hyper-saturated in contrast. Weariness colored over any expression he could have chosen at that moment.

"They released me last night," he informed me, rubbing his hands over his face. "They're interrogating all of us. Including Fé."

Rage bubbled up inside me, but I pushed it down. My father had escaped, but we still retrieved valuable info. Why were we being treated as if we were traitors?

"He's injured!" I hissed.

"Don't you think I haven't protested it? Against any of this?" he retorted, eyes glittering dangerously.

"Why did you come to me? Why not him? Or anyone else? They're likely to need you, or anyone, right now."

Valentin sighed. "You need someone too."

I started, trying to control my breathing, the tears that threatened to escape. I missed him and all his abrasiveness. His cold demeanor, sharp mind, and even sharper tongue.

"Besides," he continued, standing again. "You're my team leader, and I felt it was appropriate I tell you I'm being assigned to another group temporarily."

"What?" I cried, standing to my feet as well. "They can't do that!"

"They can…" he said, stepping in front of me and placing his hands on my shoulders. "Daux, I need you to do something for me."

"Anything," I promised around the lump in my throat.

Valentin's eyes squeezed shut for a moment and he swallowed thickly, as though he were contemplating what to say next.

"Protect the others," he said finally. "We don't know exactly who we can trust anymore. And I need you all to be safe."

"Where are they sending you?" I asked. It sounded like he was saying goodbye.

"Into the Coalition territories. Infiltration." He smiled wearily. "I'm being sent after your father."

"They should send me."

"They don't exactly trust any of us right now."

"It was my fault he got away."

One of his cool hands brushed the side of my face as if to push my nonexistent hair from my eyes. "You're no more to blame than the rest of the team. It was no one's fault. We were ambushed."

"Still…" I started to argue but was interrupted.

"I'm going to miss your long hair."

His hand was now at the base of my neck, careful to avoid the tender areas, thumb brushing my shorn hair. There were substances to help regrow hair magically, but I did not have access to those in my confinement.

"I cried when I found out they shaved it off," I admitted, heart fluttering as his eyes bored into my own.

"No one could fault you for that." Valentin laughed and pulled me into his embrace. "I'm going to miss you."

With my face pressed into the crook of his neck, I could feel his hammering pulse. It mirrored mine. "How long will you be gone?"

"We're not sure," he confessed, resting his cheek on my head. "I don't want to be away for too long."

We were quiet for a while, just holding each other as if our lives depended on it. For a while, it felt like it did.

"Do you think we're doing the right thing? NAF and Spec Ops, I mean?" I asked him, breathing in the minty scent of his clothes.

"I'm not sure what I believe in anymore," Valentin breathed, clutching me tighter. "Everything has gotten so screwed up, and it seems like our allies have turned against us."

Nodding, I pressed myself closer to him reveling in the new sensation of my buzzed scalp against his skin.

"Will you stay in contact?" I asked, knowing full well he would be unable to, even without the barrier of my holonav being disabled.

"I'll do my best," he promised and pulled back.

I swallowed. His gaze was heated as he stared down at me in his arms, making my thundering heart shudder. Any attempt to speak was quelled by the lump in my throat. I did not know what I would say anyway. The way he was staring at me, eyes so intense, made my mind go blank.

When he leaned in my eyelids fluttered shut involuntarily. I could feel his warm breath inches from my lips, smell the ozone scent of magic and mint on him. It made me shiver. And just when I thought he would press his lips to mine, I felt them brush against my forehead instead.

I waited for the relief to come, but it never did. I only felt disappointment, which grew as he drew away from me and headed toward the door. I stared after him, eyes burning, still unable to form a coherent sentence.

"Daux," Valentin called from the doorway. "I lied."

"What?" I said thickly.

"There are a lot of things I've lost faith in," he began, his hands clenching into fists at his sides. "But I believe in you."

"I…"

"I believe in you, Daux. Don't forget that."

And then he was gone, leaving me with silent tears streaming down my face. When the door shut behind him, I sat with my head between my knees, refusing to release the sobs which threatened to rend me in two.

I had become many things since I had been Placed. The leader of a successful team, a reliable friend, and a valued member of Spec Ops. I had allowed myself to become vulnerable, loving, and open. All of which had been used against me, and despite Valentin's earlier words of encouragement, I had become a failure in so many ways.

There were many things I had lost faith in: my government, the people I was sworn to protect, and even myself. But Valentin still believed in me. Perhaps I could do the same, again. Perhaps I could become something I never dreamed I could be.

I could become something worth believing in.

Acknowledgments

This book… Where to even begin? *I am Become* started off little more than a dream. A spark of an idea. An "ember" if you will (as Daux likes to refer to that little thing inside of her that keeps her going). This book is my pride and joy and I am so pleased that it is finally being shared with the world. So first and foremost, dear reader, I would like to thank you for giving it a chance.

Without Hillary Sames and Diane Tatum, my editors, I probably would have given up on this project long ago. Hillary guided me through my own world with such ease it was as though she knew it better than I did. I am eternally grateful to her for her hard work and encouragement. And Diane caught all the (very glaring) errors I missed with patience and grace. Thank you with all of my being.

My publisher Cynthia Hickey and fellow author Linda Knowles for helping me take the steps toward my dream career. And everyone at Winged Publications for their support on this journey. You all rock!

Rachel, for being one of the very best granny girls I have ever met in my life. I cannot wait to crochet with you until our wrists disintegrate. To all the rest of my grannies and friends – Kat, Stou, Kris, Holly, Jooj, Janine, Rainy, Rose, and Autumn – your love and support through this journey have been a balm to my frazzled nerves. Thank you for encouraging my stories and being my friends.

For my parents, I am blessed to have two sets who love

and encourage me in all things. From suggestions, edits, and offering comfort and support when I felt like breaking down you have all been there for me. My thanks to all of you are immeasurable. As is my love.

My siblings, who put up with my cringe throughout my life, love me with all of their hearts and build me up. Thank you. Now you get to read my stories in print instead of scrawled in journals, and I think that's pretty cool.

Pat and Tammy for raising the best man I have ever known. I could not have done this without him, and that extends to you. Thank you.

And finally, my husband. Zach, there is so much I want to say to you. But if I say it out loud, I'll just end up crying. So, here goes. I love you, and you knew that, but if I had not met you, I would never ever have become the woman I am today. You lifted me past my fears and picked me up each and every time I fell. You laughed with me about my characters and gave sound advice. But what's most important, you helped me try. And since I did that, I accomplished more than I ever could on my own. You are my light, my love, and everything I could have ever asked for. I love you.

And to my cats, Usagi and Squeekers. Thank you for not ruining my manuscript the countless times you sat on my keyboard. I love you very much.

Katelynn R. Butler grew up in East Tennessee and has been reading and dreaming up her own stories since she was a child. She procured her first library card at eight and has continued to ransack her local libraries since, reading anything she could get her hands on. She spends most of her days writing fantastical tales like the ones she adored growing up. Otherwise, she can be found baking, crocheting, researching vintage and historical dress, or spoiling her two rescue cats. I am Become is Katelynn's first novel.